MADE IN L.A.

MADE IN L.A.

Vol. 6: Hollywood Adjacent

MADE IN L.A.
Vol. 6: Hollywood Adjacent

SIXTH FICTION ANTHOLOGY

Cover design by Allison Rose

Visit Made in L.A. Writers online at
www.madeinlawriters.com

ISBN: 978-1-953954-08-4

Published by Resonant Earth Publishing
on behalf of
MADE IN L.A. WRITERS
P.O. Box 50785
Los Angeles, CA 90050

CONTENTS

INTRODUCTION

Los Angeles is a familiar sight in film and television. Look closely and you'll recognize oddly alien rocks as the setting for a science fiction blockbuster or a beachside high school immortalized in a coming-of-age cult classic. In a time before CGI and megabudgets, filmmakers valued this diverse landscape and endless sunshine, splicing together L.A. and Anywhere USA.

There is no defining L.A. without including Tinseltown. Captured on celluloid and projected around the world, Hollywood has defined its own representation, rarely allowing a glimpse behind the lens. The Hollywood dream shapes the lives of Angelenos in ways both seen and unseen. You could call it a blob and run from it in horror, or point and laugh at its absurdity. And still, it will enter your dreams and hypnotize you with visions of the possible and impossible, the hilarious and terrifying.

Geographically, Hollywood is not a city but a neighborhood. Conceptually, it is not a place but a mindset, a process, a capitalist logic, and a siren song. Ambitious creatives flock from far and wide to this urban basin, eager to one day see their name in the credits. Many are unprepared for the vastness of a city with the population of a small country. In a place of cultural juxtaposition, Hollywood's on-screen homogenization often fails to do justice to those who live here. But we are dazzled by the spectacle, too.

As adversity rattles the entertainment industry and challenges its hard-working community, Hollywood feels as though it's undergoing seismic shifts. Broken business models, accelerating climate change, and a nation falling into chaos shape our transformation. Importantly, though, people here resemble the terrain: beautiful, unique, and resilient. For every person who works in the movies, there are thousands who carve a different path. Together we complain about the traffic, the lack of rain, and the drive-thru line at In-N-Out—united as proud Angelenos. Should our city be threatened or harmed, we feel collective grief, for it is not "they" who are lost, but "we."

The Made in L.A. anthology series has historically steered away from Hollywood as a subject, the booming voice of the industry having spoken enough for itself. The business is not just the final product for your consideration during awards season. Filmmaking is a craft, a vocation, a career. For every crew member who leaves the set at the end of a twelve-hour day, there is a story of how they got there, of how they will survive the next economic shift. Sometimes the best stories come from Hollywood-adjacent spaces, where what matters is finding the best street taco vendor, free parking spots, a friend performing onstage for the first time, or a place to listen to live music.

Hollywood may not represent Los Angeles on its own, yet the City of Angels does not exist without the mythology, the symbolism, and the love of make-believe. May that passion burn brightly for decades to come.

With our best wishes,

Made in L.A. Writers

Sara Chisolm ★ Gabi Lorino ★ Allison Rose ★ Cody Sisco

WHERE SHE WANTS TO BE

RAYA YARBROUGH

For one whole year, I taught a stripper how to sing. Not exactly a stripper, more of a discount burlesque dancer. Very little clothing that never came off.

I met up with her in a high-rise condo on Wilshire Boulevard once a week. It was part of that manmade mountain range of multimillion dollar properties that line Wilshire Boulevard, leading up to the country club. Like many of them, her building was a high-end residence with a quiet air of abandonment. Every time I entered the lobby, I passed the unused, weary couches. Same pastel art on the walls. No music in the elevator up.

Entering the apartment, the first sounds of life were the intermittent soft tweets of a bird, somewhere out of sight. This sound receded under the welcome of Her Manager as he led me down a hallway into a common room. It was 2008, but the apartment retained its eighties' angular interior design. The rug used to be white, now it was giving "old Shih Tzu." It was a tight-knit rug that always looked frazzled and confused because it thought it would be 1987 forever. The kitchen bar was positioned diagonal to the far wall and almost perpendicular to the window. Long blinds connected the oatmeal ceiling to the rug, and its slats clicked like hanging dominoes.

Among these architectural angles, I waited for her to appear. I set up my keyboard between the pleather sofa and the large television and noticed every right angle had been countered by something acute or obtuse.

Anna was always prompt. She arrived in uniform: a skimpy tank top, a flouncy, schoolgirl-adjacent mini-skirt, platform high heels, and microphone headset. She had yellow-blond hair and a pale face with a bit of acne on the hairline and some dry skin at the tip of her nose, a result of skin medicine of some sort—this was an imperfection we shared. She was a work-in-progress, though she was already amply shaped and had a natural beauty, which is why she was the jewel of the whole "pop star-in-training" grift.

Anna had an airy, sweet, thin soprano. Good pitch. She took every note I gave her about breath support and tone placement and incorporated them into the rhythm of her gyrating pelvis. The gyration never stopped. For a solid hour and thirty she ran scales, puffed air through diaphragmatic aspirations, buzzed "eeeeee" and "aaaaaaah" and "oooooooh" vowel reverberations through her nasal bones. I could see she felt it in the maxilla. She chirped and exhaled, all while stirring the pot with her hips, in sling-back three-inch heels.

When we got into her performance repertoire, the singing was inseparable from the motion. She was like a pump organ: no sound without undulation. Her songs had the hot-kitten pubescent sparkle of Katy Perry, cut with the retro lust of Samantha Fox. Electronic beats and synth gave out hooky, repetitive melodies about beckoning love, teasing love, everything except giving love. The vibe was unintentionally dated. It was as if they had the budget to pay someone to write the music but not for modern drum and synth samples—like 1995 trying really hard to be 2005 with equipment from 1985.

The music matched her movements. Her body reflected the text in wave after wave of enticement and desire, with no endgame. Her hipbones formed figure eights in the air. Watching her technique, my hip sockets suffered vicariously. Despite the relentless, repetitive movement, her core—I mean the core of her disposition—was solid.

Under the turquoise eyeliner and the above the bounce of her chest, she possessed an immovable, laser-like sense of calm.

★

As the weeks rolled on, we got to know each other. Anna had come from the Midwest to Los Angeles with her mother, who had gone back home. She'd responded to an ad placed by Her Manager, the guy who now paid her rent. There were three bedrooms off to the right, for three other young women. Her Manager oversaw all of them, under strictly enforced rules about dating (none) and some sort of financial agreement for his support. At the beginning of each lesson, he would lean over the diagonal kitchen bar to observe, then he'd retire to another room to tend to the publicity machinations of soft-core girly shows.

Anna seemed oddly free within this circuitry. She had the tenacity of those who travel across the country to find Hollywood and the naiveté to believe in a thing called "pop-star training." We were close in age, and sometimes the line between friends and teacher/student felt blurry. We laughed a lot, and I was fascinated with her, a real-life Barbarella. A musical sex alien, to whom I must teach the musical ways of my people. She was a true believer in the Big Showbiz myth. My photo negative. I'd grown up in Los Angeles surrounded by the business of Hollywood, yet I never had the chance to buy the dream. You feel it, the energy of it, but it's so constant that you don't recognize the weight of it until you meet someone who has yet to bend under the pressure.

Weeks became months. Months of the pastel art in the lobby. The couches, spotless, unused, weary. Silence in the elevator. The ghostly chirps of an invisible bird, down between the couch and the TV, where Anna swiveled, and chirped, and ran scales. She memorized the saucy lyrics, written just for her, and she began to embody an alter ego, not far off from the actual Anna, but with more flip, more sizzle.

★

The day of her show arrived. The performance space was on a side street off Sunset Boulevard. I drove the boulevard slowly, remembering when my dad lived on Hollywood Boulevard, when I was eight years old. In the eighties, we would come to this part of Sunset for various stores or restaurants.

This was where the prostitutes used to walk—between Fairfax, down past Guitar Center and Famous Amos, all the way to La Brea. Some were transexual, and I remember taking note of their prettiness, mixed with their slender androgyny. As a prepubescent girl who did not yet possess feminine curves myself, they all seemed like alluring women to me.

I let my eyes wander the relatively unpopulated streets. I found the side avenue. The venue was a tiny, black-box theatre with bars on the door. I almost drove right past it, because the curbside lighting was haphazard and jaundiced. I had a bad cold. I arrived just after Her Manager, and we sat on chairs in a short hallway. Men began arriving. All men. All solo. Each one entered with the same dark countenance that darkened when they saw the other men. They'd come to be alone with a fantasy.

I sneezed. The dark herd of men shifted their eyes towards my noise. I looked down at my feet.

Once Her Manager opened the doors, the crowd shuffled through, and I found a seat in the way back. I didn't want to be too close to the stage because I knew I was going to be blowing my nose. The stage was bare. With all the work they put into the music, I expected more of a production, but Anna was to be the production. She was the product.

The lights dimmed, and the backing track began. Anna appeared from between the curtains at the back of the stage in a swish of pink, her lower half in full swing. White baby-tee under a plastic, pink, plaid, schoolgirl jumper. After her first number, she did a little monologue about herself, her likes and dislikes. Finally, she turned her back to the audience and bent over to peek under her skirt. She smiled over her right shoulder and said, "In case you were wondering, they're pink!"

Anna gyrated through four songs. It was the same dance again and again. I began to watch the crowd for signs of boredom, but they were as engaged as ever, transfixed in hulking, profound stillness. By her third song, my nose had started going like a faucet, and I'd gone through a whole pack of tissues. I tried to sniffle quietly, nobody appeared to notice. In fact, the audience, this dark block of men, was unresponsive to anything. Outwardly. The theatre seats held shadow, resembling a communal confessional.

Thirty minutes in, I was out of tissues, and my cold was getting worse. I had to go. I slowly stepped down from the black-painted theatre riser, grazing my tights on it, I tiptoed around the corner, next to the sound booth. I apologized to Her Manager for having to leave early. He nodded and walked me out.

Her Manager thanked me and followed with, "When are we gonna get *you* up there?

I laughed, as if we both knew it was a joke, and he laughed too. We both knew he wasn't joking.

★

After the show, I continued with Anna for a few more months. One of the last times I went to coach her, I heard that tweeting bird again. I asked her about it, and she turned on her heel and cheerily disappeared into her room. She came back out holding a cage containing a blue and green parakeet, chittering to itself.

"Here she is." Anna smiled.

She set the cage on the kitchen bar top, and having paused her "pop-star training," I saw a different shade of Anna. She was still. Her face was easy and natural, enchanted with the bird.

While Her Manager was out of earshot, I wanted to tell her that this life was not the road to pop stardom. I wanted to tell her that this road was a dead end. I wanted to tell her that she didn't have to give her life to this rug, and these blinds, and those straps that cut into her pinky toes, and that Lucite platform click against the linoleum. I wanted to tell her that those rows of shadow men were only a fraction of the people who could love her, if she wanted to do something more—but she was in a rare place of serenity.

"Do you ever let the bird out?"

"Sure, all the time." She opened the wire door and reached in. A tiny claw grasped her pink acrylic fingernail. She lifted the bird out, and it flew up to a bookcase, facing the window.

"Does she want to go outside?" I asked.

Anna smiled. "She's where she wants to be."

WAGWORLD

JACQUELINE BERKMAN

I looked up, and that's when I saw Will. Though of course, he wasn't yet Will to me, just another beautiful L.A. man, tall and lanky with a golden, Jesus-like mane of hair.

"Hello, miss!" he said. "Care to hear about WagWorld Rescue?" He was holding a clipboard, and although he stood next to a playpen with two pit bulls and a sad-eyed German shepherd, I was convinced he was part of a reality TV show. I looked around for cameras.

"Sure," I said. I was at the Farmers Market, loading my tote bag with heirloom tomatoes and kale and the other "salad must-haves" that my idol, Delilah, had cited in a recent *Vogue* listicle. I fluffed my hair and took a couple of steps closer. "I'd love to hear about it."

He looked relieved, or surprised, and took a breath before launching into his speech.

"Awesome! I'm Will Hinkley, founder of WagWorld. What's WagWorld? We're a foster-based rescue organization for dogs. We find our rescues in a variety of situations—humane societies, high-kill shelters—" He leaned in close as if he were about to tell me a secret. "Sometimes lying in the middle of the road. That's what happened with Daisy Duke over there," he said, nodding to the shepherd. "Hit by a car and left for dead when I found her. See for yourself."

Before I could decline his offer, a picture from his cell phone camera was in my face. Daisy Duke sprawled across the asphalt. Fur matted with blood. Her right paw was gristly and raw, like a discarded chicken bone. It was horrific.

I was moved, and my eyes stung with tears. To be fair, it was a particularly bumpy time in my life. I had moved to L.A. three months before to pursue a job as a production assistant in the reality TV world. My dream was to work behind the scenes on *Day-to-Day with Delilah*, but I was open to any gig. It wasn't exactly working out. I didn't have experience in the field, but every entertainment industry advice blog I'd read stressed that this didn't matter. Entry-level roles didn't require expertise but flexibility, a can-do attitude, and a willingness to pitch in where you were needed. I had nothing *but* a can-do attitude. It was a point I'd belabored to studio executives in my cover letters, and to the viewers of my morning Instagram and TikTok videos, which were daily reels consisting of sun salutations and positive affirmations. But I had nothing to show for my efforts except a tiny apartment I shared with two Craigslist strangers and a part-time barista job at a cafe with an impressive selection of non-dairy milk.

It wasn't a glamorous life, but it was an expensive one, and I was running out of money. At nights, toggling between reruns of *Day-to-Day with Delilah*, different losers' profiles on dating apps, and my depleted checking account balance, I'd started to wonder if I'd have to move back to Fresno, a town that could never accommodate all of the dreams I had.

Perhaps it was because I was in all this turmoil that Will's story about Daisy Duke had such a profound and unexpected effect. I felt like I had jumped into ice water, the perpetual racket in my mind suddenly gone. It was the first time in a long time I had been completely absorbed by something outside of myself.

"Aw, don't cry, miss." Will pulled me into an embrace. "What's your name?"

"Jess," I said, nestling against his shoulder. His hands felt warm against the small of my back.

"Jess," Will said, repeating it as if the name itself held wisdom, the key to life's mysteries. "It's okay, Jess," he said. He released me and stepped over to the playpen, where he gave Daisy Duke a couple of belly rubs, then showed me the jagged pink smudge of a scar running down her leg. "See?" he said. "Daisy's fine now. She got the surgery she needed; her story will have a happy ending. But there are lots of other animals out there, Jess, that unless we intervene—well, they won't get their happy ending."

"I know," I said. There was an expectant pause before I realized he was probably waiting for money. I foraged in my purse for a crumpled $20 bill that was supposed to be for gas and dropped it into the mason jar he was using for donations.

"Thank you so much," Will said. "Would you like to join our mailing list?"

"Of course," I said. Will was a beautiful man, and for that alone I would have joined the mailing list. He handed me a clipboard, and I neatly wrote my phone number and email address.

"Fantastic," Will said. "We can always use more helpers at the rescue. If you'd be interested in that."

I smiled at him and the panting pups in the playpen. It felt like a transformative moment—I couldn't remember the last time my heart had felt so open. But working at a rescue was not what I had moved out to Los Angeles to do. I couldn't let distractions get in the way of my plan.

I told Will that I was super busy with work. "But you know how to reach me," I said with a smile and an implied wink. I was doing my best to be coy. But being coy has never been my strong suit.

Three days later Delilah formally announced her Companics for a Good Cause contest on Instagram, and in a flash I could envision the winning video, scene by heartfelt scene, featuring Will and his WagWorld pups. I called him and pitched my idea.

★

At the film shoot three days later, I was energized and full of purpose. It was noon, the sky was Easter-egg blue. The cul-de-sac was quiet and guaranteed easy parking. We had been strategic about picking this North Hollywood cul-de-sac, selecting it for its proximity to the office and a freeway underpass. It had just the right amount of crushed cans, candy wrappers, and cigarette butts to convey an atmosphere of disarray without being so foul-smelling or disgusting that it would be unbearable to spend a few hours filming there.

"Ooo! Looks like we just got another $100 donation for the microchip campaign," said Heather, the high-ponytailed intern from USC. She was sitting in the back seat of the WagWorld van with Rosie, petting the sweet dog's scraggly head as she scrolled through her phone. "Do we even need to do this fake film shoot? We have so many real and *actually* exciting initiatives going on as it is."

"This shoot is not fake," I said. Even though I'd only been working at WagWorld a few days, I felt this was true: the shoot was a symbolic representation of the rescue's larger story. "We can't just be sunshine and rainbows, you know. When you're one applicant of many, you need to say something dramatic to stand out."

"It's true," said Will. He sighed and adjusted his baseball cap. "I mean, I don't like it any more than you do, Heather, but the fact of the matter is that we're entering a contest, and judges love sob stories. And we need all the money we can get."

"Ugh, but it's all so cheesy," Heather said. "And Rosie's scared."

"Rosie's fine," I said. "It's a dead-end street." Another key reason we had chosen the cul-de-sac was it reduced the danger to the dog of cars whizzing by. I looked to

Will to back me up on this, but he was sullenly staring into the distance. Clearly, tough love was needed. "Look, guys, we need to nail this," I said. "If Delilah likes the video, it could be our big break. Do you have any idea what that means?"

I looked at them and waited, though I knew they hadn't fully wrapped their heads around what a win would mean. But I had. I knew it would open so many doors that were currently closed to us. That we'd be able to team up with Delilah, philanthropist and reality TV extraordinaire, to influence minds and hearts and expand the animal rescue's impact. We'd be able to change pet adoption in a way that we previously thought was unimaginable. Most importantly, we'd be able to rise from the depths of anonymity and become people who were respected and well known. When Heather finally opened her mouth, I expected her to only reiterate the obvious $100,000 cash prize.

"Are you okay?" she said instead.

"Yes," I replied, wiping at my damp cheek like it was a pesky fly. "I just want to get going." I got emotional when I thought too much about the contest, which was embarrassing. So I jumped out of the van and clapped my hands, demonstrating the can-do attitude I imagined would make the star of *Day-to-Day with Delilah* proud.

You could say that binge-watching *Day-to-Day with Delilah* made me an avid observer of contrasts. Delilah herself was always calm, cool, and collected, even though everyone and everything around her were always imploding. I knew it was precisely this tussle between disaster and success that made the show so addictive. We'd need to employ this same kind of narrative tension in our application video to advance in her Companies for a Good Cause contest.

"All righty," I said, kneeling on the ground to tend to Rosie as Heather walked away to field another microchip campaign call. I untied Rosie's purple WagWorld bandanna and mussed up the top of her head. She slobbered on my face as I fixed her appearance. Not that I really needed to worry about the way she looked. That morning, Will and I had blow-dried her fur so it stuck out in every direction. She looked mangier than she was.

"Are you ready, sweet girl?" I said.

Rosie continued to pant as we walked across the cul-de-sac. Like many of the other dogs at WagWorld, she was a COVID puppy. She'd been surrendered when her owners had to go back into the office full-time. One of our easier ones, Rosie, some type of terrier mix, was quiet, docile, and already trained. It had been a no-brainer to select her to star in our application video.

"Stay," I said as we approached the chain-link fence. I showed her the cheese stick wrapped in my hand. Her floppy brown ears tilted with inquisitiveness as she watched me walk backward. For a moment, I envied her life. The way she was guaranteed praise if she followed a few simple commands. I turned toward Will.

"Are we good?" I said.

Will was set up with his tripod and camera about twenty feet back. If he didn't look enthusiastic, he at least seemed less actively perturbed than when we had arrived. He nodded and counted down from ten.

"Rolling," Will said.

The scene unfolded like we'd practiced back at the rescue: I beckoned to Rosie with the cheese stick. She trotted alongside the fence, the midday sun casting dramatic shadows, conjuring up the harsh binaries of good versus evil. After each take, I'd pick Rosie up and give her a treat before dropping her off at the starting line, where we'd repeat the process. Will, perfectionist that he was, didn't yell "cut" until we'd gone through the routine five times.

"I think we got it!" Will finally yelled. He seemed genuinely excited about all that was ahead.

"I knew we would," I said. I kissed his cheek.

★

Fast-forward two weeks later to a day that started as most of my days started: with a livestream from WagWorld.

"Good morning, everyone!" I said, waving to my followers on Instagram and TikTok. We'd recently submitted our Companies for a Good Cause application to the *Day-to-Day with Delilah* production team and were waiting to hear back. I remained stubbornly optimistic, deciding that the morning dispatch called for clip-on orange eyelashes. "It's a hectic day here at WagWorld Rescue."

I kept my iPhone fixed on my face as I walked across the rubber flooring. I didn't want my viewers to see the awful fluorescent lighting and several past-due notices piling by the entrance. I was grateful, too, that they couldn't smell the place, which reeked of urine no matter how much Lysol we cleaned with. "Let's go check on the puppers."

The phone rang. I ignored it. In the past few weeks, the phone calls from people looking to surrender their pets had been increasing exponentially. We were now completely full, and couldn't take another animal in.

I flipped my phone camera to focus on Rosie, Daisy Duke, and a few of the pit bulls. They lounged in a corner alongside some chewed-up toys and tennis balls, different colored rhinestone bow-tie collars clasped around their necks. "Look at these pretty pups and all their swag!" I said, my voice an off-camera but nurturing presence. "How are y'all doing today?" I scooped up Rosie, who was wearing an orange rhinestone bow tie collar. I flipped the phone camera again so it focused on me holding her. "Look, we match!"

In the background I could hear the phone ringing again, as well as Heather yelling my name from the other side of the rescue. Time to wrap things up.

"Thanks for watching, everyone. I'll check back in with another video later today," I said. I stopped recording and lowered Rosie to the ground before removing my orange eyelashes. Suddenly, I felt deflated. Maybe it was the drizzly day outside, but I grew overcome with the sense that the entire world had lost color: the rescue especially, full of hues of beige and gray, suddenly seemed dreadfully muted and ordinary. I tried to shake it off, pocketing my phone as I walked across the kibble-strewn floor to Heather.

"What's up?" I said.

Heather had unmistakable bags under her eyes. "The calls for surrenders don't stop," she said. "We're getting one practically every minute."

"I know," I said. "But we're at capacity, so you can let them go to voicemail."

Since Will and I started hooking up, he'd encouraged me to express a stance of leadership and authority as far as managing Heather, our only intern, was concerned.

"It just doesn't feel right," Heather said. "It's so sad." She stared off into space, as if preoccupied. "Does it seem like Coco has a rash?"

Coco was one of the pit bulls, and I had noticed he had been scratching himself more often than the other pups, so I'd deliberately removed his rhinestone bow-tie collar.

"Did you give him his flea medicine?" I said.

"Yesterday, but it doesn't seem like it's taken effect." The phone rang again. Heather jumped. She really did seem rattled.

"I'm sure he's fine," I said. "But are you okay? Did you get any sleep last night?"

"Yeah," Heather said.

Spartacus peed on the floor, so she grabbed a rag and the Lysol, squatting down to the floor. "Well, I did stay up too late watching *Catty Catwalk*. They released three new episodes at once, and I binged them back to back. I need to stop doing that."

"Heather," I said, shaking my head in mock disapproval. She liked reality TV almost as much as I did, although her tastes were more varied. She was a *Day-to-Day with Delilah* fan for sure, but she also liked the competitions—modeling, cooking, clothing design, woodworking, and glassblowing. I didn't care about those competition shows one way or the other. If I was honest, the relentless work ethic and the emotional backstories about the families rooting for competitors back home all blurred and bored me. What I cared about were the shows that centered around a person who may have been ordinary at one point in time but, through some mysterious process of alchemy, became extraordinary.

Delilah encapsulated this transformation. She'd left her humble beginnings behind to become a spiritual advisor, reality TV star, clothing designer, and general force for good with 100 million Instagram followers. She had people hanging on her every word, not because she acted, sang, or danced, but because she was inherently fascinating herself.

Heather's phone pinged. "Hey, what do you know, we just got another $300 donation for the microchip campaign!" she said, her face visibly brightening when she read the notification.

"Woohoo! That's what I like to hear," I said.

The microchip campaign was a regular email blast we sent out to our database that said WagWorld was addressing the epidemic of lost dogs in the United States by promising to microchip at least five dogs at the rescue for every $100 donated. Will had emphasized in my onboarding that it was one of our most popular campaigns, and clearly it was. My excitement about this update was short-lived, though, because moments later, Will parked out front and stomped his way toward the WagWorld entrance, clipboard in hand and a pissed-off look on his face.

"This place is a mess," he said as he walked inside. Heather and I exchanged a glance. The place was always, to some degree, a mess—with thirty rescues running around, it was impossible for it not to be. Will knew this better than anyone, but based on his demeanor, it seemed pretty clear that his bad mood was because of something else.

"How did the Farmers Market go today?" I said.

Will plopped on the ground and only sighed in return. Rosie climbed into his lap, and he petted her absentmindedly for a few moments before squinting at her WagWorld-customized rhinestone collar.

"You gotta stop ordering these, Jess," Will said. "Slashing the swag budget should be the first thing on our list."

He couldn't possibly be serious. Will might have known dogs, but I knew branding. And I knew that swag was a non-negotiable element of building a brand.

"Aw c'mon," I said. "That's not going to be necessary, is it?"

"I spent five hours at the Farmers Market today. I showed ten different people the Daisy Duke photo. And you know how much money I raised? Thirty. Fucking. Dollars. So yes, Jess, I think slashing the swag budget is necessary," Will said.

Heather's phone lit up and she ducked into a conference room, likely to shield herself from Will's wrath.

"Look," Will said, "something's gotta give, because we can barely afford to keep WagWorld running as is."

He was curled into a little ball, rocking himself back and forth as he ran his hands through his hair. But why was he stressed? His parents were always there to bail him out. Had something changed?

"Why don't we grab something to eat," I said, "and you can tell me what's going on."

"Wait," Heather said, emerging from the conference room. "Before you both go, I had a question to ask you about the microchip campaign—"

"Later," said Will. "We're hungry." He whisked me toward the door.

★

I liked Let Me Noodle On It because it was next door, and always open, and I appreciated a cutesy name, even if it was completely at odds with the joint's grease-splotched menus and plastic chairs. It was the sort of place I imagined ducking into incognito once I was more well known. For now, though, it was just our local hole-in-the-wall. The place for Will and me to debrief about the day's work or vent.

Though that day, sitting glassy-eyed over his towering bowl of Pad Thai, it seemed like Will needed to do more than vent.

"Will," I said, snapping him out of an extended reverie. "What's the deal?"

When he spoke, his voice was shaky. "My parents are cutting me off financially," he said. "For real this time. They said, and I quote, 'Twenty-six is as good a time as any to be financially independent.'" He stabbed his fork into the Pad Thai, staring at the squiggly mass as if it were a byproduct of a science experiment. "I mean, to be clear, my dad just bought a Maserati to make himself feel better about his whole midlife crisis; there's no doubt that's what's *really* going on here, but what can I say? Without their backing, we're screwed."

I should have been sympathetic, but I was hung up on his age. "Twenty-six?" I said. "I could've sworn when we met that you told me you were twenty-four."

Will's eyes narrowed. "It's L.A., Jess, everyone fibs about their age. And it's a little beside the point right now, don't you think?"

"You're right," I said. I was always quick to find fault with my logic. "Look, everything is going to be fine. We don't need your parents' help. The microchip campaign is doing so well—we're getting donations all the time!"

But that didn't seem to appease Will. He sighed pitifully as he rested his head on the table. "I feel like I've hit rock bottom."

"You always said that your rock bottom was the night you got arrested," I said.

For the briefest of moments, a smile flickered across Will's face. The story of Will's rock bottom was a hit at parties, and we had included it as part of our three-minute encapsulation for our Companies for a Good Cause video. In a nutshell, it went like this: as a twenty-year-old bonehead, Will and three of his friends were arrested one drunken night trying to remove a Viking statue outside a shopping center. He'd described his night in the jail cell as a "dark night of the soul." He felt like a caged animal yearning to be set free, and it was that night he realized, for the first time, how many other caged animals were out there. He'd described this night as a wake-up call to re-evaluate what he was supposed to do with his life, spurring him to open WagWorld Rescue just months later. Sure, it was a bit corny, but what nonprofit origin story wasn't?

"Eh, that night actually wasn't so bad," Will said. He was sitting upright, chewing a piece of tofu. "My parents bailed me out within a couple of hours."

I looked down at my chopsticks, my face burning up. He'd never told me that before. Or had he? I knew if I questioned his story, he'd only call me out for being unsupportive again. "You can't give up," I said. "You love this work. Lean into your passion, right?"

He nodded, not meeting my eyes, so I racked my brain, trying to come up with a specific example. "Think of all the good you did with Daisy Duke," I said. Will looked at me, blankly blinking in recognition. "You were able to raise the money to get her the surgery she desperately needed, what was it, with a Kickstarter, right? You saved her life!"

Will nodded. "I made about one grand from the Kickstarter," he said, his eyes welling up miserably, before dropping his voice. "The rest came from my parents."

"Oh," I said. I was starting to feel flushed, even desperate. Every step I was taking was leading to a dead end. "Look, things are gonna work out. You just need to believe that we'll prevail. I believe it."

On Delilah's Instagram, she'd talked a lot about The Secret, a system of manifesting the life that you want for yourself by simply believing it will happen. "I'm feeling really good about our entry for Delilah's contest, as a matter of fact."

Will snorted. "You and thousands of other entrants," he said. "Sorry, I just haven't bought into the notion that some reality TV chick is going to be our knight in shining armor."

"She's not just some 'reality TV chick,'" I said. "We're talking about Delilah. She's a pioneer, an entrepreneur, an activist." *And unlike you, she's actually a genuine person*, I wanted to add. I stood up, my heart fluttering, feeling like I might be sick. "I'll be right back."

I went around the corner and locked myself in the bathroom, where I closed my eyes and took deep breaths. Will's string of half-truths made me dizzy. I needed to talk to someone. Who could I trust to help me hash things out? I couldn't talk to Heather, who was counting on me as a role model. My parents were also a no-go. I hadn't even told them about Will. I knew they'd dislike him. They were firm believers in telling the truth, even if it was often stinging with bitterness. No, calling them would not be an option. I'd need to sort this out on my own. I nodded at my reflection as though to affirm this fact. When I felt composed enough, I returned to the counter, ready to call Will out for blindsiding me with all his bullshit. But I found him hunched over his phone, a startled expression on his face.

"Did you see the email that just came in?" Will said.

"What email?" I said.

"It's from Delilah—I mean, her production assistant," Will said. "We advanced to the next round of the contest."

I grabbed his phone and read the message. "Oh my God! What did I literally just say about The Secret? It's manifesting right now!" I threw my arms around him and jumped up and down.

"Okay, calm down, we haven't won anything yet," Will said, his face flushed. "There's a link to a personalized video message from Delilah. Do you want to go back to WagWorld and watch?"

"Of course I do, what kind of insane question is that?" I plopped $40 on the counter. "Keep the change!" I yelled, grabbing Will's hand. My angst evaporated. I reveled in the stares from the diners, how the chatter in the restaurant grew quiet: I had become someone to watch.

★

We told Heather the news as soon as we stepped back into WagWorld, and whatever had been bothering her before we left seemed to instantly dissipate. She grabbed my hands, and we squealed, provoking excitable barks from the dogs in their crates and playpens.

"Quiet," Will said, chiding us like schoolchildren who had misbehaved. We huddled behind his MacBook Pro and caught our breath as he clicked the link for Delilah's personalized video message. It was not Delilah looking into the camera, but an avatar of a Pomeranian wearing sunglasses. Once we clicked play it said, "Hey! Delilah here." Will paused and turned to look at us, his face curdling into something sour.

"Is this some kind of joke?"

"Relax," I said. "If you watched her show you'd know she's obsessed with her pet Pomeranian, Lucy." Though, to be honest, I found it a bit ridiculous. Was Delilah not even going to show her face? I kept my disappointment contained as Will pressed play once again.

"Will and Jess, I was fascinated by the WagWorld origin story," her avatar continued. "And, well, who wouldn't want to support an organization focused on finding homes for sweet dogs? You are truly making a difference. As finalists in this competition, you're now one step closer to winning the $100,000 grand prize and the chance to appear on my show as special guests. All of this will be announced at our philanthropy gala at the Palencia Hotel next week, which you are cordially invited to." The Pomeranian shook its head and slowly morphed, its reddish-yellow fur transformed into Delilah's strawberry-blonde curls. Heather and I squealed as the creature took off its sunglasses to reveal Delilah herself, in blue eyeshadow and rhinestone speckles, her wink like a magic trick. "So now that you're in the finals," Delilah continued, "you'll really need to demonstrate your tenacity and inventiveness as an organization. Every enterprise needs to have multiple irons in the fire. I want to see what tricks WagWorld has up its sleeve. Before next week's gala, submit an overview of any existing upcoming campaigns and any other high-level visions you have to scale your impact. I'll be keeping an eye on your social media as well, so be bold and strategic as to how you grow your following. And remember: more videos, more content—you can't become irrelevant. Good luck." Delilah waved and blew a kiss before the screen turned black.

"Oh my God," Will said. "All of that by next week? That's so much work."

"It won't be too bad," I said, doing some quick calculations in my head. We hardly suffered from a lack of social media content. Still, I felt that some inspirational X-factor was missing.

"You know," I finally said after a contemplative pause, "we should focus a lot of our communications around our microchip campaign. That's a really special value add."

"Great idea," Will said, nodding with gusto. "Let's lean into that."

"Wait," Heather said while holding up her hand. "Hang on a second. What's actually going on here? When I called Dr. Peters and asked if Coco's itching could have been caused by a microchip he said none of the dogs from WagWorld had been microchipped yet."

"That's ridiculous," I said, looking over at Will. "The microchip campaign is one of our biggest successes!"

"Look, we're going to get to it," Will said. "We've been in some hard times financially, but things are turning around. There's no need to get Dr. Peters involved."

"Did you know that nothing was happening on this front?" Heather asked me.

I was stuck at an impasse. On the one hand, I was seething that Will was shaping up to be a full-fledged liar. But on the other hand, I knew we were closer to Delilah's coveted world than ever before. "Look," I finally said. "We've made it to the finals. We've got a lot of work to do in the next few days. As soon as we complete the final round of materials, we'll take all the dogs to get microchipped, okay? That's the best we can do."

"Where I come from, the best you can do is actually following through on what you say you're going to do," Heather said, her voice quivering. "I mean, between the fake film shoots and flat-out lying about campaigns, I have no idea what you guys stand for. The dogs deserve better." Her blue eyes locked onto mine, appraising me coldly. "Delilah deserves better."

I stepped back, as if I'd been slapped. In my moment of hurt, I wanted to tell Heather that she was no Mother Teresa. That she spent way too much money on pressed juices and online shopping, and that her need to demonstrate her goodness and morality was an act of vanity, as selfish as anything else. But I knew that wasn't true. She was a good person who genuinely cared about the dogs, and she was one of my only friends in L.A. Who else was I going to be able to debrief with when something crazy happened on *Day-to-Day with Delilah*?

"Look, Heather, you need to calm down," I said, speaking carefully. "You don't know what you're talking about."

"But I do," Heather said. "You guys are lying, and that's a fact."

I loved attention, that much was true, but I had never knowingly lied. That accusation stung. Where did she get off telling me that? And even though a big part of me wanted to yell at Will, an actual liar, a bigger part of me wanted to address Heather, who was folding her arms and glaring at me as if I were trash.

"Stop acting like you're Delilah's friend. You don't know her, and she sure as hell doesn't know you. Nobody knows you. You have like thirty followers on Instagram. It's pathetic and sad."

"If anyone's pathetic here, it's you," Heather said. "You seem to be under the delusion that you're some kind of inspiring influencer. I feel sorry for you, I really do. And I quit," Heather said, slamming the door as she left.

★

"How could you!" I yelled at Will. "You're so shady!"

Will said, "I'm the same guy I've always been."

I wanted to tell him that who he had always been was turning out to be the problem. But then he wrapped his arms around my waist and started kissing my neck. The grazing of his lips made me momentarily forget my life story, the twenty-two years of scrimping and striving that had somehow led me to this. "Don't worry about Heather," he whispered into my ear. "Nobody's going to listen to her. She only has thirty followers on Instagram, like you said."

I pulled away. "This isn't even about Heather. It's about you. I can't trust you. We need to get the damn dogs microchipped."

"Look," Will said. "We're in major debt. Dr. Peters' rates are basically highway robbery, so we're not paying for *any* microchipping until we get another influx of cash. And I'm getting tired of all these accusations about my character. I lied about a few things. So what? Return to your barista job or jet back to Fresno and crash with your parents if you think I'm so terrible."

"Fuck you," I said. "You wouldn't have even entered this contest if it wasn't for me."

"I'm not denying it," Will said. He wrapped his arms around me again. "So let's just acknowledge that we need each other and get on with our lives. We have a lot of work to do."

That much I couldn't argue with. "Fine," I said. I broke away from his embrace and grabbed a dry-erase pen, anger vibrating through my fingertips. "Let's brainstorm."

★

For the next few days, we tried to put our differences aside and focus solely on content creation. I livestreamed Will working the stand at the Farmers Market, regaling shoppers with the story of Daisy Duke's grisly past followed by her happily ever after. We filmed Spartacus crawling out of a broken cardboard box in Canoga Park near a sad stretch of the Los Angeles River. We captured candid footage around the rescue of dogs burrowing snouts into kibble, fetching tennis balls, and chasing one another.

It was after one of these marathon livestreaming sessions that I saw the first cryptic Instagram post from Heather. In the sepia-toned picture, she was sitting in a bare room, looking off into the distance at an apocalyptic-looking sky. *There's no legacy as rich as honesty*, the caption read.

"What the fuck is she talking about?" I muttered under my breath.

"What?" Will said, but I shook my head. There was no time for distractions. We needed to make more content. But my conscience had begun to gnaw at me.

★

The day before the gala, eager to alleviate my guilt, I paid out of pocket to get all thirty dogs microchipped without Will's knowledge. Dr. Peters' prices were too steep for my budget, so I took the dogs to a vet clinic down the street from his office. I was now down $500 that I needed for next month's rent, but I felt lighter than I had in days, so I convinced myself it was all worth it.

"We took care of it. I have receipts to prove it," I DM'ed Heather, my chest bursting with moral righteousness.

I'm not sure what I was expecting in return. An apology for insulting my character would have been nice. Some general well-wishes would have worked. Even an "OK" would have sufficed. Instead, she replied, "Too little too late. There's corruption all over the place."

Moments later, a new post appeared on Instagram. She was staring at her reflection under the garish light of what was probably her depressing dorm bathroom, a tear rolling down her cheek. *Gaslight: to manipulate someone by psychological means into questioning their sanity*, her caption read. And then, a moment later, another post, this time only a fist raised in the air and the caption, *Justice will soon be served.*

"For fuck's sake," I said out loud. "At least use a better filter."

But that night, Heather's surge of Instagram activity wormed its way through my brain, leaving me unable to sleep. In the dark, I watched a *Day-to-Day with Delilah* rerun in which Delilah consoled a friend who had been strung along by a married man. Her voice, as always, was reassuring and empowering. But still the hamster wheel of my mind wouldn't stop turning: Heather's ambiguous posts taunting me, threatening to expose even more than I knew.

★

The next night was the gala, and it wasn't long until the intention behind Heather's flurry of posts revealed itself. Will and I had just stepped out of the Uber in front of the Palencia Hotel when we saw them: Heather and ten or so other protestors across the street marching with posters that said: "Companies for a good cause? Wag-World isn't one of them." One woman I didn't recognize stood on a bench and shouted into her bullhorn: "Wag-World stages animal cruelty videos! They're all a lie!" She held up an enlarged photo of Daisy Duke sprawled on the asphalt with a red circle around the scar on her leg and a caption that said, "Photoshopped."

I thought of Daisy's pink scar. In a certain light, it looked like it had been applied with a marker. That would be next-level sociopathic, even for Will. Daisy Duke's video was supposed to be the real video, the video that justified the rest of the "fake videos" that followed. I felt like I was going to hurl.

"Jesus Christ, Will," I said. "That's not true, right?"

"Relax," Will said, and he smiled, unbothered, as he brushed a tendril of hair out of my face. "She's just a hater. We'll find some way to use this to our advantage."

"To our advantage? Are you insane? How do you possibly think we can worm our way out of *this*?"

But, as it turned out, there really wasn't even time for Will to answer. It was right then that a stretch limousine pulled up alongside us and a horde of photographers and paparazzi descended from the hotel to the street.

"Delilah!" they yelled as my idol stepped out of the limo, flashbulbs igniting in unison to capture her in her ruffled gown, stilettos, and pearls.

"Delilah, who are you wearing tonight? How are you feeling about the gala? The protest across the street?"

Delilah made no reply. She rested her hand on her hip as she posed for pictures, her reddish blonde curls blowing whimsically in the wind. For a moment, we locked eyes, and her mouth curled upwards into the thinnest semblance of a smile. But I couldn't tell if the smile was one of warmth or well-masked derision.

"Will and Jess?" Delilah said. "Come with me."

Will and I obliged, though it felt as if we were in two parallel universes: he strutted, carefree, while I did my best to move one foot in front of the other and ignore the frog of desperation jumping in my throat. This was my moment. I needed Delilah to know what was in my heart. I might be flawed but essentially good.

"I have to say, I'm impressed: you've got a real knack for reality TV," Delilah said when we approached. She continued to smile for the cameras before briefly looking at the commotion across the street. "I mean, you've got strangers from the internet gathered here to yell at you! That means you're relevant. And that's the most important thing, right?"

Will smiled as he followed Delilah toward the entrance. But her question hung over me, and under the glare of a hundred lenses, I stayed outside, unable to think of anything else.

ON A SCALE OF ONE TO TEN

LAURA MCGHEE

It happened so quickly.

One minute Joanne was enjoying yet another free drink as she danced blissfully to INXS, and then …

She was wearing a groove in her favorite barstool while she hunted through her imitation Gucci purse for a usable credit card. The former bartender, Mitch, used to slide her free Cosmos, but those days, and Mitch, were long gone. The present bartender was a surly twenty-something named Cody, who seemed confused to find himself serving alcohol for a living. Yet still she frequented L'Autre Femme because it was better than sitting at home alone. But now Joanne's budget limited her to two drinks per night, and she always asked for Pinot so as not to antagonize Cody with a cocktail order. She didn't dance much anymore either. Not that anyone was asking. It wasn't that she was naïve enough to refute the inevitability of irrelevance; she was merely surprised that it was so abrupt and intractable. She thought she had a few more years. She needed more time to adjust to being invisible.

A single attempt to buy more time in the form of Botox was aborted in the clinic several months ago. Joanne was deathly afraid of needles. She also didn't have an emergency contact, so when she reached that part of the form, she placed the clipboard on the seat and walked out. Instead, she treated herself to a hamburger and a chocolate shake at In-N-Out, which she hadn't had in over twenty years, and then waddled home with a bloated belly to her two-bedroom Studio City apartment. Joanne had lived there since 1991, when she had moved to L.A. from Minneapolis with an ambitious girlfriend who was going to give supermodel Christie Brinkley a run for her money. Joanne had no plan of her own, she was just along for the ride. The girlfriend had since moved on to operate a daycare in Prescott, Arizona, and there had been a constant stream of roommates ever since. Long-term roommates never seemed to work out—male or female, but for different reasons—so Joanne entertained short-term lessees, usually actors from saner parts of the country coming in for auditions or guest roles. This revolving door of roommates was partially responsible for Joanne's lack of perspective. The roommates were always in their twenties, so she began to forget that she was *not* anymore. Plus, unlike many of her contemporaries, Joanne didn't have children, whose growth marks the passage of time.

At the moment, the second bedroom was vacant and had been longer than ever. Joanne would be unable to live there much longer without the extra income. Her dental receptionist job paid barely more than minimum wage, and she had no savings. If only memories could be monetized.

Even with Joanne's recent abandonment of personal upkeep, cash flow was still tight. Once she accepted society's disregard for her chief currency, she leaned into the notion of not being seen. She gave up coloring her hair, wearing contacts, and rarely bothered with makeup other than Chapstick. Her clothing expenses were negligible. She wore scrubs to work and, in the evenings, sported the same old Diane Von Furstenberg-inspired wraparound dress to the wine bar. She had, however, replaced the high-heeled boots with orthopedic sandals. If she was going to be invisible, she might as well be comfortable.

Entering the office on that Monday morning, still fifteen minutes late as always, despite needing no prep time these days, she was thinking about the fact she only had enough in her checking account to pay rent for another two months. She was so preoccupied with her financial situation that she failed to notice someone sitting in her chair behind the counter until that person waved at her with vigor. She was maybe twenty-two and certainly gorgeous, like Jill St. John but with longer hair and a smaller nose.

"You must be Joanne. I'm Taylor. So pleased to meet you!"

Joanne ignored the social protocol and cut to the chase. "Am I being replaced by a younger model?"

Taylor laughed and then stopped abruptly when she realized it wasn't a joke.

Her boss, Dr. Gilchrist, Dr. G, was with a patient already. Joanne could hear him delivering his usual reassuring patter. "On a scale of one to ten, tell me how much it hurts, okay? We don't want anything higher than a three."

"I think I'm supposed to help you?" Taylor looked panicked. "I'm Maureen's second cousin."

Maureen was Dr. G's wife. She had run the dental office from the time that Joanne had started working there in her twenties. Joanne thought that working with a husband-and-wife team would be a recipe for disaster, but the two had a solid marriage. Even all these years later, Joanne would often catch them smooching in the X-ray room, and Dr. G had fresh flowers delivered to the office every Friday, one pink carnation for every year together. They had both been wonderful to work for, one of the reasons that Joanne had never moved on. Dr. G was a kind, old hippie—complete with gray ponytail—who gave her time off whenever she asked for it, and didn't charge for her own dental work. Maureen had never seemed threatened by the younger Joanne's looks, which was a rarity in L.A. This work relationship had been the longest relationship Joanne had ever had.

"I don't understand," Joanne said. "Where's Maureen?"

"Um, Dr. G told me she decided to retire; wanted to spend more time with the grandkids, I guess."

"Nobody told me."

"I guess Maureen told him Friday night that she wasn't coming back."

"Must be nice," Joanne said uncharitably. "I would love to be able to walk away from a job knowing that someone else was going to pick up the slack."

Taylor made a face. "Not me. I would absolutely hate to be dependent on another person. Anyway, my mom and I were visiting from Bakersfield, so the timing was perfect. I was wanting to move down here to pursue my acting career, and now I have the ideal day job. Dr. G said that I can leave anytime I have an audition. Isn't he the nicest man on Earth?"

"He really is," Joanne admitted.

Taylor emitted a tiny squeal. "It really feels like everything in my life is aligning. Two months ago, I was starring in my high school's production of *Rent*. We weren't allowed to talk about AIDS, so we gave the characters COVID, and now I am literally in the middle of Studio City! The only piece of the puzzle left is finding a place to live."

★

Joanne had to give herself a hearty pat on the back. The situation with Taylor was working out beautifully. She was a reliable and conscientious roommate, tidy and unobtrusive, and her day job guaranteed she paid her share of the rent on time. On the rare occasions that she was home, she mostly sat in her room and scrolled on her phone. From time to time, she asked Joanne to help her film a TikTok video, but Joanne didn't mind. It was actually fun. Taylor always took her advice on looks, angles, and locations, which was flattering. It gave her a warm feeling of mentorship, like an older sister.

At work, the dynamic continued. Joanne let Taylor take care of the reception desk while she completed the paperwork and billing. It was a relief not to have to flirt with the male patients. She didn't realize how exhausting it was until she didn't have to do it. She didn't miss the attention at all.

The potential problem of being left to manage alone while Taylor went on auditions had also amounted to nothing. After two months, Taylor hadn't had a single audition. Joanne refrained from mentioning it; she didn't want to seem unkind. She also didn't want the situation to change. In fact, the only tangible inroad Taylor had made in her acting career was the scene study class that she took on Tuesday and Thursday evenings on Melrose. Her first public performance was coming up in a few days, and she was visibly jittery.

"You're still coming, right?" she asked.

"Of course. I said I would."

"I know, I know. It's just that everyone here is so flaky. Not that you are. That's not what I meant. Everyone else I've invited has bailed. And I have a potential agent coming. So, I need a papered house, as they say in the biz."

"I'll be there in the front row, cheering you on. You can count on me." It felt good to say that. She refrained from adding that the agent would likely be a no show. "Which scene did you decide on?"

Taylor clapped her hands lightly. "The *SVU* scene, you know, from the episode that Martin Short was in."

"When he was a pedophile?"

"Rapist."

"Ooh, that was a good one."

Taylor nodded vigorously. "I know, right? And my scene study partner is amazing in the role. He used to be an airline pilot in Denver, but he quit his job and moved here, away from his wife and kids, so he could pursue his dream. Isn't that brave?"

"It's something. Are you playing Mariska Hargitay?"

Taylor corrected her. "Detective Olivia Benson. I hope I do her justice!"

Joanne smiled. "No pun intended."

"What do you mean?"

★

It happened so quickly.

One minute Joanne was shopping for a new lipstick, and then …

She had a couple of hours to kill between work and Taylor's showcase, so she decided to treat herself to a new shade. Most of her older lip colors were bright or bold. She had traditionally favored fire-engine red. Now she needed something more subtle. There was no need to draw attention to the labyrinth of wrinkles surrounding her mouth. She parked on a side street, believing that she had correctly deciphered the parking sign without her glasses and wouldn't get a ticket, and sashayed into a MAC store.

The store was busy with both prom season and Pride month. Joanne tried a neutral shade on her inner wrist. She was trying a second color when she was bumped from behind and the lipstick smeared up her forearm. She turned to face a striking six-foot vision in a chartreuse silk jumpsuit. The person, gender indeterminable, slapped their hands together in a gesture of supplication.

"Sorry, hon, didn't see you."

Joanne tried a few more colors until she found one she could tolerate, called "Barely There," but the rack was empty. She looked around for a sales associate, but they were all occupied. She walked up to the busy cash register.

"Excuse me."

"Someone will be with you in just a moment, ma'am."

A mother and daughter waiting to pay glared at her. "There's a line," the mom said.

Smarting, Joanne returned to the lipstick display. A black-smocked associate breezed past her.

"Excuse me."

They kept on going. Joanne was starting to sweat. The store was even more crowded now. She wanted to leave but had invested enough time that she didn't want to depart empty-handed. She looked around. Nobody was paying attention. She opened the drawers beneath the display case and found a tube of "Barely There." Then she headed back to the cash register, but now the line was twice as long.

Joanne turned to put the lipstick back in the drawer. But then she didn't.

Instead, she clenched it in her fist and waltzed out the door.

Nobody yelled. Nobody followed. Nobody noticed. She was invisible.

★

The adrenaline rush was unlike anything Joanne had ever experienced. It was so intense that she could hardly focus on Taylor's scene. Taylor was fortunate to have a day job. She was wooden and self-conscious to the point where Joanne felt embarrassed for her. The pilot, however, was impressive. Wasn't that always the way? Some people seemed to be good at everything while the rest weren't good at anything. Joanne compiled a list of innocuous compliments that she could pay Taylor afterward: "How do you remember all of those lines?" "You really looked like you were having fun up there."

When the curtain call ended, Joanne waited patiently while a short man, slicked-backed dark hair, pressed jeans with dress shoes, approached Taylor. *Good*, Joanne thought, *the agent showed up after all*. But it wasn't good. A curt exchange resulted in Taylor bursting into tears as the man beat a hasty retreat. Joanne rushed to comfort her.

"Was that the agent?"

Taylor gulped back a sob. "He's not going to represent me."

"Why?" Joanne asked, although she knew the answer.

"He said I have no talent."

"Lots of famous actors have no talent."

"He also said I wasn't pretty enough to have no talent. He said that I may be a ten in Bakersfield, but I'm only a six in L.A." This evoked a fresh burst of tears. "I don't understand that, Joanne. How can I be more attractive in one place than another? I look the same everywhere."

Joanne gently led her into the ladies' room to clean up. "Never mind about him. You're definitely pretty enough to be a famous actor." She used her compact to alleviate the redness that had pervaded Taylor's face and wiped the smeared eyeliner off her cheeks while carefully avoiding her own reflection in the mirror. "How about this? Why don't I take you to my favorite watering hole for a nightcap, my treat."

Taylor sniffed back her tears. "That's really nice of you. That's a great shade of lipstick, by the way."

Less than a week passed before Joanne shoplifted again. This time it was an eye mask from CVS. Then it was a pair of earrings from Macy's, nail polish from Ulta, night cream from Target. She was always careful not to pilfer anything too large or too expensive. The item must fit in her palm for easy concealment and have no security tag. She didn't feel any guilt or remorse. These stores had insurance. Besides, they price gouged. It served them right. Instead, Joanne felt invigorated by her delicious little secret. She no longer felt invisible. She felt invincible.

One evening, she accidentally took a bracelet from Kohl's that had a sensor on it. The alarm shrieked as she exited the store. Her heart stopped as she heard footsteps behind her. She forced herself to walk normally and not turn around. A security guard brushed past her and stopped a group of teenage girls ahead of her. She pivoted to her Camry, where she had a massive anxiety attack. Getting arrested for shoplifting, especially at her age, would be humiliating. The risk wasn't worth the reward. She vowed to stop stealing. And she did. For a while.

Taylor brooded about her artistic trauma for a few weeks after the disastrous showcase, but then she enrolled in an improv class at the Upright Citizens Brigade and met Ryan. He was respectful of Taylor, supportive, and old-fashioned when it came to picking up the check. Joanne hoped Taylor would abandon her dreams of stardom and settle down with him. Ryan wasn't an actor. He had a solid job in advertising and took improv classes for fun. He was such a gentleman that he had even offered to contribute toward their rent since he stayed over so often. Joanne didn't feel comfortable with that, but she let him treat them to Door Dash a few times a week.

The three of them had settled into a comfortable routine until one Thursday afternoon. Dr. G was performing a root canal while she filed insurance claims and Taylor scrolled through social media.

"On a scale of one to ten, how much does it hurt?" Dr. G's voice drifted from the next room. The patient's response was muffled.

Taylor had her ear buds in, so she probably was unaware of how loud her sudden cackle was.

Joanne waved at her. "What's so funny?"

Taylor removed the left ear bud. "I can't with this! This bank robber, he got caught because he wrote his instructions for the teller on the back of his gas bill. It had his name and address on it and everything." She laughed again and tried to muffle the sound by covering her mouth. A new shiny bangle Joanne had bought her reflected the light. Taylor had loved that the initial Joanne chose was "S" for "Superstar," instead of "T" for "Taylor." "It's so much more meaningful," Taylor had said.

Joanne shook her head. "You know that story doesn't surprise me. Truly, most criminals are so dumb. They're literally begging to be caught. I once read about a guy who robbed the branch where he worked. He wore a mask, but the teller recognized his voice. Honestly."

Taylor chortled. "Stop it! You're making that up!"

Joanne giggled. "Swear on my life," she said in a bad imitation of the guy. "Empty out your cash drawer. No small bills."

Taylor played along. "Phil, is that you? Is this why you called in sick today?"

Joanne laughed.

"You have such a great laugh, Joanne, like, it really fills up the whole room."

They were enjoying themselves so much that they didn't notice that Dr. G had joined them while his patient rinsed. He had been trying to find a good time to break the news that he had decided to retire. He missed Maureen too much. He was going to close the practice at the end of the month. But he knew they would both be fine. Taylor's acting career was surely about to blow up, and Joanne was going to be retiring pretty soon, right?

★

"Oh no," Taylor said after she read the notice taped to their front door.

"What is it?" Joanne asked as she came up behind.

"They sold the building! They're tearing it down to build condos!"

Joanne grabbed the notice, reading it as Taylor unlocked the door. Oddly, Joanne wasn't shocked. The complex was a tired 1960s-style stucco motel with a wraparound walkway. The layout had a central courtyard and a small pool with algae and chipped mosaic tiles. It was only a matter of time before it was replaced by something newer and prettier. It had gone from looking good to looking good for its age to not looking good for *any* age. Joanne should have anticipated this shift and moved, but change was so exhausting, especially when your options were limited. It was the same paradigm at work. She knew deep down that Dr. G would retire soon—he was over seventy—but she somehow assumed he'd keep working.

"What are we going to do?" Taylor wailed as she collapsed onto the sofa.

Joanne beelined to the fridge and grabbed a bottle of Sauvignon Blanc. "First of all, we're going to drink the rest of this." She poured two glasses and handed one to Taylor.

"I'm still on that cleanse."

"Drink your medicine."

Taylor acquiesced. "I'm really worried, Joanne. First, our jobs, now our apartment."

"You'll get another job in a hot minute. You're young and beautiful."

Taylor was not convinced. "I'm an L.A. six."

"Don't be silly," Joanne said without hesitation. "Trust me. You'll be fine. Can you move in with Ryan?"

Taylor shook her head. "He lives with his parents."

Joanne's eyebrows went up. "Really? But he's got a full-time job."

Taylor patted her arm. "It's L.A., Joanne. Everyone in their twenties lives with their parents. What about you? What are you going to do? Could you move in with your family?"

"Um, no. No, I don't think so."

Taylor chugged the last of her wine. "I'm going to have to go back to Bakersfield. Do you want me to see if you can come? I mean, my parents are basically your age. You'd have tons in common."

Joanne couldn't repress a shudder. "I have a better idea. Let's go to L'Autre Femme and get drunk."

"We can't afford it."

"Who cares?"

They finished the bottle and toddled off to the wine bar. Joanne ordered Cosmos because Taylor was with her, and Cody the bartender couldn't drag that cranberry juice from the back of the bar fridge quickly enough. They kept the party going. Men were sending over new drinks before they'd even finished their current ones. This time when vintage INXS came on, Joanne danced, grinding and twirling in her wraparound dress, not noticing that those same men were rolling their eyes and smirking at her. Until she did.

★

The next day, Dr. G announced that he and Maureen had bought a yacht, and they were going to keep it in Marina del Rey so they could travel back and forth to their new place on Catalina Island.

"Did you know that Dr. G had that kind of money?" Taylor whispered.

Joanne did not. If she had, she might have been less reverential to the bonds of matrimony, especially in the last few years. Now it was too late. To add insult to injury, Dr. G had her go to his bank to arrange a certified check for the boat deposit. She hadn't been to a bank in ages. Even though it was lunchtime, there were only a few people in line, all senior citizens, so she reached the only teller quickly.

"Where's the security guard?" she asked the slightly built, prematurely balding man. She remembered tellers as being more attractive and female.

"We haven't had one in forever. What's the point? Most robberies now are online fraud. The only people who do their banking in person anymore are the elderly." He realized his gaffe and blushed. "Sorry. You know, you could have done a wire transfer on the app. It would have been much more convenient."

Joanne exited the bank but instead of returning to the dental office, she marched across the street into another bank. No security guard. One woman with gray hair and a shopping cart was at the teller window. Then she texted Taylor that she wasn't feeling well and was going to go home and lie down. Joanne spent the rest of the afternoon visiting bank branches. They were all virtually empty and only one had a security guard, who was so aged that he looked like a skeleton in uniform. The weight of his gun dragged his pants down.

Joanne called in sick for the rest of the week.

★

From the outside, it might have seemed unreasonable that Joanne's criminality escalated that quickly. On the inside, though, there was a sharp, visceral desperation that eliminated the intermediary steps. At her age, what hope was there? Who was going to hire her? Without a job, how could she lease an apartment? The grim reality was that nobody was coming to save her. At first, Joanne was going to walk in and hand the teller a note, which she would retrieve and take with her along with the money. But then she reconsidered. Although she could capitalize on her real-life invisibility, she wouldn't be invisible on security cameras. There was also the potential for social media viral sensations with ubiquitous phone cameras. She had seen people lose their jobs after videos had been posted. She stood to lose a lot more than that.

Joanne decided to make herself as visible as possible in direct contradiction of her everyday life. Like all older women, the polarized choices of either social specter or cosmetic clown were the only options. She embraced the latter. On Friday afternoon, right after lunch, when everyone was sluggish and less alert, an ample woman in a bright pink jumpsuit (padded) and heels (excruciating) strutted into a bank in Westwood. The woman had a mass of curly blond hair (Dolly Parton wig) and a heavy mask of makeup with false eyelashes and cerise lipstick that matched the jumpsuit. Given the usual clientele, everyone turned to gaze at her, mostly in pity.

That was exactly what Joanne wanted, the attention. She glided across the marble floor and got in line behind an elderly woman. Then a tiny face peered up at Joanne from behind the woman's legs.

"Hi."

Shit. Grandma must be babysitting.

"Hi." The little girl was not going to give up.

The grandmother tried to shush her, but she was a bored little girl in a bank. "Hi."

Joanne was conflicted. She had to remain silent. She didn't want to risk voice recognition. She tried a little wave.

"My name's Violet. What's yours?"

Thankfully, the teller called for the next customer and Violet was whisked away, but not before she called out, "You are a beautiful princess!"

Joanne couldn't help herself. She burst into laughter, which immediately calmed her nerves, so much so that when it was her turn, after waving goodbye to the grandma and her young charge, she waltzed up to the window and slid her note across the counter.

Minutes later, Joanne walked briskly out of the bank, carrying a pink tote with the money and the retrieved note and entered a neighboring alley. She crouched behind a dumpster where she'd stashed a black duffel bag. Inside the bag were a pair of polyester pants with elastic waistband, an oversized cardigan, a pair of slip-ons and makeup remover pads. She doffed the wig, changed clothes, and wiped the makeup off as best she could. She threw everything in the duffel bag and grabbed the empty Starbucks cup that she had also stashed.

She waited until the police arrived and then strolled right past the bank, sipping her Starbucks. Completely invisible. Completely invincible.

"Good news!" Taylor yelled as Joanne walked through the door. "Dr. G is getting a divorce!"

"What?"

"He told me this afternoon. He also said he hoped you're feeling better."

"Why is that good news? Wait, why is he getting divorced?"

"Mrs. G left him. I know, they seemed so tight, right? She's moving to Portugal for some reason. I don't even know where that is."

"I still don't understand why that's good news," Joanne said.

"Because now he can't afford to retire. He's got two homes, a boat, and he'll have alimony. Our jobs are saved!"

Joanne sank into the nearest chair. "That still doesn't solve our housing problem."

Taylor clapped her hands with glee. "That's the best part! Dr. G said that he can't stand living in the house now, too many painful memories. He's going to live on his boat and said we can sublet his place. Isn't that unbelievable!"

Joanne sat stunned. "It is. Unbelievable."

"I've been waiting for you to get home so we can go out and celebrate. Go and change. No offense, but that outfit makes you look like an old lady."

★

It happened so quickly.

One minute Joanne was celebrating her change in fortune, and then ...

The two of them were perched at the bar. Cody the bartender comped the first round and then left to take orders from a couple at the other end of the bar. His departure sparked the open stares of three men seated in the middle. Taylor didn't notice, but Joanne did.

"Cheers." Taylor raised her glass to Joanne's.

"Cheers."

"Hey, where were you today? I was surprised when you weren't home. You seemed legit sick earlier."

Joanne wasn't expecting this sudden need for an alibi. Taylor was usually so self-involved. "I was out looking at apartments. Nothing good."

"Well, now you don't have to look anymore. Cheers!"

"Cheers to that." Joanne thought that would be the end of Taylor's curiosity.

"What was in that bag? It looked heavy."

"Um, just income tax stuff. My accountant's been nagging me to come and pick it up for months."

"You have an accountant? That's really grown up."

Mercifully, the first of many free drinks were delivered by Cody, which clipped the conversation. The libations continued to flow. Taylor told Cody it was Joanne's birthday, so that was good for another round. Then some older gentlemen caught the alcohol altruist bug. Joanne enjoyed the irony of now having more than enough money to cover the tab, yet hadn't had to pay for a single drink. She did, however, check her phone continually for any news about the robbery. There had been a few news items immediately following the hold-up; fortunately, a tractor trailer had jackknifed on the I-5 during rush hour, which eclipsed the heist. Now a shooting on Hollywood Boulevard had overtaken the media's interest, so Joanne was confident that the robbery would be overlooked entirely.

She decided to let her guard down and enjoy herself fully. After a few hours, and a collection of empty glasses and discarded garnishes, Joanne was on the dance floor exhibiting complete abandonment. She didn't even care if those idiots at the bar were snickering. They would never guess her secret, and that gave her a renewed sense of value. She had gotten away with it and now she could probably make a play for Dr. G. For once, the rewards were commensurate with the effort.

She and Taylor spun each other around on the dance floor to "Need You Tonight."

"On a scale of one to ten, how much does it hurt?" Taylor yelled drunkenly.

"One!" Joanne yelled back. That was only because her bunion was inflamed. She indicated that she had to go to the "little girls' room" and shimmied off the floor.

Taylor kept dancing. "You're a Bakersfield ten, baby!"

Joanne guffawed. "Honey, we're *all* Bakersfield tens!"

It was her laugh.

The laugh that filled up the whole room.

The bank teller didn't live anywhere near L'Autre Femme, but he had just picked up his partner from

Cedars-Sinai Medical Center. His love was always exhausted after radiation, but the teller had been so distraught from the robbery that they agreed to stop at the bar. The couple was now camped out in a back booth, aspiring to attain physical and emotional homeostasis with the help of double vodkas on the rocks.

The police arrived with striking speed. Two officers in riot gear ran through the bar to the restrooms. They escorted Joanne out the rear door and loaded her into a patrol car. They took her to the North Hollywood station, where she was Mirandized, fingerprinted, and mugshotted. Given her gender and age, news outlets jumped on the story. Security camera footage of her in the bank was juxtaposed on screens with her mugshots.

After she was booked, Joanne was given her one phone call. She was advised to contact a lawyer. But she didn't have a lawyer or even know one. She was still in shock. The gravity of her predicament hadn't yet sunk in. The only person that Joanne could think of calling was Taylor.

Taylor answered on the first ring. "Joanne! Oh my fucking god! What is going on? You never came back from the bathroom, and then the police were running through, and everyone was evacuated. They wouldn't tell us anything, then my phone blew up. I just saw your mugshot on *TMZ*! Your face is everywhere!"

There was a very long pause.

"How did I look?"

DRIVING THE BAND

AMY JONES SEDIVY

I should not have taken the 405. I know better than to get to the airport this way. I will be stuck on the 405 all the way past the 10 and all the way to the airport. If I don't get there in time, they will take a shuttle and then I won't know what hotel they will be at, and I could call Niall's cell phone or the others' cell phones but they almost never turn them on. If I am not there to pick them up in the van I had to rent, then they will take a shuttle and they will go to a hotel and I won't know which hotel and it will be hours, if not the next day, before one of them turns their cellphone on, or someone thinks to call me and ask where I am.

So yes, I'm pissed off sitting in this traffic and not moving. And they would say, pissed, that's getting drunk, you American girl. They think I'm funny. You know, the alternative rock group called The Hyperboreans? Second album sold like 10 million copies, everyone's waiting for the third album? And they will be waiting for me, or not waiting if I don't fucking get to the airport.

Planes are coming in over L.A. toward the airport. I think one of those could be the plane they are on. I imagine them sitting in first class and the young people on the plane, when they walk through first class, see the band members sitting there and go back to their coach seats whispering, did you see? Did you see who that was?

I check the dashboard clock and their plane would have landed just a few minutes ago and I figure by the time they are off and they get their bags and go through customs, I've got forty-five minutes before they will be looking for me, and with any luck I can get from the Sunset exit, past the 10 and down to LAX in forty-five minutes.

There is no point to me. I am a pointless person. I am not a girlfriend of any of the band members. I am not a groupie, I am not a manager, a PR rep, a record company rep, or any kind of rep. I am called a personal assistant. When they come to L.A., I do everything for them, the everything kind of things that no one else will do because they are too high and mighty to do them. No record company rep will go out at midnight to find McVitie's cookies that Henry craves (gotta feed the drummer) and which are available only at one store (closed at nine) and one bar (open until two a.m.) in all of Los Angeles.

"How do you know everything?" Niall asked me the very first time I worked for them. We were standing in the lobby of a Best Western in east Hollywood—this was four years ago when they stayed in normal motels and not the upscale, high-security places they stay in now—waiting for Henry to finish his incredibly long phone call with his wife back in England. "How do you know where to buy our cookies near the ocean and how to park in Hollywood without paying anything and the best newsstand to get the British press, and it's way the bloody hell over that mountain?"

"Hill," I said. "The Hollywood Hills."

"Do you just drive all the time?" asked Michael, the bass player. "In London, none of us drive. Don't even own cars in London."

I can't imagine not having a car. I had one when I turned sixteen and drove away from my parents' home in Newhall to live with my boyfriend's family in Mar Vista to finish high school where things were happening.

"Well, yeah," I answered. "I drive all over L.A. I am trying to learn it all."

"Like a fucking London cabbie," said Niall. "They can't even drive a cab until they pass some mad test and prove they know every street."

"And hotel and restaurant," said Brendan.

"All of London," finished Niall. "You, Maggie May, are the L.A. equivalent. The driver."

"I am," I agreed with him. "And I will be driving you to all the places you have to go here, and I can get you whatever you want while you're here and that even means McVitie's in Santa Monica."

In the two days since I first met them, I had developed a crush on every one of the five guys, although Niall scared me. I wanted him to see me. His eyes were intense, his conversation intense, and he would back out of talking to me in the middle of a sentence, leaving me wondering if he thought I was not worth talking to any longer or if he had a sudden inspiration for a song.

"Too many fucking cars here. I don't know how you can even have a complete thought with all this frenetic energy around you," Niall said.

"I find it invig …" I started to say.

Niall walked away from me, across to the far side of the lobby, and leaned his pale blond hair into the sunlight streaming through the window. There, glowing like a medieval saint, he stared at cars speeding past on Wilshire Boulevard.

What about when they aren't in L.A. because they only come here two or three times a year? Then I am a personal assistant to personal assistants. I don't work with the stars, since they like beautiful, fetching young men and women to interact with them. No, the beautiful, fetching ones call me when they have too many tasks, or tasks that they abhor doing, and then I go—take dogs to get washed, or shop across town for a particular food item that can't be found in B. Hills. I even drive to Burger King for fries and a burger because the personal assistant can't bring him/herself to enter a drive-thru line.

See, when the Hyperboreans come to town, they see me. They love me. They make a big deal over meeting up with me and asking what I am doing and kissing me, and of course I like being kissed by all of them, and then while they are here in town they include me in everything they possibly can. I think I am their pet. Or their court jester. I said that once.

"No, you are not a pet or a jester. You are a friend. And we like having real friends around," Niall the genius said.

Niall said not to call him a genius. I don't call him that, but I think he is. Niall Stafford. He doesn't look like a genius, whatever one would look like. He isn't that tall. His hair is that kind of blond that two-year-old children have—bright, nearly white—but his is bleached to be that way. It's a disheveled, not-really-a-style cut that goes to his chin. His eyes are a kind of pale blue that become more vivid depending on what color T-shirt he wears. He's slender, with muscular arms, and long fingers that look beautiful when wrapped around a microphone. His voice has been described as astounding, ranging from delicate, clear high notes to powerful, head-on blurs of syllables. He rarely smiles; in magazine articles, they describe him as sullen, but really he's just thinking, he's deep in thought about things far removed from the craziness around him. That's what he does, he separates himself from the rest of us and then he writes these incredible lyrics about what he sees from his vantage point and then we are in awe at his insight. It's true and this is why he is a genius, even if I can never tell him that to his face.

The traffic starts to move, there is a car on the side of the road, no two. They are crushed and crumpled. Things look bad. An ambulance just left, I can see it ahead veering off at Santa Monica Boulevard, and as I pass, because we go so slow, I look at one car. The door has been ripped off, perhaps by the jaws of life? I can see a deflated airbag draped over the steering wheel, I can see a high heel shoe sitting upright on the floor as if the driver slipped out of it for a minute. A very sexy shoe, the kind you would wear to a dressy event. I feel terrible for this girl who is being taken away in an ambulance and hope she will be okay. I hope the airbag saved her and she is not too damaged and all this reminds me to drive more carefully, to stop tailgating, to live. Even if they go to a hotel and I don't see them for a few hours, at least my shoe isn't left behind on the floor of a car that can never be repaired.

So, I drive with my attention on the road and not on every stray fleeting thought in my mind. I navigate the LAX turn-off and the entry to LAX and follow the signs for arrivals. In front of the international terminal at the end, I pull up exactly forty-eight minutes from when I said it would take forty-five minutes, and I wait and hope and wait. The door opens, a porter with a luggage cart careens toward me and then there they are, the Hyperboreans, smiling and laughing and running toward my van, yanking doors open, and sliding in—Brendan, Leith, Michael, Henry, Niall—tumbling over each other to welcome me with a kiss.

"Hi, Maggie." They tell me how wonderful I am because I showed up on time. They'd walked into the waiting room and saw my van pull up.

Niall, the one I like the most, sits in front. We will never ever be more than friends. I tell him about the airbag and the high heel shoe and how the accident made me drive safer and I thought I would be late.

He leans over to kiss me on the cheek. "Maggie May, never get in an accident on our account," Niall says, and I nearly run into the back of a hotel shuttle bus, so everyone laughs and now I am happy.

Monday morning and I'm at the hotel for the first duty of their weeklong visit: a photo shoot for the *L.A. Times*. A week of interviews, as many as twelve a day, and photo shoots and guest appearances on late shows, and it will all end at the Wiltern on Friday night. After their L.A. concert, they leave that night for New York. This morning is just the beginning.

The guys pile in with a lot less energy than they had at the airport. They are scruffy and wearing jeans and wrinkled shirts and Niall has on his Dr. Marten boots, unlaced and falling off his feet. They are quiet. I drive in silence to downtown L.A. The address given to me is in the garment district and I wonder how this is going to work.

Parking is a nightmare, so I give up on street parking and go for a seventeen-dollar lot on Olympic. The guys trudge after me; I feel like a scout leader. I'm guiding a group of reluctant boy scouts on a mountain hike through dangerous territory. All we have to negotiate are the homeless men and the extremely fashionable girls heading to the fashion mart. No one recognizes the guys: homeless men are not big fans of alternative rock and these girls are more the dance-music type.

The address leads me to a building with bars across the door and empty windows with empty rooms behind them. It is locked. I pull out my cellphone and call the number I have and the photographer says he is looking for parking and he has the key, so just wait.

"Bloody ridiculous," says Niall.

I say nothing. I can't help what's going on and it's not my fault anyway. The photographer comes within minutes and unlocks the gate. We go inside and he locks it again, while several homeless men watch with interest.

We try the elevator.

"It worked yesterday," says the photographer, who has asked to be called Spike. He is round: round face, round glasses and kinda greasy straight hair, and there is nothing spiky about him. Oh well.

We take stairs to the roof, eleven floors. Spike is deaf to the grumbling.

The roof, however, is way cool. Very blade-runner-like.

"Gargoyles," Michael exclaims. He runs to the edge of the building and leans over to look a gargoyle in the face. Brendan, Henry, and Leith explore the roof with all its peaks and old crumbling gables. Niall stands off to the side, his hands deep in his pockets and his eyes staring off the roof, off into distance. Spike is trying to get everyone against one of the peaks and Niall is not responding.

"Isn't it your job?" Spike snaps at me. "Get him in the picture."

"*L.A. Times* photographers are usually pretty nice," I say to him. "I've worked with Scott and Mike and Anna and they ..."

"Too fucking busy for this job. I'm freelance. I don't really care if you like me, you're just the P.A. Do your job already. Get the old man to pose for his picture."

If Niall has heard any of this, he's not letting on. I go to him and lightly touch his elbow.

"Niall, the photo. The sooner you do it, the sooner I can get you out of here," I say.

"I quite like it here," he says. And he points off to the west. "There is a deep gray-blue over there. It's the end of the world."

"It's fog, on the Westside."

He turns his gaze to me. "Do you have no sense of metaphor?"

I feel like an idiot. He goes to the other guys and they all light up. They have practice in looking photogenic even if they don't feel like it. Niall keeps his hands in his pockets and his face sullen. He is beautiful and knows how to turn his body in awkward sideways poses that underscore his eccentricity. The photographer moves them from peak to gable to gargoyle and back again until he is satisfied and they are tired. And all the while, I have been formulating answers in my head to his question. I can think of a million ways to show him I have a deeply evolved sense of metaphor.

I meekly follow everyone down the stairs, back to the van. I pull from the lot only to have a guy race his little black Jetta in the curb lane and almost take off our front bumper.

"Fuck," shouts Niall. "I fucking hate L.A."

Next on the list is lunch and then an interview on the Westside, so I take the 10 west and head to Sushi on Main, where they once went and once liked and fortunately like again.

We take all the seats at the sushi bar, with me at the end, and Niall next to me. He banters with the others over what to order and debates the merits of eel and Spanish mackerel.

They are all much more relaxed after eating sushi and onigiri and sashimi and miso soup. The Kirin beer has helped too.

A young couple walks in and immediately spots the band. They walk over, their smiles wide and hands outstretched.

"The Hyperboreans," says the girl. "Wow, you're like our favorite band."

"Cool," says Niall and shakes their hands. They go down the line and shake everyone's hands.

"We were just listening to 'Not Everything' in the car," the girl says.

The guys all nod and smile.

"We're ready for your next album," says the girl with a cheerleader air, as if she will urge the guys on to more music.

"Well, we're not, quite. Not yet. But soon, maybe sometime next year," says Niall. The girl makes a pouty face and her boyfriend laughs.

"They're the creative geniuses, honey, they gotta do it when it's right." He turns to Niall and adds, "We'll be ready whenever it comes, dude. Just can't wait, that's all."

"Thanks," says Niall. "I appreciate that." He turns his body slightly and it's clear to the two fans that chat time is over. The guys want to get back to their dragon rolls and beers. The couple says their thanks and sit at a table in the back of the room.

"Sometimes," says Niall, "I wonder why so many people want something from me. Like they want a part of me."

His back is to me and he can't see me flinch. Has he picked up on my longing? I can't hear what he says next, or what Brendan says, as they keep their voices down, not wanting the two fans to overhear.

Niall turns back to his food. "But I can't be this way," he says. "I can't write songs and sing them and want people to be interested in them."

"Right," agrees Brendan.

"And I can't say to them, 'be interested but only up to this line here. Up to when I say, stop being interested in me.' It just doesn't bloody work that way," Niall says.

"You can't be famous and not be famous at the same time," I say.

Niall looks at me as if he hadn't realized I'm still here. He looks right at me, then up over my head, devising a sentence.

"It's a paradox," he says. "A paradox like an impossible object."

I poke my chopsticks at stray rice on my plate, and my brain goes, *Yes, I get it*, and so I say, "Like an MC Escher etching, where the people go upstairs and downstairs at the same time."

"Exactly," Niall says and stuffs an eel roll in his mouth. He follows it with a swig of beer and then puts his hand on mine. "Sorry about my behavior earlier," he says. "I rant complete shite sometimes."

"It's okay," I answer.

"It's not. That photographer was a bloody bastard to you. I was mad at him and what do I do? I'm a bastard to you too. Fucking brilliant. Call me on it, Maggie May. Just tell me to sod off."

"I don't even know what that means, Niall." I laugh.

"Just say it. I'll know what it means." Niall smiles at me and his lips part and I take my breath in sharply, then put a gyoza into my mouth so he won't notice that I am lusting for him in that very moment. He doesn't. He goes back to sushi and my moment has passed.

★

I'm not being interviewed and yet I'm exhausted. I feel terrible for the guys. Brendan is fighting a cold, and I keep handing him bottles of cough syrup and antihistamines. Henry calls his wife constantly, since she is eight months pregnant. Leith and Michael have reduced themselves to adolescent humor to pass the time between interviews. They manage to be scatological with the interviewers, peppering fart jokes in with the literary references the band is known for. It's hardest on Niall; everyone wants to talk to him.

We are waiting in a hotel suite for this series of interviews, well away from the hotel where the band is actually staying. Michael and Leith are sprawled across the bed in the other room watching Cartoon Network. Henry is on the balcony, a beer in hand, and he stares down at the pool. Brendan is stretched on the couch, tissues on his chest, alternately blowing his nose and coughing. I am curled in a chair with a notebook, trying to write dialogue in a story about a bizarre actress I worked for a few weeks earlier. Niall is sitting at the table in the center of the room, waiting for the next interviewer. He is drumming his fingers on the table and scratching his eyes and clearing his throat.

"Do you think I'm getting sick?" Niall asks me.

"I don't know." I shrug. "Maybe?"

"I could have caught Brendan's cold," he says and clears his throat again, tries to cough.

"Could have. Are you warm?" I would put my hand on his forehead, but I am not comfortable being that intimate.

Niall puts his own hand on his forehead. "No, I don't think so. What if I get sick? What if I lose my voice? And the show at the Wiltern, it's tomorrow."

"I'll order you some orange juice," I offer. He nods and I go to the phone. I order orange juice for everyone, along with some cinnamon bread. I know they get it from the Hungarian bakery at nearby Farmer's Market and I know it's really tasty. While I'm on the phone, the interviewer comes in.

He's a college student, Andy, from UCSB, which means nothing to Niall until I explain.

"University of California at Santa Barbara," I tell him. The reporter looks at me then back to Niall, like this was some kind of annoying intrusion.

"All right if I record?" Andy asks as he sets his phone up.

"Yes." Niall coughs and looks at me.

"The orange juice is coming," I say and return to my corner chair.

"What about my mates?" asks Niall.

"I really want to interview you. The kids at school, they gave me questions for you. From the paper's staff and from other people." Andy juggles his phone to record and to read his notes.

"What other people?" Niall asks.

"Well, my friends, people I know," says Andy. "People who like the Hyperboreans."

"All right."

"So the first question, it's one a lot of people asked. There's this class on campus, in the Media Studies department. It's called The Work of the Hyperboreans and its Signifying Factors. We want to know …"

"Jesus fucking Christ, what kind of class is that?" Niall asks.

"Well, we listen to your music, we listen to one song, then we deconstruct it. We take it apart and analyze the parts. The lyrics, each guitar, the drums, then we reassemble it and determine—"

"Bloody hell. That's an amazing amount of work for a pop song." Niall laughs. "I take it you are in this class?"

"I took it last semester."

"And what did you learn about our songs?"

Andy sits back in his chair and opens his eyes wide and spreads his arms. "We learned so many things. Different for each song. For instance, with your b-side, 'No Release,' we found that the first person telling the story was really a third person imagined by a narrator who wanted to distance himself from a bad relationship."

Niall stares at the kid. One eyebrow is raised, and his mouth is open and he couldn't look more perplexed if he tried. He finds his voice. "And this enhances your appreciation of the song?"

Andy fidgets and moves his phone from hand to hand. "Well, yeah."

Niall starts to speak, and suddenly coughs uncontrollably, that kind of cough you get when your throat tickles and won't stop. He goes off to the bathroom. And when he passes me, he mouths, "Get him out."

I stand up. "Sorry, but he's getting sick and needs to rest now. He needs to save his voice for tomorrow night. Are you coming tomorrow night?" I ask.

Andy is so disappointed; his face has fallen in and his shoulders slump. "I had a lot of questions. I can't believe I even met him, but I have all these questions. No, I don't have tickets for the show."

I go to my purse and remove two tickets from the stash entrusted to me, then decide on four, and hand them to him. "Here, he'd want you to come to the show. Really, he's sorry that he's sick, but you know. That's how it goes."

The kid leaves with mixed feelings and room service arrives with the orange juice and bread. Niall comes from the bathroom and the others move around the table to get their share.

"Studying our songs in college," says Brendan. "That's fucked up. I didn't get any shit like that in college. We did Dante and Chaucer."

"And Dickens and Woolf and Blake," says Michael.

"Deconstruction," says Niall. "Fuck. You make a fucking rock song, and people examine it like it's a rare artifact."

"You know why, don't you?" I ask.

They all look at me.

"I guess you don't. But think about it. Think how much you like the Beatles and you listen to their music over and over and you try to tease out every chord change, and time change and whose vocal comes in and goes out. Every detail."

"Musically, yes," says Niall.

"But also because you love their songs so much. You want to be *in* the song. You want to get inside it and see it from the center looking out. You want to inhabit the song." I take a breath and add, "And that's what your fans want to do. It's not enough to listen to your songs. They want to get into the middle of a song and walk around inside that landscape and be a part of it."

Niall stops sipping orange juice and gives me a quizzical look, similar to the one he gave the student reporter. "Is that it? That's what they are after?"

I shrug. "I think so. Maybe. I don't really know. I don't know."

"You're probably right," says Brendan. "Poor kid. He adored you, Niall. He looked like Santa walked out on him when you left the room."

Niall shrugs. "Not my responsibility." He finishes a glass of orange juice and pours another. "I think I'm losing my voice."

And everyone goes back to their beds, couches, chairs, and balconies to wait for the next interview.

★

The Wiltern show is almost over. Niall sings his famous ballad, "Tear Me Open." The audience, in orgasmic moans, welcomes the opening chords.

Niall sings over a lone acoustic guitar. The audience quiets after the initial applause and everyone's hearts are being pulled from their bodies. The yearning from the audience to the stage is electric and palpable.

"This is how you change," Niall sings, "this is how you tear me open. I live on the edge of your love, and I bleed for you to see me."

I start to cry. Because I love this song and because when the show is over, I will be left behind, my love for them a deflated airbag as they say their goodbyes and head into the terminal at LAX on their way home. And me, navigating the exit, already forgotten.

THE FOODIE DETECTIVE

DUNCAN BIRMINGHAM

PART I

I'm perched on my usual stool at the bar, finishing a spicy michelada and my latest review, when I feel eyes on me. A few stools down, a brunette with no make-up and hair pulled back brutally tight side-eyes me over her margarita's salted rim. Despite her best efforts, I still smell money. A natural beauty. No wedding ring.

She stands out in the Boyle Heights crowd at Los Toros Cantina. Me, I've had enough practice to blend in; I may as well be another dusty sombrero on the wall or dying fern.

"Are you ..." She pauses, hoping I'll finish for her. But I don't. "Mr. Mustard?"

I drain my massive drink by way of an answer, then paw the rim's tamarind sauce from my mouth. I make a show of snapping my battered laptop shut. My latest food column, *To Live and Dine in L.A.*, is already a day late, but that's early for me.

"Want to split a plate of molotes?"

She shrugs. In my line of work, it's rare to have someone to share with, and my waistline reflects that. I sit up straight and motion to Xavier, my old friend and the swizzle stick-chewing owner of the place. He knows exactly what I want; that's how often I'm here.

Over fried appetizers and another round of drinks, Tatiana tells me she works for a group called Animals First. I understand now why she's dressed like a communist and not touching the little chorizo-filled bombs I'm baptizing in salsa verde and shovelling away. So much for sharing.

I nod like I've heard of the group. My ex, Mandy, is also vegan. When I met her, we would be first in line on Sunday mornings for Roscoe's Chicken & Waffles, road trip to Tijuana just for our favorite pork adobada tacos, and save up all summer for dinner at Chez Panisse. Later, she cut out beef, then fish, then dairy … then me.

"My group has gotten reports about these new underground dinners in L.A. Off-menu, black-market dishes. Whale, horse, you name it," she explains. "I heard you may be able to find the person behind this; that you know the city better than anyone."

"The culinary corners of it, maybe," I say modestly. "What happens if I find this person?"

"Contact me. We'll do the rest."

She sees I'm waiting for more.

"Citizen's arrest for a misdemeanor," she clarifies. She smiles, and it's showstopping enough for me to vow not to eat that last juicy molote. "We're vegans, not vigilantes."

"There's crossover. Just ask my ex." As both a stab at humor and a way to let her know I'm single, the comment falls flat.

"So. Can you help?"

"Maybe."

I mean it to sound mysterious, but I'm thinking. If there's anything I've learned in my handful of cases, it's to keep expectations as low as possible.

My new crime-fighting side hustle was born a couple of months ago after a green-haired woman started screaming. From my stool at Los Toros, I saw her pointing to a guy hunched over in the corner booth with blood streaming from his mouth. Seems a piece of glass made it into his chilaquiles. Most people were too busy watching the Dodgers game to notice. Knowing better restaurants have gone under for less, Xavier cleaned him up and gave him nearly a grand out of the till to keep quiet.

I ended up following him when he left. Maybe I had a hunch or needed to stretch my legs or was thinking of Mandy's parting shot out the door about me watching and scribbling but never *doing* as the world passed me by. First, I tailed him to the liquor store, where he bought a new T-shirt and a tallboy of beer, and then to the best hot-chicken joint on this side of the city, where he pulled the exact same routine. But this time, I snapped his photo with my phone, which we ran with my next column. That column got a huge reader response from owners bamboozled by the phony glass eater, and my nom de plume, Mr. Mustard, earned a reputation as a go-to gastronome for help with, for lack of a better term, culinary criminals. A foodie fixer, if you will. Although, I'm still very much a food writer first, food detective second. And because Xavier likes to brag to anyone who'll listen that Mr. Mustard uses his hole-in-the-wall restaurant's bar as a de facto office, those in need knew right where to find me.

An owner with a thieving waitstaff, a restauranteur who needs a sober companion for his wild-card chef, a fried chicken magnate who thinks his family recipe's been stolen; the desperate pilgrims to Xavier's run the gamut, and that they actually believe I can help them is a much-needed ego boost. But Tatiana's the first client I'm tempted to give a discount to because she reminds me of my ex. That resemblance also makes me want to charge her double.

I split the difference and tell her my fee, plus expenses, and say I prefer Venmo. She tucks five hundred-dollar bills along with her number on a napkin under my michelada, tells me to text as soon as I'm close, and slides off her stool.

"We'll be in touch!" I feel compelled to yell. She casts a confused look back at me. I wave off my dumb comment.

Xavier, polishing a glass in eavesdropping distance, isn't shy about his eyes tracking her out the door. His place, his rules, he likes to say. We went to Catholic school together, and he gave the young nuns hell. He strolls towards me, clucking his tongue. Handsome and flirty, Xavier's used to being the center of attention when there's a pretty woman in his family's establishment.

"Aren't you Mr. Popular lately?"

"You know of any underground dinners going on where they serve exotic fare? Whale, that kind of thing?"

"Too rich for my blood. Chapulines in my tacos is as crazy as I get."

Now that she's gone, I gobble the last greasy molote.

He continues, "Considering you use my place as your office, you should really give me a cut of your fee. Hell, I'm practically your agent."

"Add it to my tab." I rattle the chili powder-dusted cubes in my glass for another michelada and stifle a hot, greasy burp. Feeling a flare-up in my chest, I fish into the pocket of my army jacket for a couple of Pepto tablets. I'm sweating as I lumber off to the restroom.

Xavier laughs. "Mr. Mustard is on the case," he says, making my drink.

PART II

The city is awash with pop-ups, illegal restaurants, and underground dinners. Lately, it seems there's more underground than above. I scroll a dozen online food boards looking for any mention of illegal edibles, like kujira or shark.

I crisscross the city, talking up contacts. A taco slinger in Lincoln Heights turns me onto his aunt's Monday night goat dinners in her co-op. A Glendale bar-back invites me to a queer Persian supper club after hours at a Knights of Columbus. A sous chef hips me to an aphrodisiac-heavy tasting menu and cuddle party every full moon in Woodland Hills.

My editor, Suki Fleck at *The L.A. Beat*, scoffs and tells me she's heard rumors of endangered-species dinners for years.

"It's the foodie equivalent of Bigfoot," she says. "Forget that. I want you to write up the new gastropub thing in the Arts District."

Despite being a food editor, Suki wouldn't know a good meal if one dropped from the sky into her mouth, which, considering her eating disorder, would be the only way it could get in there. I tell her I'm not setting foot in another trendy gastropub. I've choked down enough charred Brussels sprouts and deconstructed hamburgers under exposed Edison bulbs to last a lifetime.

"I'll bring you something better. A real kickass column," I promise. But after I hang up, I'm doubting myself. It's been a long day of nosing around the city without a scent, yet I'm already fairly stuffed.

Besides being oblivious about food, my editor doesn't know about my moonlighting either. However, it shouldn't come as a surprise. A food writer isn't that far off from a detective. Both professions are best filled by loners with impeccable memories and eyes trained for detail. Both require keeping odd hours and low profiles—floating bogus backstories and juggling multiple aliases for reservations and credit cards, occasionally even burner phones. Both entail deploying low-key attire to avoid drawing attention or even disguises for deep cover.

And both professions are hell on your personal life. I pass Mandy's vegan bakery on a Highland Park street corner. She opened it a few months after ankling me. A line snakes out the door. I can smell her baking from my truck. Almond croissants, coffee-cake muffins, braided cinnamon buns that leave your fingertips sweet and tacky all day. I loved waking up to that smell filling our apartment. Even now, in my truck, it smells like home, and I slow down, getting an eyeful of hipster families giving up so much of their morning to taste her creations.

Often around last call, Xavier will wag his head at me and say I should do whatever I can to win her back. No doubt, the first step would be overhauling my lifestyle.

Mandy was with me a year ago when, halfway through the spiciest bowl of ramen on Sawtelle Boulevard, my nose bled, and I collapsed to the tile floor, sure that I was having a heart attack. An emergency room doctor that night told me it was caused by excess stomach bile, a symptom of gastroesophageal reflux disease. He clicked his pen and informed me that, besides the GERD, I also had low-level food poisoning and sky-high blood pressure. All this is on top of my IBS, recent weight gain, and cold sores when I eat eggplant or candy corn.

"You need to make some changes," he said as my eyes met Mandy's.

"What am I supposed to do? Sit home and eat kale?"

When Mandy realized I was neither going to clean up nor slow down my act, it was the Get Out of Jail card we both knew she'd been waiting for.

During those lonely last calls at the bar, I always agree with Xavier about taking action to win her back. But now I step on the gas. A perk of my new profession is I'm always on a mission with little time to wallow in our failed relationship.

My phone buzzes. I see a text from my sommelier neighbor, the first person I reached out to that morning. Isabelle's return text is simply a shark and thumbs-up emoji. Seems promising.

Within a few blocks of driving, I get the feeling someone's following me. I recognize the boxy Subaru station wagon in need of new brake pads a few cars back. The Vulture is a little punk from the San Gabriel Valley trying to parlay some stellar dim-sum blogging into something bigger. His real name's Zhang, and he suffers from teenage acne and an overreliance on hackneyed foodie phrases like "mouthfeel" and "fork tender." He's tailed me before in an attempt to scoop my scoops, dashing off a quick post claiming my culinary discoveries as his own before I have time to digest and craft a decent review. He hasn't succeeded yet, but it's only a matter of time.

I take it as flattery. No doubt he envies my readership as I covet his youthful bowel control.

"Not today, Vulture," I mutter. "Not today."

I floor my pickup through a red light, hear the screech of brakes around me, and hurtle south on Figueroa with a little toot of my horn and a middle finger out the window. The Vulture will have to upgrade from his mom's car if he ever wants to eat my lunch.

I pull up curbside to the jazz bar in Westlake where Isabelle works—for now, at least. She has a habit of berating the customers and ridiculing their palates, carrying on dueling love affairs with staff, front or back of house, all genders. She says it's the French half of her Montreal upbringing. The plus for me is her ever-changing employment has yielded a fantastic array of contacts and intel on bistros and wine bars across the city.

When I arrive at the bar, it's still the honeymoon phase—the hip clientele still thinks her scornful attitude is a hoot, and the manager she's sleeping with looks wrapped around her finger. She waves at the customers to make room for me. She gives me a heavy pour of Bordeaux, and ushers over a plate of sea-salted shoestring fries and a chunk of tonight's special, a sweating hunk of porchetta and slice of liver, rich as fudge. I can't count on two hands how many meals I've had today.

"What would you do without me," she says.

In the past week alone, I've loaned her money, set rat traps in her apartment, and dealt with a jilted ex drunkenly banging on her door at four a.m.

"You're my genie in a bottle," is all I say, raising my wine glass.

Isabelle explains she got a call from an old flame last week trying to win her back with an invitation to some kind of exotic once-in-a-lifetime dinner thing.

"What's on the menu?"

"Omakase. You have to trust the chef and hope you don't get food poisoning." She'd turned the invite down, but only when she heard it was in the Valley.

"But, for you, I agreed to let him take me to Nobu in exchange for giving you his reservation."

She hands me a cocktail napkin with an address I don't recognize. "Tomorrow night. Dress well. Bring $1,500 in cash. Leave your phone in the car," she says, then adds, "and come over and check my rat traps this weekend."

PART III

The meal starts off normal enough. At least as normal as a fifteen-hundred-dollars-a-head dinner of seven strangers in a defunct ice cream shop in a strip mall with blacked-out windows deep in the Valley can be. The space is no bigger than a studio apartment with cement floors and bare bulb fixtures. A huge pink chunk of Himalayan salt sitting on the counter is the closest thing to decor. The chef, Kiro, is a graying Japanese man with a wheezing laugh and a patriarchal twinkle in his eye, who seems to be working all alone.

I texted Tatiana on my way that I had a lead on a journeyman chef serving an omakase menu off Van Nuys Boulevard. Since the menu was a secret, I texted her to stand by and stashed my phone in the rim of my boot. Kiro had frisked us upon entering, padding and kneading me like so much raw meat with his cold, wet hands.

Standing in his tiny kitchen at a makeshift sushi bar, the chef is surrounded by us. He has a deeply lined, inscrutable face, and it's hard to tell from his terse small talk if his English is limited or he's just soft-spoken. Like a croupier, he deals out the first few dishes—raw oyster and poached quail egg, followed by melt-on-your-tongue sashimi and pork-filled onigiri rice balls. Between dishes, Kiro fills our glasses with sake and, later, whisky, rich dessert wines, and back to sake. He drinks, too, but if he's getting buzzed, it's impossible to tell. "Drink, drink," he tells us. For a change, I do as I'm told.

During a dish of creamy uni doused with caviar and yuzu juice, I feel that familiar flare-up and covertly palm a couple of chalky Peptos into my mouth. I'm squeezed into my only suit for the first time since Mandy's dad died, and the cheap pants already feel like they could blow any second.

"Eat, eat," he commands.

The crowd is in awe. They bow in their seats between dishes. Their orgasmic faces pucker around each spoonful. Everyone bookends their compliments with "chef." There's a pillow-lipped Kardashian knock-off with a young guy who looks like some kind of prince or silent movie star. A couple of bros in monogrammed cuffs are speaking Mandarin. I know these types—extreme foodies who will eat anything for bragging rights.

Next to me, a young Black man introduces himself as a DJ based in Miami who flew in just for this dinner after a friend attended one of the chef's underground meals in Austin last month.

"The guy's a total jazz ninja. A culinary outlaw. I hear everything after course eight is seriously *next level*," he smirks. As if on cue, the chef dips into a metallic cooler, pulling up a long black eel like a magician's scarf and slams it on his cutting board. Less than two minutes pass between him driving a nail through its head, slicing it down the middle with his honyaki knife, and thrusting tiny bowls of its squirming innards in front of us with a wink. A moment later, he cracks open live lobsters with the butt of his palm, serving their carapace over tufts of crushed ice so we can pick at them as their heads are still moving. Next is octopus, sesame-oil-soaked tentacles thrashing as I chew fast enough to keep the suckers from sticking to my teeth. The meal is certainly moving to, in my dining companion's words, *the next level*, but I don't excuse myself to the bathroom to text Tatiana—it's still nothing you couldn't find in a handful of smoke-filled locals-only Koreatown spots.

"Ready for soup!" Kiro declares as he doles out steaming bowls, the scalding broth splashing onto his knife-scarred hands. The other diners nudge each other conspiratorially.

"Shark fin soup, brah," the DJ giggles at me. "Next level." Indeed, this constitutes the kind of illegal fare Tatiana tasked me to find. At least in name.

In fact, the next few dishes are basically a showcase showdown of black market specialties. "Dolphin sushi" is announced, then "kujira," before a huge platter of blubbery bites is handed family-style from patron to patron.

"We're eating Flipper and Free Willy," the DJ whispers to me through a mouthful. "It's killing me that I can't take photos!"

"Chevalier," the chef announces, and a gamey pink meat, sliced so thin as to be nearly translucent, is distributed to each of us.

"Mr. Ed," the DJ says, determined to anthropomorphize every plate. If the meal weren't already ruined, it would be by his commentary.

Despite my bulging stomach's protests, I eat everything and polish it off with a homemade mochi ball. Then, the tabs are distributed and collected, each bill folder thick with the same $1,500 in cash plus tips—except mine.

"Hit me up on Insta. Come to a show," the DJ says on his way out the door.

You bond after a meal like that.

I hand Kiro the folder with a hard look that says I know. I'll text Tatiana that this was a false alarm and call the cops myself on this fraudster. Then, I'll go straight home to the bathroom as my belly is on fire and I'm out of my little pink pals.

"Stay?" he asks. "One last sake."

Curious, I hang back, watching the envious gawks of the other diners as the door swings shut. Now the two of us, the chef beckons me to enter the kitchen and thrusts a cup of sake in my hand. He holds up his cup to toast, but I don't.

I'm about to call his bluff and remind him that omakase derives from the Japanese word for "entrust" when a large Latino in a black jumpsuit and glistening manbun rushes in the back door. The chef spins around in time for the man to crack him on the forehead with the butt of a .45 like he was hammering a nail. The chef sinks to his knees, stunned but conscious, and now the gun is trained on me, standing there with my sake.

It happens so fast that the back door hasn't even had time to close when it opens again for a glamorous woman in enormous sunglasses and a leather duster, who looks more nonplussed to see me than the chef on his knees, bleeding. She coolly sidesteps a wriggling eel on the tile floor that escaped an overturned cooler. My spastic colon churns into overdrive. I'm so focused on the gun's muzzle that it takes me a moment to recognize this is Tatiana, my employer.

She no longer reminds me of my ex.

"You're still here?" She sounds inconvenienced.

"Why did you come? Did you follow me? Track my phone?" My suddenly high, reedy voice asking all these questions doesn't make me sound like much of a detective, but it feels like Tatiana and I have reached the end of our professional relationship. The only thing I know for sure right now is this woman in leather boots is not an environmentalist with a warm fuzzy for all creatures, great and small. And I'm desperate for a bathroom. "This man stole from us." She motions to the chef without looking at him. "Hijacked a whole truck for his extravagant little dinners here."

"And I led you to him."

"Good job, Mr. Mustard," she says. "You can go now. You were never here."

The muscle with the manbun flicks the ball of my nose with the gun, motioning for me to get lost. There's nothing I'd rather do.

"Actually, it does concern me. You're pistol-whipping the wrong guy." I hope they don't notice the tightness in my voice. "Not that you should be pistol-whipping anyone."

Manbun is antsy. "Want me to fix them both?" he asks her, never taking his eyes off me.

Tatiana takes a beat, hand on her hip. And that's when I see her white lobster belt buckle and realize who she is.

Tatiana "Truffle" Vennmann.

The same lobster logo was emblazoned on the black Tesla vanity plate of a guy who picked Isabelle up one night for a date last year. We passed each other on our building's steps, her in an off-the-shoulder tight-knit number and smelling of fresh juniper, and me with a head cold, lugging a plastic bag of more pleated Korean dumplings than one man has a right to.

"You're going out with Rodney Vennmann?" I said to Isabelle, not without some jealousy, and nodded toward the vanity plate. "Be on your toes. Supposedly, he's a real player."

"Well, so am I."

She returned early, knocked on my door, and we split a couple of bottles of Malbec and watched old Tony Bourdain episodes.

"Men are such shit," is all she said, staring into her wine.

That rare white lobster is the ubiquitous logo of Vennmann Family Delicacies. Need bluefin tuna or squid ink from Spain, rare French chili peppers, Iranian caviar in bulk for a wedding, banned delicacies from salmon babies to puffin hearts to pig bladders to blowfish for the international crowd at your casino ... call Vennmann, the biggest rare-food purveyor on the West Coast. The father, Frank, handles the Bay Area; the shitty player son, Las Vegas; and the daughter, Los Angeles. In a food-glossy profile, I remember a photo spread of them big-game hunting on safari with their logo on their absurdly matching hunting jackets. I heard she got the nickname Truffle after a competitor undercut the family by passing off Chinese fakes as black French truffles to one of their casino buyers. Supposedly, Tatiana ordered her muscle to force-feed him all his own inferior product. I never believed that story until now.

"The chef is guilty but not of selling your goods," I say. "The big-ticket items were all fake. He was passing off sturgeon for shark fin. That was moose meat, not whale. And the chevalier wasn't gamey enough to be horse. I'm guessing venison."

If the chef hears any of this, he doesn't show it. He's leaning against the dishwasher like he's on the verge of passing out.

Tatiana gives me a little golf clap.

"Before I was broke, I got out of L.A. more. I tried to be a good traveler," I say by way of explanation. "One culture's beloved pet being another's delicacy and all that."

"You have quite the impressive palate," Tatiana says. "But in this case, it's to your detriment. Sorry."

Tatiana looks at manbun and nods. He clicks off the safety. I realize too late that I probably should've invested in a firearm when I started this side hustle.

"Please don't."

I wonder what kind of tribute Suki will run for me. I can imagine The Vulture coming for my job. Maybe Xavier would hang a tasteful photo up by my barstool. Who would check Isabelle's rat traps? Not much of a legacy, although I like to think a few people ate a few delicious meals that they wouldn't have without my say; that's not nothing.

I think of Mandy, a smudge of flour on her cheek when she looks up from the oven to hear the news I'm gone. Will a teardrop cut through the flour, or will she simply sigh over the inevitable? At least she'll scratch her head when she hears I didn't keel over mid-meal from a heart attack but from a bullet in the face in a random kitchen in the Valley. If that isn't the world's smallest victory.

I should beg for my life, but my mouth is dry. There's little doubt I'll shit my pants. Then manbun screams.

I look down and see the chef has used the same knife he opened the eel with to deftly slice across the big guy's stomach. The jumpsuit fabric hangs like torn wrapping paper, revealing a deep, long gash gushing blood. He grapples to keep his insides from falling out. Blood rains down on the eel, still writhing.

With a bloody knife in one hand and the dropped gun in the other, the chef backs towards the door.

"Follow me, and I kill you," he says to Tatiana, who has inched up against the wall, looking pale and shaken. He swings the gun in my direction.

"You, driver."

The patriarchal twinkle in his eye from dinner is long gone. I walk towards him with shaky legs, averting my eyes from the big man groaning for an ambulance. Even an excess of myoglobin pooled around a rare steak can make me a bit queasy.

PART IV

Despite my protests that I've had too much sake, the chef orders me to point my truck east and drive. I covertly unbutton the top of my pants and comply. The knife gleams under the passing street lights, same with the gun in his lap. I could still really use a bathroom, but it feels like we're in a rush.

"Someone following." He nods at the rearview as we cruise down a deserted Ventura.

I know before I even look. "The Vulture."

"Who?"

"It's—it's just some punk kid. He's got a dim-sum blog, but he's desperate to widen his readership."

"What?"

He's confused. I don't blame him. It's madness what we spend our days pursuing.

Kiro is fully pivoted in his seat, clasping the gun.

"He's only a dumb foodie kid!"

"Lose him," he says. "Or I'll end him."

I accelerate till the cab of the pickup shakes and don't let up until we're on the 10 Freeway. I'm almost sad to see Vulture's shitbox recede in the rearview. He has no idea how close he came to getting his mom's tires shot out, or worse, in pursuit of a scoop. Kid should be in bed anyway. I know I wish I was.

Kiro's chain-smoking, busy texting on his phone, and clearly doesn't want to chat, but when the city's disjointed skyline is far in the rearview, I'm compelled to bring up the obvious.

"Once they poke around the kitchen, they'll understand you didn't jack their truck," I say. "So why run?"

The chef looks my way for the first time. Passing under a street light, I see he's staring at me with scorn, waiting for me to figure it out. Another mile or two goes by.

"Vennmann Foods *is* counterfeit?" I venture.

"Bingo." Kiro goes back to texting on his phone. "I was surprised, too."

"That's why they wanted to find out who jacked their truck so bad."

The fact that Vennmann is charging exorbitant sums for phony shark fin or whale sushi would not only bring personal and financial ruin but also incur the wrath of countless connected casino owners and fat-cat restauranteurs who'd spent fortunes with them all these years.

"Why did you cook with their food if you knew it wasn't the real deal?"

"I already stole their truck," he shrugs. "A good chef makes do with what he has."

"It wasn't about the food at all. It was about you knowing their secret."

The chef gives a gruff chuckle as he texts. "And now you know their secret too."

Tatiana was right about a great palate being a liability.

The chef waves at me to pull off the highway and swing into a derelict gas station. We're in the middle of the desert. There's nothing but darkness for miles.

"You sure?" I ask him. He's clearly made arrangements with his people; whatever shadowy forces helped him jack the truck and shuttle him from city to city.

I suddenly don't want him to go. "Here?"

He kicks the door open without a second look and jumps out. The blood has dried on his forehead.

I say, "Good luck, you need it."

When I hesitate, he kicks the bumper of my truck like it's a stray dog following him.

"Go."

I do as I'm told and watch him glowing red behind my taillights, enveloped by my exhaust, growing smaller in my rearview until he's gone in the darkness.

Driving through the desert, I see manbun holding his guts standing among the passing cacti. I pass him again and again. I stop at the filthiest truck stop toilet in the Coachella Valley; the stall is tattooed with obscene graffiti, and the toilet seat is chipped and as discolored as a dead tooth. I stop counting after five courtesy flushes, vomit in the sink on my way out, and get back behind the wheel, shaking and empty in every way. As I approach the city an hour later, the sun is starting to grope its way up through the marine layer.

Despite everything from a fifteen-course meal to almost being killed last night, my stomach growls. I've never been so ashamed of being insatiable.

It's so early that not much is open.

I find myself parking in front of Mandy's bakery. The closed sign is up, but I see her ten-speed chained by the kitchen door and know she's in there, baking something hearty and delicious. I want to sit on the counter and eat coffee cake fresh out of the oven and tell her everything that happened and how scared I feel.

"Jesus, Gordon," she'd say.

I stop short, stand by the back door, close my eyes, and inhale the fresh baking bread. It smells like her embrace and calms me.

I start thinking of the review I could type up about last night's meal and everything that followed. It will be a hell of a column, if I live long enough to write it. I take one last deep breath, turn around, and then I'm off to work again.

Acknowledgment
"The Foodie Detective" by Duncan Birmingham was previously published in *Mystery Tribune* (Mystery Tribune, 2021) and *The Cult in My Garage* (Maudlin House, 2021).

BECAUSE JIMMY WORE IT

MELIZA BAÑALES

"Pop-quiz," he says. He sits back on the living room sofa, the TV remote in one hand and a Budweiser in the other. He still has his work boots and pants on, and his hair lies flat under a black fishnet cap.

"C'mon, ask me any question about Jimmy. I bet you my dick and balls I know the answer."

He keeps going like this until one of us—either me, my older sister Linda, or anyone else who happens to be around—answers him. Mario is Linda's husband, and he loves Jim Morrison. Often, we are subjected to more Jim Morrison trivia than any of us cares for. It usually comes when he's drunk, which is every day.

There's a leather jacket hanging delicately in the hallway closet. His "secret jacket," I like to call it, because he only wears it when he thinks he is alone. The jacket, Mario claims, is Jimmy's. Stolen right under the nose of a thrift store owner on Santa Monica Boulevard back in 1977. Mario always talks about how the store owner was "dumber than a donkey's dick," how he didn't even know it was Jimmy's jacket, but Mario was smart enough to have recognized it from when he first saw The Doors at the Whisky a Go Go back in 1968. The jacket was all fine and good. I always wished it would end there, with the "secret jacket" hanging on a special wooden hanger. But it was only an ornament for the elaborate Jimmy shrine, an obsession that Mario harbored for almost twenty years.

"Missy," he says to me, "ask me a question, chica. If I get it wrong, I'll give you five bucks. But if I'm right, and you know I'm always right, you gotta rub my feet, on your knees."

"Mario, don't make her do that," my sister says.

"Spshh—shut up Linda, you ain't playin' today. Now Missy, pop-quiz chica."

"Okay," I say, my sigh of annoyance always inaudible to him. "In what year did The Doors first play at the now-historic Whisky a Go Go?"

"Oh, dammit girl! You ain't even tryin' to challenge me!"

He takes a big sip of his beer and answers, "1967, you fucking losers! It was 1967—now rub my feet."

I kneel down and begin to take off his boots. I spend much of my sleepover time at my sister's rubbing Mario's feet, kneeling below him. I never know if any of the answers to the questions are true. But I don't know anything about The Doors or Jimmy or the '60s in general. I figure if he's crazy enough to steal some cheap-ass jacket from the thrift store, then he must know the answers to every question. And I will be his little foot slave for as long as he can milk it.

"Stop doing that to her, Mario. I'm serious."

"Hey, dumbass," he yells back at my sister, "mind your own fucking business. And get me another beer."

His feet are long, and his toes always curl under my fingertips as I rub.

★

The Doors movie is playing on a Friday night at the Gardena Theater, the one-dollar picture show, two weeks after my birthday. Mario gets off work early so that he can be the first in line for the six o'clock show. My sister, her kids, and I pile into the cargo van, and we head to the movie theater.

"Mario, I don't think it's safe for me to hold Little Mario in my lap," Linda says.

My youngest nephew is only eight months. His chubby body squirms against my sister in the front seat. The rest of us sit on the floor of the van, no seat belts, our asses hitting every bump and curve the van encounters.

"Linda, don't bother me with this shit right now! We're gonna be late."

Mario's van is a Jimmy shrine. Pictures of Jim Morrison in concert, or wearing only a beaded necklace, are plastered against the interior of the van. Jimmy's torso stretches long against one door of the van, and if you lean into it, you can imagine Jimmy is holding you. Right now, from the van's stereo, Jimmy is crooning "Riders on the Storm." Every time it comes to the part about loving your man, Mario turns to Linda and says, "See—you hear that? Jimmy knew what he was fucking talking about. You gotta love your man, Linda."

"Mario, what if a cop pulls us over?"

"Dammit, Linda! We're almost there! Just shut up about the goddamn car seat!"

"Mario, we could get arrested."

"I said shut up about it!"

And that's when he smacks my sister across the mouth. He uses the back of his hand. The blow is quick. It barely misses the baby in my sister's lap. I sit with my niece and nephew in the back of the van. They huddle against me, like usual, and keep quiet. Little Mario is crying, and I can't tell if it's from the yelling, my sister's bloody lip, or Jimmy singing too loud. My sister sits still, puts her hand to her mouth, and shrinks back into the seat, her legs bouncing to try and calm the baby.

"You get it now, Linda! You see why I always have to do this shit to you? You just never know when to shut up! Now you're bleeding, and we're gonna be late to see Jimmy!"

We continue down the 405 freeway, approaching the exit to the movie theater. My niece begins sucking her thumb, while my other nephew curls into my chest, my arms around them both. I stare straight ahead.

"Now, we're almost there, and when we get there, you better stop bleeding. You fuckin' hear me, Linda? Take care of your shit! You're not gonna ruin this day for me."

We exit the freeway and turn into the parking lot of the shopping mall where my mother bought me my flower-girl dress for Mario and Linda's wedding. He swerves the van into a space, then turns to us kids in the back of the van.

"Get out," he says to us.

We quickly get up and head towards the van door. Mario comes around the other side. "Not you," he says to me, "you stay and deal with your fucking sister. Tell her she better stop bleeding, or I'm leaving you all in the fucking van, you got that?"

He grabs the kids' hands and runs across the parking lot to the ticket window. I find some napkins in the glove box and place them on my sister's lip.

"Thank you, mija," she says.

I hold them in place and remember that applying pressure to a wound will stop the bleeding. The sun falls against the Sears and Mervyn's buildings, while Jimmy's voice stays stuck in my head, *riders on the storm.*

★

"Pop-quiz," he says. He puts the bottle down long enough to look in my direction. "I said pop-quiz, chica," he repeats, "go on, ask me a question."

My sister stands, her back to me, hiding in the dishes. I knew how many nights her tears mixed with the dishwater, me never asking her if she was okay, never wanting to cause trouble. But as I watch her wash the same plate for the third time, I finally allow myself to feel what has been building in my chest all those nights.

"Okay," I say, "pop-quiz—what is my sister's favorite color?"

"What?"

My question wipes the smirk off his face.

"I said, what's my sister's favorite color?"

He takes a swig from the bottle, turns to my sister, "What the fuck is she talking about, Linda?"

My sister falls deeper into the water. "I don't know Mario. I don't know."

"Look," he says, "ask me questions about Jimmy. If you're not gonna play the game right, then I'm not gonna play with you, stupid."

"Just answer the question, and I will."

"What?"

I stand up from the table and stand next to my sister. I'm not counting on her for protection. I just want to be near her, for her to hear his answer with me.

"Maybe you didn't hear me—I said, what's my sister's favorite fucking color?"

"Linda, she's yelling at me. You better tell her to lower her voice."

"Just answer the question!" I scream. "Or how about this: what's her favorite cereal, her middle name, her favorite anything!"

Mario stands up and throws the bottle against the wall, "You see, Linda! You see! This is exactly what happens when you raise a child in a pocho house. If she was raised in a real Mexican house, like me, she would have gotten her ass kicked for talking to me like that."

"Just answer the question—you know what happens when you don't answer," I say.

He stands from the table, throws his chair, and comes toward me. He stops just short of my face, the whisky from his breath between us. He's trying to make me flinch. I don't. I'm waiting to see who will throw the first punch.

But my sister breaks a dish. The sound echoes and sticks to me.

"It's purple," I say. "Her favorite color is purple. Her favorite cereal is Rice Krispies, with brown sugar. And her middle name is Maria, after our mother."

I fight back tears because I will never let him see me cry. I know this, too, is my sister's daily victory, crying in the dark bathroom or hallway or backyard when she thinks no one is looking. But I'm always looking, always listening. Mario still stands before me. I'm the one who threw the first punch. And he knew I beat him.

Her face still in the sink, clutching the broken plate, my sister finally speaks. "If you do anything to her, I'm telling my dad."

It's her blow that stings him the most. I feel glorious. We're a team—the team I always knew could take him on. I wait for war, for my sister to take a flag, hold it to her chest, and claim herself. I wait for her to tell him we are leaving and never coming back. But the script changes. Right when I think it's over, Mario says, staring at me, "Linda, take this little bitch home. And when you come back, clean up this fucking mess."

He walks away into the darkness of the hallway, then slams the bedroom door. I turn to my sister. I want her to know that none of that matters, because tonight we won. She goes into the living room and gets her purse.

The car ride home is long, even though the drive is only ten minutes. It's two in the morning, and I'm wondering how we are going to explain my coming home so late.

"Linda?"

"Not now, mija. Please, shut up."

"I just want to know what we're going to tell Mom and Dad. About my coming home."

"You're sick," she says. "You don't feel well."

When we reach the driveway, I cry. I think she will cry with me, but she just says, "See you later, alligator."

As I enter the house and slide into sleep, I worry about what my sister might come home to. I later found out that he left and spent the night at his girlfriend's house. My sister slept in the big bed, her young children wrapped around her.

85

REFUNDING HIS DICK

KEN FUNSTEN, CFA

Tony Chapin felt *gobsmacked*. It was a word he'd learned only recently from the new redhead down in marketing. But now, driving "this dangerous and heavy piece of equipment" on Sepulveda Boulevard on the way to the costume store, Tony knew his wife Ellen expected him to control his urges, set a positive example for their son Zack, and not yell at the boy. That was going to be tough, however, because Zack had just told him that he wanted to be a dick for Halloween.

"You can forget about that one, big fella," Tony jokingly drawled, imitating John Wayne. "An' I'll tell ya why, pardner. It's because Halloween stores don't sell penis costumes."

Mardi Gras stores maybe? Tony Chapin pictured his own flabby, middle-aged body squeezed into a pink sheath and the wild parties he might wear it to. Then he began fantasizing about who else he'd like to be at that party—certainly Colleen, the younger woman in marketing who'd taught him the new word.

"And even if they do sell 'em," he continued to Zack, as much to kill his own fantasy as to stare down the boy's, "they're *not* gonna have 'em in *your* size."

However, once they were inside the store, much to his surprise, his now fourteen-year-old led him directly to a full rack of the coveted penis costumes. And, as Zack pointed out, there were even a half dozen in his size.

Tony knew he shouldn't give in. No good parent would. And he knew what the boy's mother would say.

Just say no, she would say. He pondered this as he took in the retailing frenzy around them: Yes, actions have consequences; that was the essence of the science of economics. It's what he taught his students. Caution should always be applied to market decisions to make sure one's choices didn't lead to bad outcomes.

"Have you considered what the neighbors will say?"

For once, Zack's response wasn't awkward. He didn't care what the neighbors said—or what they thought. "I just wanna be a dick for Halloween. That's what *I* want. It'll be funny."

For a while, both Chapins huffed and puffed, facing off against each other in the crowded aisle of pink tubes, like they were a couple of gunslingers at the OK Corral, neither wanting to give an inch to the other.

Then Tony had an idea.

"All right," he said, feigning defeat by pushing out his lower lip to the boy, "you can have your cock costume. But on one condition. You have to pay for it with your own money."

He'd seen the store wanted twenty-nine bucks for the flimsy thing with hoops, and he figured Zack wouldn't spend that kind of dough on a Chinese throwaway. Instead, he figured his son would make a rational decision. Rational economic actions are all about self-interest. Therefore, he would decide—even *if* he had the money—to alter his personal preference to any other costume in the store and use his father's money to pay for it.

But Tony watched in amazement as his little banker tugged two crumpled twenties from his back pocket and held them up to his father's face, waving them. "Yeeeeee!" he squealed in the way only boys at that age can squeal. "I'm gonna be a dick for Halloween."

★

And so it was that Ellen Chapin came home that afternoon from the brokerage firm where she worked as an office manager to find her son dressed in a pink penis costume—with her husband snapping photos of him.

Of course she was furious, even after hearing about the challenges Zack had met and won. Ellen—only a couple of years younger than Tony but in far better shape—tried counting to ten. When she didn't make it, she turned on their son.

"And you? Are you listening? I'm not having you dress up like some penis and then go out trick-or-treating. Not on Halloween or any other day. N-O. Out of the question. Understand?"

She looked at both her boys—the younger and the older. She could tell neither was going to fix the problem. So she would have to.

"You're both staying home," she ordered, stuffing the pink costume back in the store's bag. "*You* make some dinner, why don't you? I'll be back."

Twenty minutes later at The Party Store in Sherman Oaks—where three-quarters of the retailer's annual sales came during the forty-five-day period preceding Halloween—Ellen was glaring at the same cashier who'd sold the penis costume to Zack. He, in turn, was pointing up at the sign above the register. *NO REFUNDS*, it said.

But Ellen wasn't about to be intimidated by a sign. "How can a responsible business sell *a dick costume* to a fourteen-year-old? Tell me that."

The cashier—who was also the store manager—calmly explained that the boy's father had been with him.

"That's no excuse. *He's* more immature than the boy." She jabbed her finger into the manager's chest. "*You* have to take responsibility. *You* weren't thinking, buddy. But you better start thinking now. Or you'll soon be out of business."

★

Tony always paused at this point in his story to let his listener ask, "So what happened next?" Hal Wolin thought it was a charming habit Tony had.

Forty-six years old, never married and with no children of his own, Hal Wolin was Zack's godfather. He still had the old photo of the trio of Chapins—Tony next to Ellen showing her baby bump—framed on his coffee table, which he'd recently moved from Mar Vista to Austin. He had said no at first when he was offered the job managing a Texas insurance company's securities portfolio. Then they'd offered him so much he couldn't say no. Nevertheless, he still missed LA. All his friends were there—friends like Ellen, Tony, and little Zack. My God, did he miss them! Austin seemed halfway around the world, instead of only halfway across the country. The lack of a state income tax left him enough extra money to visit L.A. twice a month; even so, he still missed them. As he ate his lunch—the braised beef Wellington that was the Wednesday special—in the company cafeteria across the plaza from his office, he replayed the cute story Tony had told him the day before, envisioning each scene, each actor's performance in the family's little drama, Hal began to feel the loneliness of Texas even more.

Later, back in his twelfth-floor office, Hal twitched the mouse until his screen lit up. Half of the new emails he received while at lunch were spam, but one of them was from another L.A. crony, Bob Barrett, a business journalist until the local newspaper decided to eliminate business news. In the old days, when Bob had needed a quote or an idea, he often called Hal, who would devise pithy comments for him. The arrangement had been win-win, especially for the journalist when he was stuck for copy, which was most of the time.

Opening the email from Bob, Hal saw it was about the out-of-work journalist's new blogsite *Barrett's Blasts*: "Welcome to my new gig! And with your help, friends, I might eventually get paid to do this. At least in theory! Please click on www.barrettsblasts.com and contribute whatever you can."

Hal looked at *Barrett's Blasts* and started reading commentary about two of the more obscure and misleading California ballot initiatives up for a vote the following week. They were, Bob Barrett wrote, "wolves in sheep's clothing." But as Hal kept reading, he realized he didn't care about California ballot initiatives now that he lived in Texas. Instead, his mind wandered back to the story Tony had told him about little Zack's Halloween drama and the refunded dick costume.

He clicked *reply*, then typed in the story as he remembered Tony telling it: The money, the purchase, and the refund Ellen got. He tried to tell it with the same enthusiasm—but even greater reverence. It was a guy thing, Hal figured. And he was sure Bob would appreciate that about it too.

★

Bob Barrett was having a bad day. Pre-election jitters and raw emotions had aggravated the journalist. He wasn't sure he could keep going like this for another ninety-six hours through to the election, not while dealing with internet trolls, among them Skully, who kept lobbing his obnoxious shit-bombs onto Barrett's blog. He could kill that asshole. Then, he noticed an email reply from Hal Wolin. Hal was usually good for a laugh, so he clicked to see what he had to say.

It was a long, rambling story about a kid who wanted to be a dick for Halloween, but his mother just said no. Bob read how the mother got the money back by returning the dick. And there was a photo, too. Bob figured it was clever enough to use someday, so he tapped *print*, and a few moments later, the sheets rolled off the cheap printer he'd bought from the Target on Jefferson. Then he put these in the tray marked *New Ideas*.

Two days passed. It was Saturday, and the election was only three days away. Bob Barrett already felt like he was running on empty. That damn Skully continued to screw with him, interrupting serious online interactions with his juvenile idiocy. Bob could no longer ignore it. Skully must be neutralized. But how? It would take a point of view so all-American, and yet so funny, that Skully couldn't respond seriously. The story of the dick costume and the weird photo Hal Wolin had attached to his email came to mind. He fumbled through the stack of papers in his *New Ideas* tray until he found the pages he'd printed. Then he got to work.

The moral of the story—for all stories have a moral, right? —was that perseverance gets results, even allowing a mother to get a refund on her son's penis. Hah! What could Skully have to say about that? Bob assured himself he knew how to handle the matter.

"Congratulations! Here's our Barrett's Blast hero of the day. This mom won her battle hands-down, refusing to bend over, while getting a full refund! Her teenager, Zack, may have had to dress up like a clown for Halloween, but that's nothing compared to how she made Dad feel."

"Well," thought Bob as he posted this strong family-values story, "that seems light enough to outdo Skully."

★

But Monday morning, when Hal Wolin sat down in his large glassy office in downtown Austin, the first thing he noticed was the new mass mailing from *Barrett's Blasts*. It was very troubling: MOTHER GETS REFUND ON SON'S DICK—A Victory for "The Little Guy."

With dread, he read the posting.

There, under the headline, was the photo of Zack in the pink costume. Bob had rubbed out his face and somehow squished the picture, so the boy in the penis costume looked like some pink weasel with venereal disease, not like little Zack.

Still, Hal felt guilty and immediately picked up his phone to dial Tony at home. He had to warn his old friend before he saw it himself. Such a surprise, Hal figured, would be hard to forgive.

But Tony didn't answer.

"Hello," Ellen Chapin mumbled groggily, and Hal almost hung up.

"Ah, Ellen? Ellen, sorry to wake you. Is Tony home? It's Hal. I need to speak to him for a moment. Is he up yet?"

"No." She sounded grumpy. "It's early, Hal. Tony's at some investment conference in San Francisco. What time is it? Is something wrong?"

Hal hesitated, but his guilt hammered inside him, then he began to sputter, and then told Ellen everything, exactly what had happened. And that woke her up instantly.

"What do you mean"—she was shouting now—"the story of Zack's penis is on the internet? Hal, how did it get there? Hal?"

Hal explained how Tony told him the story and emailed him the photo. How he then emailed both story and photo to his friend Bob Barrett, just to share, but Bob had posted it all on his blog. Hal hadn't given him permission to do that. Hal hadn't intended harm. And he was sure Bob hadn't either.

"Why don't I call the guy, Ellen, and politely ask him to take the photo and story down? That'd resolve everything, wouldn't it?"

"No," the boy's mother fumed, defiant. "I'm calling this prick myself. Give me his number, Hal. And after I tell him what I'll be doing to *his* penis, he'll take the story down—or else."

"Ellen?" Hal pleaded with her.

★

Much later that morning—in fact, it was almost afternoon—Bob Barrett was waking up. Exhausted, he'd snoozed through the first half of the day. He felt worn out blogging back and forth with Skully, like he'd been playing tennis against someone much younger *and* in better shape. Sooner or later, he'd lose. He never remembered having to deal with trolls like Skully at the newspaper.

So, it was late when he finally poured his first cup of joe and settled in behind the computer. The first thing he noticed were the three emails from Hal Wolin—the last two stating in the subject line: "*Urgent—Not Happy!!*" He clicked on the first, and then the second, and then the third. Each related how the wife of Hal's friend Tony wanted to murder him because of yesterday's penis story, feeling it was an invasion of their family's privacy. She was contacting an attorney to sue Bob Barrett, *Barrett's Blasts*, and even Hal Wolin. She'd already called her husband who was at an investment conference at the Fairmont in San Francisco. She'd gotten him out of bed, or something, so now he was livid too.

"Great!" Bob's anxiety rose. "First the election, and now I'm getting sued!"

In the last email, Hal proposed Bob take the story down. He said it was the *only* solution. He said it was making life real tough for everybody. After all, Zack's parents were only trying to protect their little guy. And Hal felt terrible, too. The boy's mother said her young son might interpret the article as making fun of him, and that it might permanently damage his self-esteem. Hal couldn't bear being the cause of that.

Bob tried staying calm, sipping his coffee, cracking his knuckles, reading over the email once more. Then, like the great Zubin Mehta when the curtains rose on the L.A. Philharmonic and he lifted his baton, Bob put his fingers to his keyboard and replied: "Hi Hal, I just sat down. Let me cop a cup, and I'll think about all this." He didn't sign it. Then he clicked *send*.

A few minutes later his phone rang.

★

Election day, and junior high schooler Zack Chapin found himself in Tuesday's usual computer lab. He'd finished the assignment early so had time to goof around. He liked having free time, surfing the 'Net, finding blogs, and jumping into their discussions, seeing how obnoxious he could be, signing his own comments with a pen name he'd made up, never his own. He had half a dozen or so of these alter egos. And some were pretty harsh—like Skully.

That day, right away Zack noticed the article about Mom getting the refund on his dick costume and one of the photos Dad had taken before she got home from work. He couldn't believe it. He, Zack Chapin, on the internet—like a regular Hollywood celebrity!

At first, he could only stare. Then it hit him what he should do.

Zack emailed all the students sitting at the other desks in the computer lab. "Check out www.barrettsblasts.com," he mass-mailed the room. "That's me. I'm the dick in today's posting."

Slowly, the buzz grew in the roomful of thirteen- and fourteen-year-olds. A boy they knew, someone actually at the school with them, right there in the same classroom, was on the internet. He was suddenly more famous than any fourteen-year-old they knew. Look at him!

Though the face wasn't clear, no one doubted it was Zack. The two parents described were certainly his. Or, in fact, could be any one of theirs. But the story was a good one, the way he'd beat his father fair-and-square, even using his own money. Of course, it was too bad his mother had returned the costume. But she had gotten a refund for him. And there was the photo to prove it had happened. Turning around, they compared the photo to their new hero sitting in the back of the room. Yes, those were certainly Zack's arms, hanging out the sides of the pink fabric with the wrapped baggy feet and the large mushroom cap on his head. No one else at school ever had their photo on a blog, unless you counted those sappy family sites their mothers and grandmothers kept on Facebook.

"Computer scientists! What's going on?" Mr. Gordon, a twenty-something would-be actor who'd drifted into education, looked up from the glossy magazine he was reading, his feet still on the desk. "You've got your assignment. Are you done already?" He craned his neck to look at the clock on the wall behind him. "Do some of you need extra to do? Only fifteen more minutes. Let's settle down and finish strong today."

So, Zack waited. Then, a quarter of an hour later, between second and third periods, he told everyone: "Just go to www.barrettsblasts.com and look at me. Yeah, two *R*s and two *T*s. Write it down then. You'll see me. No, I'm not kidding. Yeah, on the internet. Sure, I'll bet—if you want me to take your money, dummy. Just go look, okay? It's cool."

By the end of third period, Zack Chapin was known throughout Hollywood Middle School as "the-eighth-grader-who-tried-to-be-a-dick-for-Halloween-but-his-mother-wouldn't-let-him." Soon emails were flying, even forwarded outside the school, and suddenly Zack Chapin was famous all over LA, with friends and friends-of-friends knowing about his short-lived life as a dick. The rush Zack got from his sudden celebrity was huge. It felt life-changing.

Now he was looking forward to lunch period.

★

At about this same time, Harold W. Wolin wasn't looking forward to anything—certainly not lunch. He'd had a Texas-sized headache since Monday morning. His whole body ached as if he were coming down with something. Ellen called him every few hours. Evidently, she and Tony were having some other trouble with their marriage—something about his room at the hotel. Or perhaps about someone *else* answering the phone in his room at the hotel? In any event, Tony had emailed Hal the day before, then called him. They'd talked about how stealing family memories to post on a public website was unacceptable. That he and Ellen felt violated, "legally speaking." That Hal should put a stop to it. If he didn't, Tony warned him, Ellen would likely kill them both. "She may kill *me* regardless."

That was the moment a light at the bottom of Hal's monitor pulsed, and he saw he was receiving an email from his former friend Bob, the tardy journalist. Hal almost fell off his chair, lurching to pick up his handset, hitting the speed-dial button labeled "BBarrett."

★

Bob Barrett felt like he'd walked into a shitstorm that week. Reporting on the election wasn't easy. But mostly it had nothing to do with reporting or the election. It was all about that cutesy-wootsy penis story he'd drummed up Saturday night, where he'd had to use a fine touch. Many readers of his were church-goers who seemed wound up over the off-color story. But even *they* weren't his real problem. His real problem was the kid's mother. She'd seen the posting and gotten so mad that poor Hal Wolin had become suicidal.

Sure, Bob thought, he *could* take the story down, but why should he? The face was smudged, the background was totally nondescript, the names—except for the boy's first name—had all been deleted. So, what was the problem? "It's not about *them*," he'd told Hal when they last spoke. "The story's bigger than that now." He paused, to let that sink in. "It's getting lots of hits."

"Come on now," Hal bellowed back. "What's more important here? It's affecting a little guy's life. The whole family knows it's about them, and Ellen doesn't want to run the risk Zack will see it and it'll harm the boy. He'll wonder how his parents could have let this happen. He might end up in therapy—all because of me." Hal moaned. "I'd feel horrible if anything happened to that little fellow."

Bob grumbled. If it had not been election day, he'd have made time to take on this mother, made an example of her. Stomping on First Amendment rights! Who did she think she was? But soon, he forgot all about the diatribe he'd been composing, obsessed instead with writing another response to that moron, Skully, who had again written *in support* of Proposition 90. What an idiot! But he couldn't let Skully's faulty logic go unchallenged. Bob gulped down his morning's second cup of joe as he furiously typed a response.

★

Lunchtime at Hollywood Middle School came after fourth period, and that's when Zack first became aware that he wasn't a dick anymore. The website was still there, blabbering away about election stuff, but there was no penis story. No Zack. No celebrity. He was gone, a girl told him.

Some of the jocks who didn't even *get* the internet tried to tell him he'd never been there, but enough other people swore they had seen him when he was a penis so that a fight about whether he actually had been a dick didn't break out during lunch period. Still, Zack had really loved being a Hollywood celebrity. On one hand, he wished the photo was still there showing him dressed in the pink costume. But having everyone talking and almost fighting was almost as good. In fact, maybe it was better, because now his parents wouldn't see the blog post, or the strange picture, which would have only made Mom madder.

And Dad? Well, maybe someday Zack would tell Dad about how his photo got posted on the internet for a day, which made him famous at Hollywood Middle School and beyond. It had been a rush being a celebrity, one like he'd never experienced before. Then he'd tell Dad that he figured the feeling was even better than sex. Or maybe he wouldn't say that. In fact, maybe he'd better keep his mouth shut and exercise that same cautionary economic principle Dad talked so much about—paying attention to the consequences of present actions regarding future outcomes. Because if Zack understood what he'd overheard correctly, Dad was in so much big trouble with Mom—"gobsmacked," whatever that meant—that he had to stay in a motel now. Evidently, being a dick had gotten Dad in trouble too.

THE BILTMORE GIRLS

M. LOPES DA SILVA

"Time isn't real. It's an artificial construct," they say. I look around the lobby of the building we're standing in, a monument of Los Angeles artifice, and wonder at its reality. The old Millennium Biltmore Hotel crawls with revival: resurrected Renaissance and Mediterranean and Beaux Arts movements lumber down the halls, embodied in frescoes and murals. Dead eras live here. Too many peculiarities peer out of painted wooden frames, twisting wooden necks to watch us walk by.

"Are all artificial constructs fake?" I ask, but they've already turned away and taken out their phone.

"Let's take a picture together!"

I never remember to take a picture. They squeeze me close to their side and aim the rectangle of the phone at us.

I'm forty-one. Hair a short crop of gold and red wires; eyes blue enough for my driver's license, but actually yellow-ringed gray. The fox ears I'm wearing on a headband complement my hair. I've lived in Los Angeles almost all my life, and the pinball of myself has entered this scoop many, many times before.

It's taking too long for the phone camera to focus on our faces; the lens keeps selecting faces on the walls. The reality of their features is more concrete than our own, it seems. When they've taken several images, their finger slides across the phone screen, moving photographs back and forth. I think I feel the floor beneath me slide forward, then back.

Time isn't real. Recorded bass tunnels down the barrels of my ears. It's dark. Masked guests peer down at us from plastic wisteria-decked balconies in the Crystal Ballroom.

I love them. I feel like I've loved them for years, even though it's only been months. I've been going to this masquerade ball for over a decade, sometimes, as a special treat, letting myself imagine the moment of a romantic partner approaching me and asking me to dance. I have dreamed about that outstretched hand, the song from the film *Labyrinth* that inspired the masquerade's very existence, lethargic and cruel, dripping like wine as our fingers met.

That song is playing now.

I'm in their arms, and the world is falling down the way it should. It feels like I've always wanted this moment, to dance with this particular partner. Time gathers at my shoulders, eager to tell me: *you are living*.

I lift my head to whisper the good news in their ear, but they're gone. They probably had to run to sound check, but it's not like them to leave so suddenly. Time isn't real. The room has reverted: the Crystal Ballroom is down the hall where it belongs. The lobby feels emptier, a little lighter of people than I remember only minutes ago. Or hours? Or is it months? I'm a bit sad that they didn't say goodbye, but I shouldn't be; they're standing right here at my elbow.

"Time isn't real. It's an artificial construct," they say. We're outside in a small, concrete alley festooned with fairy lights. We've been together for over a year. They're standing next to someone they're interested in dating. I'm meeting her for the first time tonight.

"That's the first sentence in a story that I'm writing," I say. There's an awkward pause. I rush to fill it. "It's about you. It's about this place, the hotel. You're in it."

"I'm in it? Like a character or something?" they ask.

"Yes, as yourself. I'm myself in this story, too. It's about things that have happened to me here, and Los Angeles, and time travel."

They laugh. The person they are interested in dating watches them laughing with a quiet joy that I know well.

"Let me read it when you're done?"

"I always do."

On the other side of South Olive Street, their car is waiting in the parking lot. Pershing Square traps the sky. A patch of black bubble gum snags the sole of my Docs. I try to scrape it off and keep up with the conversation. I can't hear what they're saying, but they're laughing, so it must be funny.

When we get to the glass door of the hotel, they have to go. It's call time. The peck they leave on my cheek is so light I could have imagined it. I turn to ask them a question, but I'm alone with my thoughts again. The Crystal Ballroom is seeping through the walls. I close my eyes. I let it happen. I don't resist. Time isn't real, after all. I go back.

They're onstage playing their flute at the Labyrinth of Jareth Masquerade Ball again. For years they played their flute while I danced by myself or with a friend in the dark of the audience. I have danced in front of them many times while closeted, wearing the femme mask of my gender so precisely that no one could see any part of myself peeking out. A mask on a masc. I don't wear masks anymore. That person is gone, and I promised myself I'd never have to pretend anymore. No more masks.

When the world falls down, I'm forty-two, and we can't kiss because my top surgery is only a couple days away. Our mouths are covered with surgical masks, and our love is a secret we hide underneath the N95s. I'm laughing. Someone else is laughing. I frown because she looks familiar. She's wearing a dress I haven't seen since the late nineties, a morose swirl of moldy greens, occasionally iridescent when the crushed velvet catches the light. I become marble, cold and finite in her presence. She's very young, a teenager. I turn back to them, but they're gone, the Crystal Ballroom receding. The child lingers in my memory. I didn't get a proper look at her, couldn't see her face. Who was she? I feel like I should know. Her laugh is something I can follow, so I do.

I follow the hallway carpet, my eyes chasing down the pattern of polite diamonds (or flowers) in the weave outside the bathroom. Heavy bass precedes her laughter. I haven't heard these songs in years.

Of course, it's my senior prom. I wore that dress. I called it my "garbage dress" because it looked like a beautiful prism-dipped trash bag. I glance at her hair, as big and golden-red as a lion's mane. I know what it feels like when she shakes it and the curls skim across the cups of her ears.

When I could not be a man or simply be, I pretended to be many things, all at once. I pretended to be a girl, every flavor of pixie; my neurodivergence masked behind cute things, elf ears, big hair, long claws, why not? Why not one more mask?

Not built for such heavy scrutiny, the teenager of myself falls apart underneath shards of mirrored disco light. Silver bright sparks flare into the depths of my optic nerves, burning. I flinch.

The Crystal Ballroom oozes through the carpet, through the walls. I am forty-one again. I'm smiling because I'm so damn happy. Their hand extends to lead me to the dance floor, and I accept.

Time is syrupy between the notes of the masquerade music. David Bowie's canned seduction beckons us closer, hip to hip. I hold them. When we kiss, invisible light spills out of our mouths and lifts us up to the ceiling, and we are floating, we are believing in forever. It's hard to remember that in *Labyrinth*, Bowie played the villain. Someone is wearing a wig that perfectly mimics Jareth's boldly teased hair. The person wore the same wig at the last ball, too. I'm getting distracted.

They're gone. They don't know me, and I'm wearing a skirt like a galaxy, LED-starlit, gyrating in a lonely corridor of self-love, waiting to come out (or die). I don't know them yet, but I believe in something better, so I follow the hallway carpet, my eyes chasing the pattern of polite flowers (or diamonds) in the weave outside the bathroom.

Time isn't real, but it splits nonetheless. It fractures. The world is falling down but they're not falling with me. Weeping, I fall, and the world falls through me like a cold wind, a moribund harbinger, and then she's there. Inescapable. Suspicious.

My mother sits at a table in the tearoom, smirking. I've spilled tea on my skirt.

"I can dress you up, but I can never take you anywhere," she says.

I'm irritated. *I* was the one who invited her to the Biltmore for afternoon tea.

She serves herself a piece of pale cake from the tiered tray between us, blueberries trembling.

"Why did you ask me out here anyway?"

"I thought you'd like it."

She stares down the busy décor as if it might suddenly vacate the walls. "I love it here."

I let her wax warmly on sugar and caffeine and carbohydrates. She doesn't know that she's dead, so I don't tell her. Instead, I decide to try coming out again.

"I'm bisexual," I venture.

"Oh yeah?" she says and then makes a crude joke. I take a sip of tea I can't taste through the bitterness of her biphobia. I never get to the part about being trans or polyamorous. I don't know what I was thinking. She never was much of an ally.

We finish tea while she rattles off a list of suggestions for stain removal. I am patient. In my heart, I record every method. I don't tell her that in a few years that skirt won't be hanging in my closet. I don't tell her that in a few years her ashes will be sitting on my bookshelf, facing the television set. Tonight we have baking soda, then she's gone.

The future, uncertain but joyful, takes me up the stairs again. The Crystal Ballroom returns to consume me. Time, unreal, offers me a dance.

I see them. I see us. I see myself. Balcony lips painted blue with plastic wisteria. The world is falling down, and I am a man, and I am dancing with myself. Or I am a man and dancing with a partner, but I am still a man, beautiful and whole, believing in forever.

MEAL PENALTY

KATHERINE TOMLINSON

It was the hottest day of the year so far. By the time Andrea made it to the set with lunch, Sonja already looked harried, her dark hair plastered to her forehead and her motions jittery like she was jonesing for a cigarette.

"We're running out of water!" Sonja wailed as she helped Andrea unload the folding tables, the giant coolers, and two hot boxes from the van. "They keep opening the bottles and then leaving them around half empty."

Andrea sighed. Her cousin Marisol, who usually handled crafty, figured out long ago that actors were like California almond growers—didn't really think about where the water came from until it stopped flowing. Marisol worked around that thoughtlessness by handing out refillable water bottles at the beginning of every shoot and bringing in massive thermoses of iced water that she replenished with a few surreptitious trips to the nearest bathroom. L.A. tap water was fine to drink, in Marisol's view, and no one had ever noticed her substitution for pricey "artisanal" water.

Unfortunately for Andrea, Marisol was working a ten-week gig on a Fox show, so she recommended her girlfriend as a fill-in. Andrea preferred not to hire unemployed actors for on-set jobs, but no one else had been available on such short notice, so she agreed to take a chance on Sonja, who was crap in a crisis. To her credit, Sonja was hardworking and wasn't constantly trying to slip her headshots to the producer every day.

"Do you want me to go buy more water?" Sonja asked.

"I'll handle it," Andrea said and mentally added it to the list of things she needed to worry about, chief among them how to keep the cast and crew hydrated in triple digit heat. They couldn't run the A/C when the cameras were rolling.

After a quick head count, she realized there were at least double the number of extras she'd been told to expect. Andrea would have a word with with the assistant director about that, but in the meantime, she had forty people waiting to be fed. Fortunately, chili was on the menu for both the vegetarians and omnivores. She'd made triple batches of both, intending to use the leftovers later in the week as the base for other dishes. Although she was required to provide a cooked entrée for lunch, it was so hot out that Andrea wondered how many people would actually eat it. A cold option would be better. Andrea thought, *Lots and lots of pasta primavera salad with chopped vegetables and vinaigrette dressing.* No parmesan, though, because then the vegans would complain. And there was nothing like a pissed-off, hungry vegan to make things a nightmare for a production caterer. *I'll put the parmesan on the side,* Andrea decided, *and provide a shaker of nutritional yeast.*

★

Andrea had just set up the big jugs of iced tea and pre-sweetened lemonade when a hipster kid with a worried look materialized at her side. "I'm Devin," he said.

"Hi Devin," Andrea said. "Can I help you?"

"I'm Jack's assistant."

"Okay." She wiped a splotch of dripping tea off the plastic tablecloth.

"*Jack's* assistant," he repeated.

"Okay, how can I help Jack?" she asked. She hadn't recognized anybody's name on the call sheet. Perhaps the makers of the low-budget, no-cast movie had somehow blackmailed an actor with some name recognition into making a cameo. *Jack Quaid? Jack Black? Jack Nicholson?*

"He wants to know if the chicken in the chili is free-range and hormone-free," Devin said.

On a budget of $1.80 per person per meal? Are you fucking kidding me? She kept a straight face. "Absolutely!"

"And is the cornbread gluten-free? Jack can't eat gluten."

Of course he can't, Andrea thought, but said, "There's no gluten in cornbread, Devin, cornmeal doesn't have any wheat in it."

The kid looked relieved, and she decided not to mention the smidgen of flour that also went into her cornbread. Jack would have to deal.

Andrea turned away from Devin, and reached for the cold pack with salad greens. To her dismay, she saw the shredded red leaf lettuce had started to wilt. Thank goodness for this meal she'd also made coleslaw—Ina Garten's recipe—with blue cheese crumbles mixed into the dressing and set the bowl inside a larger bowl filled with ice, which was melting before she could set it out on the table.

Coleslaw didn't exactly go with chili, of course, but it was too late now. She ripped open the giant bag of blue cheese crumbles she bought on the cheap at Costco, and started to mix them into the cabbage dressing. At home, she'd have used her hands instead of two large spoons, but she didn't want to give anyone the ick. The people who were lactose intolerant—except when it came to ice cream—wouldn't touch it. So she'd have plenty of leftovers for her kid, who inexplicably loved blue cheese.

She put out a tray of shredded romaine hearts, which she bought in bulk. Romaine stayed crisp a lot longer than other salad greens, and it looked fancier than iceberg lettuce. Frankly, Andrea thought romaine tasted like crunchy water, but it looked nice, and presentation was everything in on-set catering. People being fed for free wouldn't hesitate to mention a wilted lettuce leaf. Or anything else that bothered them. Andrea had grown to hate the words "special dietary needs."

So far, this gig had been mostly drama-free. She'd been working with Nico since the first film he financed through Kickstarter. He figured out that hiring a caterer to feed his cast and crew was cheaper and easier than ordering a bunch of pizzas come lunchtime, and her inventive menus pleased him. She liked the director, but the diva acting-school students who populated his sets made her want to puke. Very few people ever seemed to have legitimate medical issues—like diabetes or celiac disease or a peanut allergy—but everyone had food preferences.

On her last job with Nico, one lunch break descended into chaos when his star started screaming that Andrea was trying to kill her. When the actor was calm enough to explain what had happened, it turned out that she had been served a plate with a pat of butter touching her (homemade) roll. "I'm lactose-intolerant," she'd said, her big green eyes glittering with rage. "I could have died."

If only, Andrea had thought at the time, but she knew Nico was sleeping with the woman, so she swallowed her anger and made the little princess another plate. Last Andrea heard, the actress was playing the mom on a *Stranger Things* knockoff running on ABC. Andrea hoped her wardrobe consisted of lime green and chrome yellow A-line skirts and empire-waist dresses.

★

"One of the grips just took five cheese sticks!" Sonja said.

Andrea rubbed her temples attempting to relieve the stabbing pain of her migraine and sighed. Everybody always snarfed the cheese sticks, and they were probably the priciest thing she had on the craft services table. On Nico's shoots, the crew was always young and hungry.

"Get out the Ritz crackers," Andrea ordered, "and start making little peanut butter and cracker sandwiches." She knew from experience the snack was a crowd pleaser, yet cheap and easy to make.

"But we were going to make those for the afternoon snack."

"We'll make popcorn," Andrea said, wondering if she had enough clean bowls to pour the popcorn into.

Meanwhile, people were going back through the food line for seconds. As usual, no one touched the green salad and the fruit salad was almost gone. On hot days, Andrea always brought a big fruit salad. Producers wanted fresh produce, but Andrea had found ways to cut costs by adding tinned peaches and apricots to make the fruit salads filling and tasty, without reminding people of the canned fruit cocktail they used to get in their grade-school lunches. One of her most requested dishes was what she called "chai fruit salad," which was a festive blend of orange and yellow fruits—pineapple chunks and diced apricots, and mango slices—jazzed up with curry spices. Sometimes she threw in golden raisins for a little extra sweetness or stirred in brown sugar, which she bought in two-pound bags from Amazon. "Yes, that's raw turbinado brown sugar. Organic and gluten-free," she would say in response to inquiries about the provenance of the sweetness. If the questioner seemed particularly earnest, she would add, "Sourced from fair-trade vendors."

She once had a publicist who wore half-a-million dollars' worth of diamond jewelry lecture her about the ethics of serving chocolate cake and thereby aiding and abetting heinous child labor practices in West Africa. Andrea bought her chocolate from an ethical brand sold at Whole Foods and didn't see the point of into getting into a conversation on mindful shopping.

★

"Excuse me?"

Andrea turned to look at the young woman, who'd broken into her reverie. She was a waifish white girl with impressive boobs and, if set gossip was accurate, Nico's latest bedmate.

"Yes?" Andrea asked pleasantly, even though she had a headache forming.

The girl thrust out her plate, which held about an ounce of chili, a square of cornbread the size of a postage stamp, and a massive cupcake with a bite taken out of it.

"There's coconut in the cupcakes," the girl said. "I have a nut allergy."

"Coconut isn't a nut."

"You're supposed to provide food that everyone can eat."

Andrea looked at her for a moment. "There are also vanilla cupcakes with lemon icing."

"The extras ate all of them. You didn't make enough."

There was an accusatory whine in the girl's voice, and Andrea wanted to slap her and force feed her almond butter. She looked over at the dessert trays and, sure enough, nothing was left but crumbs and a smear of lemon frosting. Andrea sighed. She had some packets of oatmeal cookies in the van that could pass for homemade, but she'd have to be careful bringing them out because providing store-bought anything was considered cheating.

"I'm sorry," Andrea said, and she meant it. She hated running out of food. But the girl wasn't placated.

"You suck," the actress said. She threw the mostly uneaten cupcake on the ground and stomped on it before prancing away like a show pony.

"No, *you* suck," Andrea said under her breath and thinking, as she often did, that movie sets were not unlike elementary school playgrounds, only the mean girls were prettier.

An hour later, as Andrea was packing up the lunch remnants and updating her supply list on her "Mighty Grocery" app, little groups of interns and production assistants started to drift by. That was her cue to pull out the plastic storage bags. She always brought tons of them so she could send leftover food home with "the kids." She knew they'd make the leftovers last a couple of meals. She felt bad there weren't any cupcakes left. Dessert always made a meal seem more like a meal, somehow.

"Less to put away," she said, as she handed out care packages, which she did so they didn't have to ask for doggie bags. She remembered being twenty and living on scrambled eggs and liters of highly caffeinated off-brand soda while working as a sous chef in a third-rate French restaurant hoping to learn enough to open her own place one day. The restaurant never happened, but catering had, and it was the kind of job that let her be at home with her kid most afternoons. She took him with her when she had to work nights or deliver a "walking breakfast" at the crack of early. He was a good kid, and all in all, they made it work. She got wistful sometimes, then she would watch a couple of episodes of *Top Chef* and counted her blessings.

She was finishing loading the van when Nico's assistant, Taylor, walked up. "Andrea? Hi. Listen, we won't need you tomorrow."

"You're not filming tomorrow?" Andrea asked.

"Um ..." Taylor looked down.

Oh, hell no, Andrea thought.

"It's just that we found someone who's ... cheaper."

She flicked a glance in the direction of the girl with the nut allergy, who had a smug smile on her face as she lounged in Nico's chair while Nico conferred with the cinematographer about something and pretended he couldn't see Andrea.

No, you didn't. You so didn't, Andrea thought, but said nothing because, really, what was there to say?

"And we'll be okay on crafty too," Taylor added.

"So, Sonja is out too?"

"Yeah."

Andrea nodded. "Okay. I'll be by the production office tomorrow to pick up my final check."

Taylor looked confused. "There is no final check."

"I bought food for the whole week, Taylor, out of my own pocket."

Taylor wrinkled her nose. "Well, we can have the new caterer come by and pick that up."

"No, I paid for it."

Taylor, who had worked for Nico ever since she graduated from the Peter Stark program at USC a month before, sighed at Andrea's stubbornness. "Okay, fill out a form, and I'll have business affairs reimburse you."

"No," Andrea said. "Have one of the producers write me a check out of petty cash."

"But petty cash is just for important things," Taylor said.

Andrea almost wanted to laugh but instead, she turned away and headed to the craft services table and said, "Pack it up, Sonja. I'll help."

Taylor followed. "What are you doing?

"Leaving," Andrea said.

"But we're still shooting—"

"Don't let us stop you." Sonja grabbed the big jar of Red Vines and walked away.

"Hey," one of the production assistants said to Andrea, totally oblivious to the vibe between her and Taylor. "We're out of lemonade."

"Hang on," Andrea said. "I'll get you a refill."

Andrea went to her van, leaving Taylor to stand guard on the craft services table as Sonja boxed up the fun-sized candy bars, the big bowls of gummy bears, and the leftover corn chips and salsa. Closing the door behind her, she dumped two-gallon jugs of ice and water and a whole canister of lemonade powder into a large thermos. Then, balanced over the open mouth of the thermos in a graceful pose her yoga teacher would have admired, Andrea peed into it. She'd been drinking water all day, so her urine was colorless. It mixed right in.

"Here you go," she said, handing the heavy thermos jug to the PA. He looked at it and then at the folded tables now stowed in the back of the van.

"Where should I put it?" he asked.

Andrea smiled. "Taylor's in charge of that. Text me when my check is ready."

Nico's assistant bristled.

And with that, she turned and walked away, followed by Sonja. She could hear Taylor saying something, but let it fade into the ambient noise.

It was going to be a hot afternoon, and Andrea hoped there would be enough lemonade to go around.

METALLIC HEART OF A DISTORTED GHOST

A. J. PAYLER

Jesus fucking Christ.

How many times had they run through "Metallic Heart" before—had to be at least a dozen, maybe more? Not even counting the initial time Sato had demonstrated it for the rest of the band, taking pains to make it clear the song's delicate melodic structure would require some degree of finesse.

And yet, there was Jerome: totally oblivious, head down in his corner of the sweaty El Cajon rehearsal room, blasting away at top volume, slathering riff after riff atop the song as if Sato had written it specifically as a vehicle for his guitar work.

Sato sighed, knowing no one could hear him until the tune came to an end. Cutting it off mid-flight would only annoy Rich, the drummer, who'd inevitably argue that the option wouldn't be available in a week, not once they were out on the road opening for the Artery Boys. Better to plow through to the end, knowing the crowd at the gig wouldn't know the difference.

Sato knew, though.

And Jerome should, too. He'd been told more than once, though it clearly hadn't sunk in. Jerome brought the song to an unearned crescendo and squealed away with his whammy bar until his amplifier fed back upon itself, shrieking deafeningly while Sato and Rich waited him out. Finally, the song came shuddering to a stop after a cacophony of dense shreddage.

"Cool," Rich commented once Jerome's assault let up. "Let's move on to 'Blank Banners.'"

"Whoa, whoa, whoa, hold on." Sato unstrapped his bass from around his neck. "No, not cool."

Jerome looked at him quizzically. "What's the problem, bro? We've only got a week until the Artery Boys tour kicks off, and a whole setlist to get through."

"The problem, bro," Sato snarled, "is that you're wheedly-wheedly-wheeing all over the end of 'Metallic Heart' like it's the eighties again and hair metal suddenly came back into fashion. Don't you—"

He paused, noticing Jerome looking at his feet—not in shame at his musical narcissism, as Sato might have prayed, but simply staring at the tuning pedal at the head of his signal chain while he made minute adjustments to the tuning pegs on his headstock.

"What?" Jerome said without looking up. "Go on, I'm listening. Don't I what?"

Sato took a deep breath, and gave a *c'mon, man, help me out here* look to Rich, twirling his drumsticks idly behind the drum kit.

Rich nodded and cleared his throat. "I think Sato is concerned you're going to go all guitar hero on that one when we get on stage, and then the song is going to stick that way. Is that right, bruh?"

"Yeah," Sato agreed. "All that decoration and filigree is kind of stomping all over the melody. Like I said, when I showed it to you, it needs a little space to breathe, but you're filling up all that space with extraneous licks that don't have any relation to what I'm singing."

Jerome rolled his eyes. "All right, all right, I'm sorry. That's what you get for bringing me something in E minor. So, sue me for trying to have a little fun while we're slaving away in this tiny fucking room. It's got to be a hundred degrees plus in here, for fuck's sake. I thought this place was supposed to be air-conditioned?"

"It is air-conditioned," Sato protested. "I kicked it on twenty minutes before you arrived. But that thing …" He gestured at Jerome's towering amplifier stack. "That thing eats up so much wattage and pumps out so much heat, the AC can't keep up. The places the Artery Boys have booked, the soundmen aren't even going to run you through the PA once they see the size of that thing. You know nobody hauls those dinosaurs around anymore, right? Even on arena tours."

"Pfft," Jerome sneered. "And that's why there are no real guitar heroes anymore. Everyone's all soft and lame these days with their digital modeling and in-ear monitors and boutique signal processors."

He slapped the top of his amp stack. "None of that for me, dude. Just this axe, a few choice time-tested pedals, and two hundred watts of classic British power give me that creamy brown sound."

"I know, I know," Sato acknowledged. "But does it have to be turned up so goddamned loud in here? It's only the three of us."

Jerome's face wrinkled up like he'd caught a whiff of something terrible, as though Sato had suggested he replace the vintage handcrafted Mockingbird replica strapped around his torso with a ukulele.

"Come on, man," Jerome said. "Are we here to play, or are we here to jerk around? Time's a-ticking, and we've got an entire set of material to iron out."

Rich looked at Sato and gave an *I tried* shrug.

Sato bit his tongue, trying to tell himself that he'd said his piece and maybe it would sink in enough to keep Jerome from splooging all over his songs.

But Jerome was going to be Jerome. And nothing would ever change that.

★

Later, slumped in their usual booth at Kathy's Place on Fourth, Sato hunched over his bitter cup of coffee, restlessly drumming his fingers on the chipped Formica tabletop.

"I don't know, Rich," he grumbled. "Maybe we made the wrong decision, trying to bring Jerome into the band for this tour. Distorted Ghost has never been a heavy guitar band."

Rich raised a single eyebrow. "Distorted Ghost has never been a lot of things, bruh. Stable. Successful. Popular. Well-known. Profitable. Bottom line, we need a guitar player to get on the bill; we can't go out just the two of us. And Jerome's playing is head and shoulders above anyone who's ever filled that slot before."

Sato lifted his head. "So, what are you saying?"

"Nothing, man. What I said was what you heard." Rich looked off, searching for their server. "But I don't see any point in getting all caught up in some idea of what the band is or isn't or wasn't or couldn't be. This tour is the biggest thing either of us has ever had a chance to play. And it's not like there's some huge audience out there carrying around a ton of preconceptions and expectations, right?"

"I guess not," Sato conceded.

"Right. They're coming for the Artery Boys reunion, not their opener. No one is going to blink an eye if there's more guitar up front than on the EP we put out five years ago."

Sato's fist clenched around his ceramic cup. "So, we roll over and let this newcomer stomp all over everything, parading his ego around like he's the cock of the walk?"

Rich rolled his eyes. "You know that's not what I'm saying, bruh. But I also don't think that's necessarily what Jerome is doing, either. He's still finding his way into the material, trying things out to see what works and what doesn't. If anything, you might want to consider that maybe you're the one injecting your ego into it a little too much. Like the way you came at him after we played 'Metallic Heart' earlier—it was a bit much."

Sato's eyes bulged. "Me? I'm the one who wrote that song, and most of the others too. How is it ego for me to show the new guy how my song's supposed to go so it can be as good as it can be?"

Rich touched his finger to his chin, eyes still seeking the server. "All I'm saying is, the next time you're tempted to get into it with Jerome, you might want to consider if you're really trying to make the song as good as it can be, or if you're trying to make it what you want it to be."

"I—" Sato said, then stopped, unsure how to respond. Was he getting hung up on his own preconceived notions of what he thought Distorted Ghost should be, as Rich seemed to be suggesting? Or was Jerome the self-involved, wannabe-virtuoso prima donna Sato was beginning to fear he might be?

"Ah, there she is. Fucking finally," Rich muttered under his breath.

Sato shook his head, mouth watering and stomach grumbling in sympathy at the scent of the hot pastrami sando topped with deli mustard he'd ordered forty minutes before. He always got a little crabby when he was hungry; maybe what he was feeling was nothing more than a lack of fuel.

"Here you go, boys," their server said, depositing Sato's plate before Rich and placing Rich's buttered lobster roll in front of Sato. "Sorry about the wait, but two of the kitchen guys called out at the last minute, so we're a little short-staffed."

"I know the feeling," Sato said, switching their plates.

★

Coming off the stage at the Colombo Theatre in Los Angeles, Sato wiped the sweat from his brow with the sleeve of his T-shirt, legs still tingling from adrenalin.

"That was spectacular, bro," Jerome enthused, slapping hands with Rich. "Great way to kick off the tour."

"Definitely," Rich replied, glancing at Sato under his brow. "Things are really starting to come together."

"Starting?" Jerome snorted. "Man, we had them in the palm of our hand. Those L.A. schmucks standing around sipping their fifteen-dollar IPAs had no idea what was about to hit them."

"Neither did I," Sato murmured under his breath, quiet enough that Jerome wouldn't hear—it would take a few hours for his hearing to recover from playing directly in front of his monolithic amp stack.

Rich's glare was unmissable as he slapped Jerome on the back amiably. "Listen man, why don't you run on ahead and get your guitar safely stashed away while the crew changes out the stage. Me and Sato will catch up and help load the van in a few. Okay?"

Jerome grinned. "No problem. Save me a beer or two, yeah?"

"You got it," Rich said, watching as the guitarist disappeared into the labyrinth of hallways of the Colombo before wheeling around on Sato.

"What the fuck, dude," Rich snarled.

Sato shrugged. "What?"

"You know what, bruh. You're out there with all the charisma of a dead carp, shooting daggers across the stage at Jerome every time he does the slightest little thing that doesn't meet with your absolute approval."

Sato cocked his jaw. "Not like he noticed. Dude is so into his own thing; a fucking rocket could go off ten feet in front of him and he'd keep wailing away."

Rich grabbed Sato by his shirt, pulled him up close enough to smell the black coffee on his breath.

"I noticed, man. Believe me, I noticed every. Fucking. Time. And the audience noticed too. You're killing the vibe stone dead, and if you keep this shit up, you're going to get Distorted Ghost kicked right the fuck off this tour."

Sato knocked Rich's hands away. "Who gives a fuck? This isn't even Distorted Ghost any longer. I don't know what this is, but it sure isn't anything I recognize. Not anymore."

Rich's eyes rolled skyward, and he let go of Sato. "God damn," he said. "I fucking knew this would happen."

"Well, sure," Sato protested. "If you'd have helped rein him in, maybe there would have been a chance. But now here we are."

Rich shook his head. "Not that. You. You pulled this with Marty, with Jason, with Allan. It doesn't matter who it is, you always find something to complain about."

"Well, yeah," Sato admitted. "None of those guys were right, either. Not for what Distorted Ghost is supposed to be."

Rich paused, seeing the Artery Boys' rhythm section coming down the hallway toward them, heading to the stage.

"Good set tonight, guys," their drummer said as he passed.

"Thanks, bruh," Rich called after him, injecting his voice with false enthusiasm. "Knock 'em dead out there."

Sato braced himself once they were alone again, expecting Rich to renew his assault. But instead, the drummer's shoulders slumped.

"Look, Sato," Rich said with a deep sigh. "I've been doing this shit too long. And I'm tired of fighting every step of the way. This tour is the best shot I've had in a long time, and I told myself when this whole thing started that I wasn't going to let anything get in the way. I can't afford to, not anymore."

Sato smiled, putting his arm on his friend's shoulder. "Of course not. That's why we make such a good team."

Rich pulled away, shrugging off Sato's hand. "Nah, bruh. That's what I used to think, too. That's why I let it get this far."

Sato's brow wrinkled. "What are you saying, man?"

"You know what I'm saying. What I've been saying for a long time. You just can't hear it."

"No," Sato whispered, clutching his bass tightly to his body. "They're my songs."

"Only as long as it takes for us to work up enough new material to fill out the set," Rich said. "Don't worry, 'Metallic Eyes' is all yours again. Jerome has some tunes, I have 'Blank Banners' and the others. We'll jam it out."

"Without a bass player? You said the band couldn't join the tour as a two-piece."

Rich shook his head. "There you go again, man. What I said was we couldn't go out just the two of us. Bass and drums only works for noise rock and that powerviolence shit. But guitar and drums? I can name a dozen bands like that off the top of my head from the Peppermint Twins and Shaded Locks on down to Chinabots and Legion J, and so can anyone who's going to be in the audience. No one will blink an eye. No one knows or cares who's in Distorted Ghost, and no one ever will unless we do something to make them care. And when I say 'we,' I mean me and Jerome."

"But ..." Sato trailed off, at a loss.

"But nothing," Rich said. "It's done."

He turned and headed back to load out the equipment the stage crew had offloaded to the side of the stage. Standing alone in the wings of the theater, Sato hugged his bass to him.

He stood there for some time. Eventually, he walked back to the tiny dressing room with "Distorting Ghost" handwritten on a yellow sticky note on the door. For a moment, he considered what he'd say if Rich and Jerome were inside. Maybe if he apologized, promised to turn it around, agreed to go along with Jerome's embellishments, he could salvage the situation.

He pushed open the door. Inside, it was empty, save for his amplifier, empty bass case, and suitcase. The others were probably on their way back to the hotel already, or even on the road to the next town. Hell, maybe they were hitting a late-night rehearsal spot, working out their set for the next night in Reno.

He noticed an envelope on his amplifier. For a moment he allowed himself to fantasize it might be an apology, maybe even an invitation to meet up with them for an after-hours reconciliation. But it was a check for his third of the night's fee; barely enough to buy a bus ticket.

Somewhere far away, the audience roared at the familiar intro of one of the Artery Boys' biggest hits. For a moment he felt like joining them, stripping off his instrument, diving into the crowd and losing himself in the collective celebration of familiar music being paraded on the stage after too many years away.

But he couldn't afford to miss the last bus back to San Diego. If he did, he'd be stuck in L.A. with nowhere to sleep until service started up again in the morning. And if he crashed out in the bus station, he'd wake up to find his belongings gone.

His face expressionless, Sato snapped his bass back into its case and hoisted it over his shoulder with an involuntary groan. Pushing his amp on its casters ahead of him, he headed towards the rear of the theater.

It was a ten-block walk to Union Station, so he might as well get started. At that point, there was nothing to gain by waiting.

THE SECRET FISHING SPOT

CHRISTINE HERIAT

Henry steered his emerald BMW 2002 around the last hairpin turn and squeezed the car into a parking spot further down the hillside. The uphill slog to the Kleiners' front door was more strenuous than usual. He enjoyed Bruce's parties, but the thought of mingling work and pleasure at this one weighed on his shoulders.

"Henry! Great to see you." Bruce grasped Henry's shoulder, leading him inside. "Alice isn't with you?"

"She sends her apologies. Her morning sickness lasted all day, but she'd love to celebrate Ruth's milestone over lunch."

"First kid is always the hardest. Ruth is in the living room. Give her the invitation yourself." Bruce gestured behind him. "You'll know most of the faces, plus my new colleagues are here." The doorbell rang. "Duty calls. Grab a drink, Ad Man, then go drum up some business for yourself."

As Bruce turned to the door, Henry moved in the direction his host had suggested. The party was well underway. Scattered groups of fashionably dressed guests chatted, laughed, and drank, spilling merriment throughout the space and into the pool area, where a band played rock and roll.

Turning right, Henry entered the cantilevered living room. The combination of the location high on the Hollywood Hills and sweeping windows created the illusion of floating in space above Los Angeles. The fragrances of mahogany paneling and Chanel perfume infused the room with luxury. Although he appreciated the beauty of the house's interior, its opulence drained him.

Henry spotted Ruth standing by the windows, back to him. She held the rapt attention of a group of elegant ladies, all members of the Philharmonic Women's Fundraising Committee to which his wife and Ruth both belonged. He eavesdropped before interrupting.

Ruth was sharing sensational details of interactions with Hollywood stars from her job with prestigious Apex Talent. Henry didn't want to be pulled into her bragging. He slipped towards the sunken dining room, where a wave of nausea washed over him. The air, thick with cigarette smoke and cologne, smelled wasteful. The bright colors exploding from a tropical fish tank screamed of exhibitionism. On his way to the bar, he passed two men engaged in vigorous debate.

The tall man in the blue wool jacket said, "Shouldn't society focus on alleviating poverty and inequality?"

His shorter companion adjusted his glasses. "No, and anyway, Nixon is right. We can't make any progress on big issues without restoring law and order."

Henry, despite his passion for political debate, resisted the urge to ignite further conflict by placing his foot on the scale. He understood the importance of networking while other guests remained clearheaded. Mr. Weinberg, the firm's founder, emphasized expanding the client base as crucial for Henry's advancement to partner. Without Mr. Weinberg's pressure, Henry would continue to prioritize his favorite aspects of the job: scripting and campaign strategy.

He scanned the room for Bruce's colleagues and spotted one near the bar. The man, who wore a dated suit and worn tie, moved with an awkwardness reminiscent of Fred Flintstone. Based on the man's lack of style, Henry concluded his connection to Bruce had to be through Bruce's current role in the airline industry, rather than his prior Hollywood career. Mr. Weinberg's desperation to land an airline client had driven Henry to attend the party, despite his urge to skip it.

The situation required lubrication. Henry made his way to the bar and ordered a gimlet. As he waited, he assessed the Fred Flintstone man, his shifting eyes and tight body. Henry read a sense of unease with extravagance and an inability to fit in.

Henry extended his hand toward him. "Henry Jareb, long-time friend of Bruce."

"Walter Huxley, colleague of Bruce's from Air West." Walter's sweaty hand gave him a limp handshake. Henry heard a tinge of a Canadian accent.

"How long have you lived here?" Henry discreetly wiped his hand on his pants.

"Is my otherness that obvious? I moved with my wife ten years ago from Detroit."

Henry noted Walter's clipped response and wondered whether he had offended Walter or if Walter was naturally awkward. Mr. Weinberg's advice rang in Henry's mind: build rapport by putting the client at ease and find an angle by asking smart, engaging questions.

"Thought I heard a hint of an accent, Walter, that's all. Me, I was born in this city of angels and grew up as it grew up. The marvel of freeways, the growth of Hollywood, and the post-war building boom transformed us from scattered villages to a metropolis. I look forward to the next phase of change, driven by aviation. But you're at the forefront, working at Air West. What direction do you think commercial aviation is heading?"

Walter stared at his feet, then his glass. An uncomfortable silence hung between them. Walter broke the pause. "Well, we established Air West to meet the growing demand on the West Coast. But my passion is airplanes more than air travel. My background is in aerospace engineering ..."

Walter kept talking, and Henry nodded along to the monotonous tone, though he struggled to follow what Walter was saying through the loud chatter around them.

Two women to his left contemplated the meaning of the large, ocher-hued acrylic painting on the dining room wall. The painting, which depicted a party in a setting reminiscent of an Eero Saarinen design, was Ruth's proudest acquisition and the inspiration for the Kleiner home's interiors. However, Henry knew the women were pretending to have depth to cover their lack of true understanding of the painting. They were another empty display of wealth, like Lamborghinis parked in front of a Beverly Hills restaurant.

The raised voices of two men arguing about cars overpowered the women's discussion of the painting. Henry became distracted by the men's escalating argument. Then, another pair of voices grew even louder, as a woman screeched about the colors of the new silk Pucci bags. Her voice oozed with materialsm, devoid of any substance.

Henry felt an urge to escape from the banal conversation he'd trapped himself in, as well as those surrounding him. Fortunately, Walter's monologue wound down of its own accord.

"Hey Walter, why don't we admire the view outside? I could use some fresh air and would love to share with you what my little ad agency does," said Henry.

"This atmosphere is a bit much for me too, but I'm waiting for my partner to come back. I can't disappear on him." Walter looked at his feet as if he could uncover the mysteries of the universe if he stared longer. "He's better than me in these settings. I'll come find you once he returns."

"Can't wait." Henry was relieved to escape work-related talk. He went outside.

Henry's friend Charles, who stood by the pool, waved him over. Henry and Charles were colleagues who had advanced in the industry together, starting when New

York was "It" and Los Angeles was Siberia. The growth of Hollywood and its impact on advertising changed the perception of assignments in Los Angeles from detested to coveted. Both he and Charles had grown professionally as a result.

Charles was engaged in a discussion with a recent New York transfer, whom Henry called Slick because he couldn't be bothered to remember the man's name. Slick puffed on a cigarette, his white teeth reflecting the pool's light.

"Hey, Henry. Nice jacket." Slick fingered the lapel of Henry's deep green sports coat. "How's old Weinberg treating you? Were you involved in creating that sharp Gino's ad?"

Slick's blinding grin widened. He'd deduced that Henry's involvement in the most brilliant campaign of the year was minimal. Mr. Weinberg had controlled every aspect. Henry couldn't bring himself to admit his lack of involvement.

"I'm proud of that piece. Mini pizza sales have doubled since the ads started airing. As I'm sure you've seen, Mr. Weinberg has been too busy on the talk show circuit to run the agency. He's also working on a play."

Mr. Weinberg started in entertainment and drew from it to craft campaigns that had transformed the advertising industry. Henry hoped to capture this skill, along with Hollywood connections, by continuing to work with him. Connections were essential to selling Henry's screenplay, which would allow him to escape advertising.

Slick said, "Wait until you see my latest ad. Fasten your seatbelts because it's going to take off. It'll give your ad competition for the Clios." He formed his hand into an ascending airplane. "The New York boys say it'll soar. If I land another new client, I'll be partner in the agency by early next year."

Henry didn't understand how Slick, whose main gifts were terrible puns and nice hair, landed any clients or how he stayed on the partnership track. Who would want to hire the guy known best for those boring ketchup ads?

"Well, boys, would you look at that," Charles said, averting conflict by redirecting their attention to two ladies. One possessed the looks of Raquel Welch and the confidence of Anne Bancroft. "Bruce certainly has an eye for setting."

"He's stocked the pond, and this angler is ready to cast. I'll catch up with you gents later," Slick said. He slithered off toward the two women.

Charles and Henry traded industry gossip as they sipped their drinks. Charles suspected Slick of landing an aerospace client, given his addition of aviation puns to his tired repertoire, but Henry couldn't imagine it.

By then, the festivities were heading toward the debauchery typical of Bruce's parties. One group shook to the band's spirited rendition of Montez's "Let's Dance" while another played Twister. Three heavily intoxicated men stood near the fish tank, playing truth or dare, with each task growing more outrageous. Henry noticed Walter, alone at the bar, observing the trio with a mix of fascination and disgust.

Charles suggested going inside for another drink. Henry understood that Charles wanted a better view of the daredevil trio. Charles found inspiration in indulgent fun if he observed it from a safe distance. Henry, more exhausted than energized by that prospect, opted to remain outside.

The party's sounds receded as Henry headed to the pool's rear to take in the city lights sparkling below. He took a deep breath, allowing the crisp herbal air to fill his lungs and tickle his nose. He wished for a railing to lean on at the concrete patio's end so he could better appreciate the view. Instead, the patio fell away, plunging unobstructed into the abyss below. The openness of it, the endless darkness, unnerved Henry, so he turned to the pool. He removed his shoes and socks, rolled up his pants, and dipped his lower legs in the cold water, which created an initial shock that jolted his mind from thoughts of business. Sitting on the edge, he rested on his elbows to survey the scene.

The calm, chilly pool contrasted with the vibrant, hot party. The distance created a detached feeling, like viewing a film from the theater's back row. Slick, who was in the dining room, was making a move on the Raquel Welch look-alike. He leaned in as he wrapped his arm around her waist, but she slipped out of his grasp and stepped outside. She stopped at the edge of the pool opposite Henry, the water's surface twisting her reflection into a succession of surrealist images. Henry stared at the reflection until its source moved. She walked toward him, hips swaying, daring him to move with her eyes. Her high-heeled shoes clicked on the tile, and a sly smile played on her mouth.

"Mind if I join you?" The words rolled off her red lips with the heat of lava.

Before he answered, she removed her shoes. She sat next to him with her short dress pulled up to expose her flawless legs. Henry pondered whether it was an unintended result of sitting or a deliberate act of seduction.

She raised her eyebrows. "Are you some kind of voyeur, sitting here watching everyone?"

"More an observer of human behavior."

"Isn't that the same thing?"

Henry shrugged. "I needed a break."

"If you don't enjoy parties, why did you come?"

"Bruce is an old friend." Henry caught her attention. She forgot about her sexy pose and sat forward. "I like parties. It's just … it feels so extravagant sometimes. I'm here to network and generate business for my firm, but I can't get into it in this atmosphere." The woman leaned back again, watching the crowd out of the corner of her eye. "What about you? How did you end up here?"

"Ruth invited me, said mingling with the Hollywood types would give my career exposure. But it's been a bust. So far, I've only met a pair of airline guys and a grabby ad man who promised a spot in a commercial, clearly a ploy to extract more from me."

Henry now understood her connection to the party. She was one of Ruth's aspiring starlets, invited to enhance the scenery. She differed from the typical starlet because she hadn't fallen for Slick's fake promises of commercial stardom. The hint of depth in her interested Henry.

He asked, "What inspires you?"

"Film, obviously, but not only that." She gestured towards the large ocher painting, which Walter was now standing in front of, speaking with a shaggy-haired man who sported a handlebar mustache. "Take the painting in the dining room. It either inspired the house or was commissioned for it. But if you look beyond the surface, you notice bored facial expressions and dissatisfied postures. It's questioning whether wealth is making the people happy."

It never occurred to Henry to analyze the painting. He'd dismissed it as a useless extravagance. Her words made him long to examine it, to draw parallels between the painting and the real-life scene before him. But even more, he wanted to spend more time with The Starlet. Her intelligence was a beacon in the abyss.

"Have you read 'The Affluent Society'?" he asked.

She shook her head.

"It concerns the issues of unhappiness and consumerism, advertising's role in generating unnecessary demand, and the importance of prioritizing public goods over private consumption."

She shifted closer to Henry and brushed against his arm. "That's why you're here, observing consumerism from afar?"

Henry felt renewed when he realized his ideas interested The Starlet. "You could say that. I needed a breather and space to plan my next move, and then you came along, and my evening improved."

"Although I appreciate your kindness, I'm a distraction if you stay with me rather than mingle."

Henry debated what to do. While he preferred to stay with her, Mr. Weinberg's words echoed in his mind. He decided she was the type of woman who respected a motivated man.

"You're right, I should focus. Let's talk later, after we've each wrapped up our business. You're fascinating." The Starlet winked as she wished Henry luck. Henry's eyes followed her as she headed inside.

Henry's improved mood meant he looked forward to finishing his networking so he could talk to The Starlet without his job trailing him like a pungent odor. He put on his shoes, then stood at the end of the patio again and talked himself through his approach to Air West. This time, rather than an abyss, the void took on the air of endless possibility, which motivated Henry to explore his ideas, trying them on in an imaginary conversation until he found the perfect fit. He needed to stand apart from other Ad Men.

Henry, confident in his pitch, returned inside. The party's noise was unbearable, driven by the game of truth or dare. Henry felt disappointed that he didn't see The Starlet but encouraged because he didn't see Slick either. Slick had slyly swarmed into a prior deal of Henry's, turning a lock into a competition. He had no intention of giving Slick an opening to grab Walter's business, especially if it would make Slick a partner. Henry struggled to tolerate him as a colleague. The thought of Slick as his senior twisted his stomach into a knot.

Walter said, "Henry, this is the partner I mentioned earlier." Walter's social incompetence prevented him from finishing the introduction, so Henry took over.

Henry held out his hand. "Henry Jareb, ad man and Bruce's long-time friend."

The man pumped Henry's hand with a solid, dry grip. "Heroic Hank, aviator, Walter's colleague." Hank laughed at his own joke.

What kind of person introduces himself as Heroic Hank? In Henry's experience, aviators didn't sport the small stature and disheveled appearance of this man. Henry masked his surprise at the contradiction by redirecting attention toward the game of truth or dare. "What do you make of that?"

Walter said, "It's over the top. We should stay out of it. Let's go outside." Henry and Hank agreed.

Outside, Henry began his pitch, highlighting the ethical angles of his work and his approach to building brand trust over empty demand. He elevated his own role in the agency even further than he did with Slick. It was the only option he saw to close the deal. Someone who calls himself Heroic Hank only negotiates with the boss. Hank and Walter asked questions as they followed along, but then the crowd behind Henry roared, distracting them.

One daredevil stood on a chair, leaning into the fish tank, his jacket still on. He yelled, "It's here, the secret fishing spot. Come to Papa, fishies." The fish scattered from the invading arm in an explosion of color.

Walter snorted with disgust. Hank's expression read repellent fascination. People climbed on furniture to gain a better view, which blocked their line of sight. Bruce, with his John Wayne swagger, cut through the mess to rescue his precious fish.

Walter shook his head. "I don't want to watch that. It's disgusting, drunken behavior."

Hank laughed. Naturally, an aviator was the greater thrill seeker.

The Starlet pulled herself from the crowd and headed outside, joining Henry's group. Henry turned to her. "Hey, let me introduce you to my new friends."

Henry hadn't caught her name earlier. He still didn't, since she said, "Nice to see you boys again."

Her voice was huskier than he remembered. She directed her sparkling eyes towards Hank.

Hank wasn't unattractive, even with his disheveled appearance, but he wasn't as good-looking as Henry, and he was bouncing on his feet as if he stood on springs. *What an odd, rumpled man*, Henry thought. But despite Hank's inferior looks and strange behavior, The Starlet moved closer to him. She turned so that her shoulder nudged Henry in the chest. He moved back.

The Starlet touched Hank's arm. "You having fun out here alone?"

Henry didn't understand why she was laying on it thick with that oddball. Henry made small talk with Walter while also following The Starlet's conversation with Hank. Despite the challenge of listening while speaking, he caught enough of what she said to detect a flirtatious tone. Henry's eyes narrowed. Then Walter mentioned his wife's interest in music, which shifted Henry's attention. Music was an angle Henry could leverage.

Henry offered to connect Walter's wife with the Philharmonic Women's Fundraising Committee. Alice and Ruth's sponsorship ensured she would be a lock for the prestigious group, even if she turned out to be a dud like Walter. Walter's flat decline of the generous offer surprised Henry.

Henry overheard an opening in the Starlet and Hank's discussion and inserted himself. "You talk about that painting yet?" Henry nodded towards the dining room, then pulled his shoulders back. His goal was to make a smart comment so The Starlet would redirect her glow toward him. The comment would also allow Henry to expand his earlier pitch and show off his knowledge of consumerism. It was perfect.

The Starlet pursed her full lips. "The one in the dining room? Well, it's a party, of course." She wrapped her arm around Hank's.

Henry failed to decipher her game, so he pressed on. "Have you ever thought about the questions of wealth versus happiness, of conspicuous consumption versus public investment and the role of advertising in meeting demand rather than creating it?" The Starlet's focus remained on Hank, but Hank and Walter nodded along with Henry's words. Henry's mood lifted, and he delved deeper into the topic. He had found like-minded individuals in this extravagant wasteland, people who appreciated profound thoughts over material wealth.

A clap on Henry's shoulder jarred him out of his manifesto speech.

Slick said, "The professor pontificates on the existential questions. Let's spare these gentlemen the communist quotes. Lighten up, man; it's a party in a beautiful place." Henry shrank with an involuntary cringe. Slick, seeping slime, had spoiled his scene.

Walter turned to Slick. "Thanks again, Don, for that intro for my wife. She's wanted to join the Philharmonic Committee for years, but lacked connections."

Slick had bested Henry by making the introduction first. Slick had probably spoken to Walter while Henry was thinking through his pitch—he couldn't think of any other time when he didn't have his eyes on Walter.

Hank stopped bouncing and leaned forward. His hair dangled in his eyes. "Also looking forward to our meeting next week. My plan is to make it productive by strategizing and initiating action. I also can't wait to see how you'll get this lady on screen in an Air West hostess uniform." He squeezed The Starlet's waist and pulled her closer.

Henry's head spun with questions. How did Slick bamboozle these two gentlemen to land the Air West campaign in such record time, despite being the antithesis to everything Henry talked to them about? Why did The Starlet join forces with this strange aviator? She deserved better than a small part in a lame commercial. A gulp of martini did nothing to quench the burning sensation in Henry's throat. He needed to escape. He headed to the bar, unaware that he left without excusing himself.

Bruce stepped in front of Henry as he crossed the dining room. "I saw you with Hal Herbert. Good work networking with him. Walter won't move without Hal. Hal isn't what you expect based on how the magazines portray him, is he?"

Henry shook his head, confused. "Hal? He introduced himself as Hank." Hal Herbert was a Big Deal, a founder of multiple airlines, the father of modern aviation. Henry couldn't reconcile the stylish Hal who graced magazine covers with the strange, sloppy man he had met.

"It's Hal, you heard wrong. It's funny to see what a magazine stylist can do for a man even when he lacks raw material, isn't it? Anyway, I'm sure you closed the deal with your smart talk. He's a flashy guy, despite appearances, and would have enjoyed hearing your Hollywood stories and meeting that foxy girl you picked up. Although his appearance may suggest otherwise, he's quite a ladies' man."

Henry's stomach turned as he thought about how unsuitable his pitch had been, focusing on ethos instead of glamor and the childish game he'd played, attempting to win over The Starlet with smart comments.

Bruce said, "You don't look so good."

Henry's lungs constricted as he thought about the ruined opportunity and Slick's imminent partnership. "I should get some fresh air. Excuse me." He pushed through the crowd and out the front door. He leaned against the house and took deep, controlled breaths.

Hal emerged from the front door, his arm draped around The Starlet's shoulders to claim his latest acquisition. Henry shifted deeper into the shadows. Once Hal disappeared in search of his car, The Starlet's body exhaled out one persona and breathed in another. She sauntered towards Henry.

She said, "So."

"So?" The word came out harsher than he'd intended, but it didn't matter because she had made her choice.

She sighed and peered into Henry's soul. "Henry, what do you expect me to say? Our conversation was lovely. Those thoughts of yours are beautiful. They're meaningful, capital 'I' important. But like you, I am here to do a job. And that job was to make connections that will make me a star.

"Where do those idealistic thoughts get you, anyway? Fishing in the wrong spot and coming back empty-handed. We're all actors and fans, consumers and shopgirls, winners and losers. We're striving in a city of dreamers, scratching for our big break. You missed yours, with your smart but unappealing talk. I didn't miss mine. So what if it required me to compromise a bit?"

Henry closed his eyes to concentrate on his breathing, reopening them as he heard an engine roar up the hill. The weight of his failure made it difficult to think of anything other than his ruined future.

"Take my advice: abandon idealism if you want success." She turned towards the car, leaving Henry watching from the shadows.

NOT PERMITTED

THEA PUESCHEL

Everyone knew Tessa. She sat in front of the old Army Surplus on Sunset Boulevard, the one with Jimmy the Big Mouth Bass on the wall. She wore her bleached blond hair cropped short and sported bright pink four-inch press-on nails. On her good days, she dressed in crop tops and jean skirts like she did when she emceed the Sunset Junction Street Festival. She announced the bands to eager fans and drunken neighbors for fifteen of the thirty years it existed, before the fiasco with the forgotten or pulled permits and her personal issues became public.

On bad days, she wandered. Yelling. Screaming. Trapped in a prison of chaos in her own mind, at least to onlookers. The NIMBYs reported her to the police for violently arguing with invisible forces. She battled her bands, and told the *pigs* to fuck off, and snarled that "the event was permitted." Some days, even by some bystanders' accounts, it seemed she had won after a litany of vulgarities in English, Spanish, and the bit of Armenian she had picked up at Jon's Market on the corner of Vermont and Hollywood.

★

In the days before those days, mostly the third week of August, the festival took shape and form. Tessa loved the sweet plastic smell of kettle corn, sugary whiffs of funnel cake, the musky scent of sweaty leather daddies in chaps, the jasmine or patchouli waft of women dressed in sheer tops with their nipples covered with electrical tape. She loved the Aqua Net or Tres Flores scented locks of the next incarnation of Mexican Goths, clad in black Joy Division shirts with thick eyeliner and fishnets. They, among others more neutral in wardrobe and smell, filled the space between both sides of Sunset Boulevard. For two whole days every year, she was queen of Sunset Junction and held court on the corner by the *Welcome to Silverlake Sunset Junction* sign. She had her pick of drugs and balladeers.

"How 'bout that guy?" Chuy asked, appearing out of nowhere. "Or that chick?"

Tessa laughed. "You only like them because their fashion sense is the same as yours."

Chuy shrugged. The crowd moved around the two of them as if they were an intoxicated reveler sleeping it off on the sidewalk. Tessa, indie rock and punk royalty, gave Chuy shit for wearing the shirts of bands scheduled to perform. Inevitably, someone would give her a dirty look after she issued judgment, likely because they too were wannabees or losers wearing the same shirt. Though Chuy's fashion choices irked her, she could always rely on him for accurate scheduling.

★

"Better luck next year," she'd say to the sneaky high schoolers that were shooed out of Circus of Books onto Sunset Boulevard, the random porno mag snatched out of their waistbands by the clerk as he showed them to the door.

"Hey, Ralph, let a few slip through next time."

Ralph threw up exasperated hands in her direction.

Tessa laughed so hard she snorted before merging into the crowd and heading to the stage near the papier mâché phallus propped up outside the leather fetish shop. The owner waved from the brand-new sex swing he sat in, dangling his legs. He showed off its sturdiness by occasionally shifting his weight dramatically. Cotton candy made pink tangled cobwebs in his beard.

Later, toward the close of the festival each night, hetero-flexible men slid behind the bookstore into Blood Alley (the space between Sanborn and Manzanita inhabited by derelict clapboard houses) with a bit more frequency. Men cruised past the No Cruising signs and pressed into consenting strangers, finding dark corners or the sides of ungated homes to hold congress.

★

"How many swings you think he'll sell this year?" Chuy asked, pointing at the owner of Rough Trade. "What are they, like six hundred and fifty bucks a pop?"

Tessa shrugged. Her mood was always lifted by the heightened sexuality and chaos that only the festival could bring. She knew how to handle it all and managed the disarray efficiently. Chuy was on standby in case the overwhelm consumed her or her lips were locked with another's too long between sets when it was time to announce a new band.

★

Families, fair snacks, silver foxes in short shorts, musicians hoping to be added to the lineup one day, and all the rest of the inhabitants milled about, blending into a smoothie of Eastside representation. The festival had been an attempt to quell the fears of gentrification and bring the Gay and Latino neighbors together in mutual celebration. It worked until it didn't.

Tessa's no-bullshit attitude and comedy chops, along with her impressive lineups, brought attention to the festival. The quirks and kinks of the neighborhood served as additional flavor. Her body, mind, and spirit were woven with the fabric of music, arts and crafts, games, and fair food, which had kept her grounded until the brightly colored neighborhood transformed into a muted version of itself.

Slowly, the colorful houses and sagging clapboard Craftsman homes were replaced by buy-me-beige/gray/white with industrial fences and boxy Soviet-inspired multi-family unit block homes. This shift in inhabitants —and poor festival management—ejected Tessa from her fiefdom.

★

"Are you ready for your next performance?" Tessa asked. The crowd went wild then, as the demons in her head did now. She could get big headliners, local indie bands, crust punks, Mariachis, and Reggaetón bands to play. The music switched from English to Spanish, with the occasional theremin, accordion, or organ. The panadería, now inhabited by Intelligentsia, gave her free conchas and café de olla, at least at the beginning of her reign.

Mohawks, faux hawks, liberty spikes, and abnormally long beards made their appearances, no matter the decade. Sometimes the freaks outnumbered those with braids, buzz cuts, and ordinary hair. Whips, chains, chinos, Dickies, bell-bottoms, flannels, and band shirts. Fashion of then and fashion of now merged, adding to Tessa's loose grasp on time and space.

"Did you notice the girls are wearing spaghetti strap satin dresses with Docs again?" Chuy rubbed his hands together in excitement. "Always a favorite."

She went to elbow him and hit her elbow against the large painted window of the surplus. The glass shook and bounced.

"Come on, Tessa." Carmichael looked up from behind the customer counter. "Can we not, today?"

She furrowed her brow, channeled her best Sid Vicious with a nihilistic lip pucker and sneer, then flipped him off. He returned the gesture, laughed, and then pressed the button on the bass. Jimmy the fish came to life and sang "Jingle Bells" by the Chipmunks. She threw her arms in the air, gave him double middle fingers, and slid to the ground.

★

Toddlers, teens, abuelas, and grandpas were equally likely to visit booths, no matter the wares. Small children begged their mothers to ride on the Tilt-A-Whirl or the Ferris wheel or for their cherubic faces to be painted. Little hands sometimes reached for cock rings, mistaking them for bracelets.

"That's not for you!" A booth attendant would rush up, remove the inappropriate toy from small hands, and offer a redirect. "Hey, did you see that—?" they said, attempting to channel attention to something bright, colorful, and age appropriate. Children wandered away from the tables in directions that promised more fun or snacks and were replaced by hipsters that milled about during breaks in sets, whose facial features melted and loosened from the mixture of sun and Molly coursing through their veins. Those too sober sought blow in the ninety-degree heat as they chugged their Stellas from plastic cups and tossed their empties into the street.

Tessa would give the nod to one of the two coke dealers who were simple to spot. Either the Vanilla Ice look-alike with the long blond dreads or the guy in the polyester suit and the 1960s mod hairstyle. The former always whipped his dreads over his shoulder and headed her way, while the latter typically motioned for her to come to him to avoid swishing his polyester pants through the crowd. After they handed her a freebie, she'd slide the small plastic baggie of white powder into the pocket of her tight jean skirt and make false promises to share it with a certain band.

★

Now, the crowd walked in wide circles around her. Musicians with their instruments strapped to their backs did not stop to ask questions. They headed toward the Conservatory of Music or gigs at the Silverlake Lounge, not realizing she once had the power to make or break their success. They were too young or too new to the area to remember her old buddy Rodney on the ROQ.

The drug dealers avoided her, too, and no longer provided free samples.

She sat in front of them all, on the ground, tattered and torn, talking to invisible bands. Her white-and-black polka dot jacket was brown with the grime of Sunset. "STOP!" she screamed at a newly implanted Westside hipster walking past the band-only area. "Stop!" Like gentrification, they never did, and they never looked back.

Waiters from the local diner a few doors down dropped Styrofoam boxes next to her. She opened them and eagerly ate their contents, only to spit out the food and curse the demon that made it taste like piss. If a beardo walked by, the spittle might hit him. She was never a fan of beards.

To the outer world, she was chaos. In her own mind, she was catering to a world of live events, testy musicians, and overly concerned parents. Sometimes she sang aloud to compete with the blasting of her internal PA system and then stepped away from the crowd to smoke a discarded cigarette butt she had found on the sidewalk. She smiled when things went right, but with musicians, they rarely did.

★

"Stop! That doesn't go there!" she screamed, but the roadies of her mind didn't listen.

"You need to get help," Chuy told her. "You've gone too far."

"FUCK YOU, CHUY!" she yelled. He was always trying to get her back on her meds. "I have this, I have this."

"I'm not Chuy," responded a random pedestrian. She couldn't hear them; Chuy's voice was too loud.

★

There were so many bands, so many personalities, and she could only do so much. She formed a line of sub-conscious cocaine, chopped it, then snorted the invisible grains with a dirty, discarded plastic straw and rubbed her nose.

"Damn! It's been cut with baby laxative!" Tessa stood in front of the Surplus, squatted in the gutter to take a dump, and lamented the porta-potties had yet to arrive. She wiped with a crumpled up El Pollo Loco napkin she sourced from her jacket pocket and threw it next to her feces, then rubbed her hands together.

Carmichael looked up from the counter and away from his crossword puzzle. "Fuck! Come on, Tessa, that's gross."

She looked at her long-dead watch and made a concerted effort to avoid Carmichael's gaze. "Chuy, did they find the sound equipment?"

The bass stopped singing Elvis's "Fairytale." She didn't know why he kept the damn thing. The songs it sang were never hits or cult classics.

Chuy tilted his head in disapproval.

She sat back down in the shade. "Fuck roadies."

"Yeah, fuck 'em," said a woman in a satin spaghetti strap dress, Docs, and a cello strapped to her back. Tessa looked at her and squinted, twisted her mouth, and nodded.

The roadies, the roadies, were always a problem, trying to lure unsuspecting girls (well, women mostly) backstage with the promise of beer. It was always shit beer, too, and Tessa confessed very few of her headliners were interesting enough to chance hanging backstage with the thirty- and forty-year-old men, whose sweat-drenched shirts clung to them. She shivered at the idea of their sweaty hands gingerly flicking a young woman's hair off her shoulders.

It had been over a decade since the last festival, but the gigs, they kept coming. Chuy and Tessa worked tirelessly together along with the singing bass.

"Who's on next?" Tessa asked.

DESIGN INSPIRATION

PAULA BERNSTEIN

Being an interior designer in Beverly Hills is a competitive business; there are only so many celebrities to go around. It's not that I enjoy working for celebrities. Most of them are more trouble than they are worth, but you don't build a reputation and have your work in *Architectural Digest* by designing tract homes in Simi Valley. All you need to become a prestigious designer is a few high-profile clients: a kitchen design for Barbara Streisand, a bedroom for Lady Gaga, or a media room for David Geffen. Once your reputation is secure, you can attract the clients you want: ones with unlimited budgets and more manageable egos.

I had reached that stage in my career where I had more prospective clients than my firm could handle, and I could happily pick and choose those I considered worthy of my attention. I had a few ground rules for my clients and refused to work with anyone who wouldn't obey them.

I began each job with a "design inspiration," chosen by the client. It could be a favorite rug, a painting, a ceramic piece, family photo, souvenir of their favorite vacation, or a hideous piece of furniture inherited from Aunt Maude. Whatever it was would have pride of place in the new room, and I built the design around it. The client got to specify the budget, tell me if there were any styles or colors they hated, and to stay out of my way until I was done with my creation. I am too old, cranky, and intolerant to put up with other people's bad taste or any meddling with my designs.

Occasionally I would have a client sophisticated enough to request a Viennese Secession dining room or an Art Nouveau bedroom, but most of them couldn't get beyond telling me that they liked "traditional" or "contemporary" furnishings, never mind Art Deco or Louis XIV. They were too busy making money to care about the fine points of design.

To be on the safe side, if it was a high-budget job, I'd show them my portfolio (while specifying that no two clients ever got the same room) and let them pick the style they liked best. If a client insisted on getting involved in the process, I'd politely hand them over to one of my junior employees, fresh out of design school, who still had the time and patience to shop with a client at the Pacific Design Center.

Most of the clients played by the rules. The prestige of having a room designed by Blanche Himmel far outweighed the possibility that they might have preferred a different coffee table. It was a statement that money was no object.

As a rule, I take great pride in my work, but after completing my most recent commission, I was left with a bad taste and a nagging suspicion that I had somehow been had.

It began one morning with a call from Lola Oppenheim, the socially prominent third wife of Barney Oppenheim. Barney was a major player in the industry and the L.A. philanthropic scene. There is only one industry in Los Angeles, namely the movie business. Barney's studio was hugely successful, producing the kind of summer blockbusters that excite teenage boys and are the despair of any adult with a modicum of intelligence.

He had a humongous mansion in Beverly Hills, a whole stable of unctuous hangers-on, and made a name for himself as a mover and shaker on the cultural scene, donating money to build various entertainment venues, particularly those beloved by sports fans. He was known for his golf game, his passion for travel, and his habit of wining, dining, and seducing young actresses. He'd been through three wives and two divorces, and was still paying enough alimony to run a small country. Having reached his late seventies, he was rumored to have slowed down in the seduction department and had been married to Lola for almost five years. His recent retirement party had been the social event of the season.

Lola explained to me that Barney had left town on a long, "guys only" African hunting safari, leaving his bride to her own devices. She thought that, while he was gone, she'd surprise him by decorating his study. My gut reaction was that this was a bad idea and could lead to a divorce. However, I was curious to see the inside of the Oppenheim mansion so agreed to consult.

The large exterior was California Mediterranean. This means the architect couldn't quite figure out if he was doing Tuscan, Spanish Revival, or Greek so he threw in elements of all three, topped by the mandatory red tile roof. The well-manicured landscaping was full of native plants, gifted to Barney for having contributed generously to environmental groups. Bougainvillea draped over the courtyard walls and was in full bloom.

Like a thirties movie, I was admitted by an attractive maid dressed in black and white. She escorted me through the two-story foyer with its marble floor, curved stairs, wrought iron railings, and chandelier, to a living room resembling the interior of Versailles. The adjacent dining room was contemporary chrome and glass with art by Andy Warhol and LeRoy Neiman. The effect was schizophrenic.

Lola greeted me effusively. She wore tight white jeans, a sequined tank top, and teetered on very high platform Manolo Blahniks. Of course, she was blond with the careless streaks only a skilled colorist knew how to achieve. She wore day jewelry, a modest pair of diamond studs, and a diamond tennis bracelet. I complimented her on the beautiful marquetry work on the French cabinet. She beamed.

"I picked it out myself," Lola said. "Unfortunately, I couldn't talk Barney into letting me re-do the dining room. It was done by his first wife's decorator. He doesn't think the Warhols will look good with Rococo furniture."

"He's probably right on that," I said. "Would you like to show me the rest of the house so I can see your tastes and preferences?"

She acceded with alacrity, and I followed her lead. Our first stop was the enormous kitchen. It had white vinyl cabinets, black granite countertops, gray granite floors, stainless steel professional appliances, and all the warmth and charm of a morgue. A staff of three was busily preparing for a large dinner party. The scent was seductive, but no one offered me a snack.

We proceeded from the kitchen to the family room, an English country symphony in chintz. There was also a media room as well as a workout room the size of The Sports Connection.

The second floor consisted of two wings; one contained eight guest bedrooms, two of which doubled as quarters for the housekeeper and maid. The other was the master suite. The style was Victorian Gothic Revival. A huge king-sized four-poster bed was draped in red velvet with a fringed canopy.

"Oh my," I murmured, eyebrows raised.

Lola sighed. "I see you've grasped the problem. Barney did not get to be a multi-billionaire by spending money wastefully. Before our marriage, he had two other wives and a host of live-in girlfriends. All of them wanted to decorate the house to their taste. Barney refused to spend the money on an overhaul every time he changed women, so he'd keep the peace by letting each one do one room. I got to re-do the living room in French antiques, but he wouldn't let me touch the bedroom.

"Second wife?" I inquired.

"Worse," Lola said. "He selected everything for this room himself, years ago and he loves it."

"I see the problem," I said. "It's like that HGTV show, *Designing for the Sexes*. Are you sure he won't mind your redoing his study?"

"The study is different," she explained. "It's the one room in the house that was never decorated. Barney can't complain that I threw out expensive furniture for no good reason. Let me show you."

She escorted me down the hall and opened another door, with a flourish. I took two steps backward. It was like a giant college dorm room, run amok. I couldn't assess the desk because it was shrouded in piles of paper, with a large computer teetering on top. The floor was likewise covered in piles of papers and magazines with a narrow aisle leading to a faded leather swivel chair. The place smelled like a combination of cigar smoke and mildew. The crowning touch was a stuffed Cape Buffalo head above the fireplace.

"He never allows the maids in here," she said.

"Does he work here?" It was hard to believe.

Lola shrugged. "He does most of his work in the office. He comes in here when he wants to smoke and doesn't want to be disturbed."

I bent down and picked up a magazine from one of the piles. It was dated 1974. I'd read about people like this, unable to throw anything out. Eventually, they died, and the police only found them when the neighbors complained of the smell.

"Quite a contrast," I said, "between this and the rest of the house."

"I imagine if he ever lived alone for any length of time the whole house would start to look like this, but no woman would stay here and put up with it. Fortunately, we have a large staff. It's not that he hoards; he just forgets to throw things out," Lola said.

"I see." I didn't understand but I didn't want to admit it. I didn't want to be within miles of this place when he came home and discovered a pristine study. "Have you given any thought to how you are going to deal with all these papers?" I asked. "He might be a bit annoyed if you threw them out."

"Of course, I won't throw them out. I've rented a storage unit and hired an organizing team. They'll sort them, put them in labeled boxes, and provide me with lists of every item so that Barney can retrieve anything he wants. There might be some papers he needs, so you'd better build in some file space," Lola said.

I thought quickly about what I could say to change her mind about hiring me. "You may be familiar with how I work with my high-profile clients. I need an unlimited budget for furnishings and labor, and my fee is fifty thousand per room. That pays for my time supervising and selecting the items. I assume everything in here will be gone?"

"Everything except the Cape Buffalo," she said. "It's his pride and joy. He's hoping to kill another one on this trip."

I winced. "So, is that our design inspiration for the room? An African safari study?" I asked.

Lola smiled. "I do want you to do an African-themed room, but the buffalo is not my inspiration. I bought something special. Why don't we go into my study? I'll show you the centerpiece, give you the architectural plans, and write you a check for a hundred grand to get you started. I'm so thrilled you'll be helping me," she said.

What could I say?

Lola's study was more of a sitting room in restrained mid-century modern taste. She sat down at a small rosewood desk, wrote me a check, and handed me a roll of drawings. Then she got up and went to the corner of the room, where a large wooden crate lay on the floor. It had been opened previously. I helped her lift the top and place it on the ground. Inside, resting on a bed of packing popcorn was a four-foot tall, bronze canopic jar with the head of a giant Eland. It was stunning.

"It's a William Morris," Lola informed me. "Usually, he works in glass, but lately he's been doing bronzes. He's going through an Egyptian phase. Isn't it gorgeous?"

"It is," I said, my admiration genuine. That piece of art must have set her back at least seventy-five grand. "It will be a stunning focus for the room. I can visualize it already." My opinion of Lola had just ratcheted up a notch. She wasn't the bimbo I'd assumed. The woman had great taste.

Lola beamed. "You'd better get to work then. I should have the room cleared by the end of next week."

"When is your husband due back?" I asked.

Lola shrugged her shoulders. "He'll be on safari for at least six weeks and plans to stop in Switzerland on business for another two. Is that enough time?" she asked.

"Certainly," I said, knowing that money can purchase speed as well as furniture.

"I'll plan to have my contracting crew here in a week to start on the walls and floors. Are you sure he won't be angry?" I asked.

"Absolutely sure. I'm positive Barney will be spending an enormous amount of his future time in this room," Lola said.

She escorted me to the front door, smiling all the way.

I left Holmby Hills and drove to my modest 4000-square-foot home in Santa Monica. Some years ago, I'd converted the garage to a design studio. Now I wouldn't go so far as to say that the studio was as cluttered as Barney's study, but it was certainly not a prime example of obsessive-compulsive disorder. I confess that there were papers everywhere and catalogs all over the floor.

I thought about what I would have done to my husband if I came home from vacation and discovered he had put everything in storage and redecorated it as a surprise. It was inconceivable; if not grounds for divorce, certainly grounds for assault. I was astonished at Lola's certainty that Barney would love the surprise.

From every piece of random gossip I'd gleaned from my many industry clients, Barney Oppenheim was a control freak and a micromanager. Either Lola knew a side of him that he kept well hidden, or she was stupid. Although third trophy wives are not known for the size of their intellects, stupid had not been my initial impression of her. Perhaps she just had a taste for danger or enjoyed a good fight. Their marriage, however, was not my problem. I had been hired as the designer, not the couple's therapist. I went back to my drawing board.

A week later I returned with my crew. As promised the room was empty, which was a vast improvement. We refinished the wood floors with a dark stain, and I proceeded to turn the interior into a tent.

I found some lush silk fabric, which I used to create padded panels on the walls and draped from the center of the ceiling. I suspended three camp lanterns for lighting and found torch sconces for the walls. With the drapes closed, the room had an intimate golden glow.

The stone fireplace was an appropriate rustic touch with a rough, wood beam mantle. I hung the Cape Buffalo head over it with a shudder. Sometimes one's good taste must be sacrificed on the altar of the client's preferences.

I commissioned two display cabinets, flanking the fireplace. On one, I placed the bronze canopic jar. For the other, I purchased some William Morris glass pieces with a similar funereal theme. A brown leather loveseat faced the fireplace, flanked by two camp chairs and anchored by a genuine zebra-skin rug; head attached. The final touch was a large custom desk and chair, which occupied a corner space. When I finally allowed Lola to view the space, she beamed.

"It's perfect. I couldn't have done anything that imaginative myself!" Of course, she couldn't have; that's why she hired me in the first place. I smiled graciously and handed her the bill for the balance, which she paid without blinking. One thing I liked about the obscenely rich is that they didn't quibble over a few thousand dollars.

I put the job out of my mind and moved on to other things. A few weeks later, I read in the *LA Times* that a tragic hunting accident in Tanzania had ended the life of the prominent Hollywood mogul Barney Oppenheim. There was a two-page story about his life and many accomplishments in entertainment and philanthropy. The grieving widow wore a fashionable black Chanel suit to the funeral.

★

Lola phoned me a year later. She was marrying again and needed to start her new marriage without too many remnants of the old one. She intended to refurnish all the major rooms of the house with French antiques and wanted my services. The offer was too lucrative to turn down.

We met at the house the next day. The movers had emptied the dining room, the master bedroom, and the den. It was all going to Butterfield's for auction.

"What about the study?" I asked.

"We're keeping that as is," she said, opening the door. "Ron, my fiancé, just loved what you did. We thought we should keep it intact, in Barney's memory, except for the buffalo head. Ron's going to replace it with an antelope he shot."

"Ron hunts?" I asked.

"Oh, yes. He loves it. He introduced Barney to the sport a few years ago. He was on that last trip with Barney when the accident happened," Lola said.

I couldn't restrain my curiosity. "The paper didn't give any details about the accident. What happened?"

Lola shook her head sadly. "Barney had a Cape Buffalo in his sights and fired, but he must have missed because the buffalo charged him, and he panicked. By the time Ron and the others shot, it was too late. Barney was trampled to death."

"I'm so sorry," I said.

Lola wiped away a tear. "At least he died doing something he enjoyed."

I glanced around the room, noticing how the soft golden glow of the lighting and fabric brought out the highlights in the bronze canopic jar. I walked over and admired it once again.

"We used it for his ashes," Lola said. "It seemed like the most appropriate place. This way he can spend eternity at home."

"I see," I said with a sudden understanding. No wonder Lola had been so sure that Barney wouldn't be angry and would spend much of his future time in the study. You can learn so much about people from the objects they choose as their design inspiration.

LITTLE EGYPT

GEORGIA JEFFRIES

Miles of Mother Road stretched ahead, hot pavement shimmering and sashaying like a crazy asphalt goblin on crack. Thirty-nine hours since the driver crept out of downtown L.A. toward Interstate 10 in a battered baby blue '95 Corvette with the only man she ever loved. Her bloodshot eyes were still fixed on the rearview mirror like there'd be no tomorrow. This was not the time for Mr. B's words to start banging inside her head again.

When do you intend to claim your potential, Julia Mae?

She had stood silent under her teacher's fierce gaze, unsure in the moment what her potential was or where it might be. Perhaps it lay buried deep with some pirate treasure in a subterranean lagoon waiting to be dug up by a friendly sailor? That was how she thought about life at sixteen.

Mr. B knew better. His shoe-shine eyes looked at her straight and level, not up and down like the foul-mouthed boys in class. Different. He always looked at her different. Kind of the way she peered at a dead butterfly under the microscope in biology lab, curious how this wondrous creature came to such a sad end.

On the car radio, Tim McGraw crooned goodbye and good riddance to the bad girl that done him wrong. He held the low notes long and hard just so the bitch knew he meant business. Goodbye, goodbye, goodbye—

"HELLO TRAVELER! YOU ARE ENTERING LITTLE EGYPT—HOME OF AMERICA'S ANCIENT PYRAMIDS!"

A gaudy Technicolor billboard stamped with the imprimatur of the Land of Lincoln winked at the driver speeding by. Against a far horizon, the thousand-year-old Cahokia Mounds loomed big and bold, mute giants from another age with nowhere to run. Local legend speculated that the prehistoric Cahokia might have been Mayan, voyagers from another hemisphere who built the tall pyramids of dirt and rock to bury their society's elite. Relics prized by archaeologists but not by her. Not since a long-ago tour guide pointed out the mound where one old chieftain's bones lay atop a bunch of shells and the remains of three hundred young females killed in ceremonial sacrifice. A steady supply of virgins for the great man's afterlife, the guide explained. No doubt the maidens were happy to be chosen.

Soon black-and-white highway signs began jumping in her path: CAIRO … THEBES … KARNAK … HELIOPOLIS … PALESTINE. Villages spat out of green rolling hills watered by the Mississippi, baptized by Old Testament believers over a century before. Grand monikers promising more riches than the region's soil or people could deliver.

The boot of Illinois masqueraded as the North with a mendacity that anybody with an ounce of sense saw through on the first visit. Most of the locals spoke slow and easy, similar to their border brethren in Kentucky, and liked their patriotic politics leaning to the right. It was no secret some pioneer families—including her own—once owned slaves and defied upstate Illinois law to raise arms for the Confederacy. Even in this century, bad blood feuds ran rampant among hard-nosed Egyptians who never forgot an injury or a slight.

What the hell. She was coming home anyway. No matter how much grief her high-and-mighty old man threw down. Lord knows they both delivered offenses to humankind that would take seven generations to forget.

Maybe here she'd be able to finally take back ownership of her Christian-born name and suck in a clean breath again.

She jerked a sideways look at her passenger curled on his side in the shotgun seat, his eyelids quivering in a fitful sleep, skin glistening in cold sweat, his breathing shallow and labored. More goddamn hurt. Hurt so bad it could make you stab somebody in the heart to make it go away …

★

"Hey Ginger, give my friend, Herbie, whatever he wants." Mr. Shapiro grinned and slapped his buddy on the back before he Uber-ed to LAX to catch the red-eye to Cancun. "On the house." Five days in a row, the two of them had been behind closed doors huddling on some big deal. She watched as they sauntered downstairs from the executive offices and saw her boss slip something into his friend's pocket—a flash drive?—as he headed out. Not that it was any of her business. After she got a better look at Herbie, she decided it might be.

Ginger never wanted to disappoint her boss. Mr. Shapiro gave her a steady job in this high-class Hollywood watering hole, and she was grateful, she really was. Polite enough not to ask her about the gap of missing years on her resume, he complimented her on the fact that he'd never seen anybody, man or woman, serve up a gin Ramos with more fizz and hired her on the spot. A family guy with manicured nails and pictures of twin granddaughters in sleek bamboo frames on his chrome-and-glass desk, he reeked of respectability. Not that she hadn't heard stories. After one too many appletinis at the Christmas party, a young waitress named Tiffany, a nice kid who always pooled her tips, implied their boss's retro cocktail lounge was more than a savvy downtown investment.

"Blow," she giggled, wobbling a little in her high-heeled silver sequined peep-toes. "That's his real business. He's one of the top dogs around. We're working in a laundromat keeping his stacks of green clean." If there were facts to support such an allegation, they disappeared a week later along with Tiffany.

"She wanted me to tell you how much she'd miss everybody," Mr. Shapiro announced to his remaining staff. But when the girl's dear mother suffered a massive coronary, she had to move back to Stockton to help out. This troubled Ginger for a time because she remembered Tiffany bitching about her mom being in prison down in Chowchilla for passing bad welfare checks. "Stupid!" the cocktail waitress said, at the same Christmas party. "How stupid can a woman be?" But there was rent to pay and medicine to buy and lean times still knocking at the door, so Ginger decided "see no evil" was the best policy in questionable circumstances.

And then Mr. Shapiro's pal, Herbie the Blue Serge Suit, climbed on one of her barstools, his reptilian gaze doubled by the gold-veined mirror behind her. He scooped up a fistful of Spanish pistachios and eyed the attractive bartender with the red hair.

"We've met somewhere before."

"I don't think so." Ginger poured the premium Chivas Regal reserved for special clientele and placed the glass on one of the recycled cocktail napkins her boss favored.

"You sure? I got a memory like a bull elephant. Never forget a face." He tapped his temple with a lascivious grin. "Or anything else. It's a gift."

"More pistachios?"

"Tasteless," he shook his head. "I like 'em salty. You?"

"Excuse me?"

"Like 'em salty?"

"Absolutely." She turned away, slicing chilled limes into perfect wedges for club sodas no one had ordered. A good safety knife, quality German steel. She'd never cut herself, not once.

"You need salty nuts. A fancy establishment like this needs to do right by its investors."

Ginger watched a cluster of tipsy singles leaving the corner banquette. Hunter-green leather smooth to the touch. A comfy cradle for upscale asses after a long day. Sit, savor, spend. Mr. Shapiro knew what he was doing when he designed the place. No doubt about it, she was lucky to be here.

"You a dancer? The way you move … maybe I saw you dance someplace?"

"Not in this lifetime."

"What's that mean?"

Ginger's tight "the customer is always right" smile twitched, splintering at the edges. "Dancing is for folks with time on their hands."

She polished the Philippine-mahogany bar top with a linen cloth. No scratches, her boss warned, no scratches to mar that fine finish.

"Maybe I should speak to Fred. Make sure he's not working you too hard?" He licked his lips. "Anything I can do, say the word."

She'd listened to his kind before. The come-ons, the promises, the oily seductions as slick as the spill from the Exxon Valdez. Over two decades had passed but TV images of those dead seabirds still flickered in her mind. Smothered, the reporters said. Wings crushed, feathers blackened, so much sweet life snuffed out.

"I'm not complaining."

"Don't bullshit a bullshitter." He gulped down his Chivas. "Hell, who wants to be on somebody else's payroll, right? Me, all I want to do is go sit in Tahiti and knock back a couple highballs while the sun sets. How about you?"

She said nothing.

"Don't be shy, honey." He wiped his mouth with thick fingertips and leaned forward. "What would you do different if you had your life to live over?"

"Everything," Ginger blurted, her face flushing hot at the revelation.

"A girl like you?" His voice oozed more than lust. Something more dangerous. "A lot of females would kill for what Mother Nature handed you."

Did she say she wanted to *be* different? No. Be and do, two separate verbs that this son-of-a-bitch could never understand. Her grit and good looks (plus brains when she used them) had gotten her this far, which wasn't nearly far enough, true, but she wasn't throwing in the towel yet. Her son needed her.

"Hit me again, por favor. A double." Pulling out a monogrammed lighter, Herbie lit up a sleek Cuban and did not bother to ask if she minded.

"California law," Ginger informed him. "No smoking in bars or restaurants. Maybe you want to take that outside."

"After hours, babe." He sucked the smoke into his lungs, then exhaled. "Your boss and I agree the rules don't apply."

She made no mention of her allergy to cigar smoke. Instead, she flipped on the bar fan and prayed to God this would be his last drink.

They were alone now. Even the regulars had moved on to the late nightclubs or crawled home to unhappy wives. She glanced at the face of the Mickey Mouse watch on her left wrist, the one she bought when they went to Disneyland to celebrate Dante's fourth birthday. Maybe that was one day she would keep, that one perfect day when her precious child was still healthy, and his daddy was still in their lives.

Fatigue swept over Ginger the way it did so often. As if she were one of those Valdez seabirds floundering in the dark waves that sapped every ounce of strength needed to survive. She filled his glass, and he puffed on his cigar, bushy eyebrows frozen in phony consternation.

"Tough life, huh?"

She turned her face away from his stinking smoke. "Did I say that?"

"Well, if you'd do everything over."

"I'm tired of being on the short end of the stick is all. Doctors, hospital bills …"

"You look in fine shape to me."

She went silent, feeling naked and dirty in that awful way she thought was gone.

"You know how to protect your assets in these unpredictable times?" Herbie drilled Ginger with meaningful eye contact.

Only fourteen minutes until two. Fourteen minutes until Dante arrived and she could lock up.

"Diversify," he smirked, his Scotch cigar breath making her want to puke.

Was there a fucking brain above his Johnson? Any fool could figure out the basics of financial investment with half a chance. That was another course she could teach if she ever went back to UCLA to finish her degree. She didn't need condescension, thank you very much, all she needed was Capital with a capital "C."

"A girl with your assets deserves to be happy." He was jabbing his finger at her chest now. Crass bastard.

Happy? She didn't even remember how to spell the word. Not that there weren't nice moments now and again. But the most she could say about the last few years was hey, she showed up. A good day happened when the other shoe didn't drop. Which reminded her of that catchy commercial selling some antacid-something-or-other. (She didn't believe in over-the-counter garbage herself. Best medicine she knew was Suck-It-Up, the giant economy size bottle. Bad day? Suck it up. Things could be worse. A lot worse. Hang around long enough, and worse was a sure thing.) How'd that old TV jingle go again? Oh yeah. How do you spell relief? Ginger knew. R-e-l-i-e-f was when the other shoe did not drop. That was as close as she knew to happy.

"Where're you from, Ginger? You don't look like the L.A. type to me."

"No place you ever heard of."

"Be a good girl now. Didn't Fred tell you to be nice to his best buddy?"

She hated being called a good girl. Even when she was a kid, the phrase riled her natural sensibilities.

"Illinois."

"Chicago?"

"Downstate."

"Gotcha. Some burg like Peoria."

Richard Pryor came from Peoria. She found that out the only time she saw him perform in person, at a dingy club off Sunset where he did his first comeback gigs after torching half his body. He made her laugh so hard she peed her pants. It was the last time she could remember laughing like that. Laughing so hard she cried. But the crying got big and loud and out of control and she could not stop. The bouncer told her it was time to leave because she was disturbing the other patrons. Pryor went right on trash talking while security escorted her out. She admired that kind of talent. The show must go on.

"You know what plays in Peoria, Ginger?" He blew twin rings of cigar smoke out of the corner of his mouth.

"No, I can't say I do." She shifted her burning eyes from the tobacco's downwind.

"That's the joke, honey, nothing plays there. No wonder you got out of town. Who the fuck wants to die in Hicksville?"

Who the fuck wants to die in L.A.? she wanted to scream. But why bother saying anything? A shithead like Herbie lacked the sensitivity to appreciate any existential point of view.

"Let's you and I have a nightcap together upstairs."

Nausea twisted her insides. She gripped the bar towel tighter and turned away to wipe down the counter. His clammy hand slid across the slick surface and trapped hers.

"I don't drink." She slid away, glancing at her watch again. Twelve minutes until two.

"You're kidding, right?" He reached for her hand again.

She eluded his grasp. "Not even with our special customers."

"Sweetheart …" His voice deepened, a harsher edge now. "I'm the man that keeps your boss in business."

"Is that right?"

"Right as rain." He gulped down half his drink and flashed a cocky grin. "Who do you think keeps the IRS from breathing down his neck?"

"Let me guess. You?"

"Now you're cooking with gas. Your boy Freddy—"

"Mr. Shapiro is not 'my boy.'"

His tongue scooped up a chunk of ice, crunching it between sharp incisors. "That's not what I hear."

Ginger could feel the short fuse she inherited from her old man sizzle and spit, hijacking good sense the way it always did.

"There ought to be a law against malicious gossip, don't you think?" Her eyes met his straight on. *Fuck with me again and I'll staple your balls tight and flat, I don't care who you are.*

Herbie chewed on his cigar, trying to puzzle out the answer to a different question. And then his face lit up and his left hand, the one with the gold wedding ring, flew through the air and slapped the bar like he'd won an easy million in the California lottery. "October 1995!"

There it was. Ten months she'd worked here, and only one other guy had recognized her. The past was the past, and that's where it belonged. She was comfortable in this place, catering the way it did to the young, hip crowd who was still in grade school when her centerfold graced the newsstands. This job she would not screw up. She promised herself and Dante that much.

"September." God hates a liar, her father used to say. As much as she despised the old man, there was no forgetting the childhood lessons of right and wrong he seared on her backside.

"Virgo the Virgin." Herbie clapped and pointed, as if she were some freak in a carnival sideshow.

Ginger winced, her breathing constricted all of a sudden, but she covered it with a taut smile.

"Do me a favor, will you?"

He licked his lower lip and waited.

"Don't tell me your sign."

Guffawing, he parked his cigar and grabbed her hand between his two fat paws. "So, what was it like?"

"What was what like?"

She felt him finger-fucking her right palm, the one with the orange and purple phoenix tattoo on her inside wrist. Inked deep and ragged the first time Dante was in the hospital. For years, the needle took her mind off things. Different needles, different "doctors," depending on the time of day and night. All substances welcome, ingested or swallowed; she was an equal opportunity addict until God and the social workers took her son away. That's when she got sober. Ginger swore on her dead mother's soul she'd never lose custody of her son again.

"You know, posing in the mansion … skinny-dipping in the grotto with Hef and his pals … whatever shit you gals do."

The drunker they got, the more profane and disgusting. She stopped taking it personally a long time ago. Four minutes to go, the white-gloved Mickey Mouse hands on her left wrist promised, only four minutes.

"You mean with all those men watching?" She pulled out of his grip and removed the empty glass, taking perverse satisfaction in making him sweat. "All those bright lights on my bare tits?"

He sucked in his breath, blisters of perspiration erupting across his forehead like a bad case of teenage pimples. Pop. Pop goes the weasel. Ginger's outlaw instinct reared up with reckless vengeance. This time he would not get what he wanted.

"Well, I'll tell you. It was cold. Damned cold. My nipples stood up like little tin soldiers and my pussy hummed 'Summertime' to keep me warm."

And then the other shoe dropped.

He jumped without warning and scrambled across the bar to trap his prey. She was strong and tried to knee him, but Herbie was stronger and just as determined. Pulling her left arm free, she grabbed a bottle of Stoli and slammed it across his jaw. Reeling, he howled like a pissed coyote too slow to corner the juicy meal he'd lined up under a full moon.

"You bitch!" He twisted her arm so far back she thought she was going to pass out. "You goddamned bitch!"

The Stoli slipped from her grip, smashing a wall of fine spirits shelved on the mirrored display behind the bar. Shards of glass exploded into a waterfall of 80-proof alcohol.

A scream came from somewhere. Did it belong to her?

When she was in the maternity ward panting through twenty-two hours of labor, she never heard her own voice. The other mothers were moaning, wailing, pleading for painkillers, but not her, not then. When her boy was born, she closed her eyes and transported herself to another planet far, far away where there was not a weak-willed woman in sight.

Another scream wrenched the air. Deeper this time. Primal.

Herbie looked over his shoulder as the young Black man attacked, pummeling his body like a speed bag at Gold's Gym. Ginger fell back. By the time she found her balance, Dante lost his. Her son lay on the floor, his limbs jerking like a mad marionette.

The first time she saw such a sight was in Vegas. A high roller on a winning streak had tipped her five-hundred bucks, then suddenly whirled around like a spinning top, and collapsed on the poker table. Chips sprayed across a surprised dentist from Des Moines who held a full house, but thanks to Lady Luck, was about to win big because the guy with the royal flush suffered a seizure. What were the odds?

The second time Ginger saw that same strange dance, her only child almost died because she was too stoned to know what was happening. Tonight, she knew. Kneeling next to Dante, she turned him over like they had taught her. Grabbed the bar towel to elevate his head. Pressed her ear to his heart to make sure he was breathing. And then she felt her hair being torn by its roots as Herbie dragged her from her son's side.

"Please," she begged. "Please!"

Herbie said something she couldn't make out. His voice slurred, his head bloodied, he let go of Ginger and staggered toward Dante, the jagged neck of the Stoli bottle in his fist. She lunged for the paring knife next to the limes and thrust it into his chest. He fell forward, impaled on the blade, his aorta severed.

Once Dante stopped seizing, his mother held his hand, helped him to his feet, and explained what needed to be done. Together they carried the body outside behind the brick building that housed the bar. Next to the recycling bin for plastic and empty glass, a dumpster stood ready to be filled with organic garbage. At the shadowed end of the alley, mother and son laid the corpse on top of last week's lettuce. Still weak, Dante stumbled when he climbed out of the dumpster, so she told him to go wait in the car while she finished. She would drive them home as soon as she had a little more time to think everything through.

Ginger worked quickly. Rifling through Herbie's pockets, she pulled out a wad of cash for future emergencies and dug deeper. That's when she struck gold: her boss's flash drive, ready for the taking. Insurance better than any benefit package. Then she went back inside to sweep up the broken glass and wash down the indigo-blue tile where Herbie's blood had spilled. His cigar still smoldered in the empty bar glass next to his monogrammed butane lighter. When she returned to the alley, she carried both, along with a brand-new bottle of Chivas. One more for the road.

After anointing his body head to toe with twenty-five-year-old Scotch, Ginger re-ignited Herbie's last cigar and tossed it along with the lighter into the dumpster. The kindling fire flickered, then burst into flame. Crackling. Consuming. Burning garbage and human remains together in one lovely funeral pyre.

GIDEON, 10 MILES, the highway marker announced.

Shielding her eyes from the glare of the late afternoon sun, she stared straight ahead, refusing even a passing glance at the Indian burial mounds. After Ginger's mother was killed in the accident, the old man ordered Ginger to cart the urn over a moonlit path and pepper a trail of white ashes around ancient rocks to appease the gods. Through drunken sobs, her father had begged her to help him, so they would not take his soul too. The day Ginger graduated high school she headed west to college on a drama scholarship and never looked back. Until now.

In her junior year of American history, when she still believed what she was told, Mr. B informed their class that the South was the only part of the United States ever occupied by a foreign power—that foreign power being Northern troops under Sherman's command. Mr. B, fifth generation Atlanta-born, knew about such things. Occupation can warp the human mind, he warned. It'll drain natural spirit and initiative until the defeated take any humiliation visited upon them. That's how shame takes aim at the occupied heart and never lets go.

Even as a teenager, Ginger suspected personal liberation could be tricky business. With bitter years of life experience under her belt, she knew it for a fact. Nobody with the upper hand ever handed out road maps with escape routes marked in bright red pencil. This way to Freedomland, motherfucker. Still. She and her son were alive. Out of L.A. Perhaps hope was too wild a thing to be held captive after all.

She flinched at the sight of a peeling billboard shaped like a super-size piece of cherry pie announcing, "Polly's Piece of Heaven, large enough to serve you, small enough to know you … only eight miles ahead!" She reassured herself this was the smartest move she could make in their extreme situation.

If there was one thing she understood, it was how to hide. Even if it meant hiding in plain sight, a vision of soft curves and parted lips on a white bearskin rug. Her boss had no evidence, no trail, and no way to identify her or Dante. She was already using a phony ID so guys like Herbie wouldn't embarrass her, Lord have mercy on his rotten ass. He had a mother too, and Ginger regretted that he had to die on her watch. In fact, she'd already asked for the good Lord's forgiveness. Still, never having made the acquaintance of forgiveness in her "family of origin" as they said in her twelve-step meetings, how would she know the fucker if it came knocking on her front door? Not that she had a front door now. Homeless, that's what she was. Why else would her old Corvette head east of its own accord? Maybe she'd find some kind of compensation along the way for all those damn shoes dropped from a falling sky.

"Mom?" Dante stirred. His eyes drifted open, still heavy lidded with drug-like sleep. It was always this way after an episode.

She placed her hand in his. "I'm here."

A bigger cross than a lot of kids had to bear, being the way he was, with no dad to show him how to grow into manhood. Even before he got sick and fell behind in school, classmates teased him without mercy. His father's chocolate skin, with her freckles and pale blue eyes.

She caught sight of it coming out of nowhere, racing up her bumper like a bat out of hell.

"Shit." She yanked her hand from Dante's, gripping the wheel.

"What's wrong?" Her son twisted toward her.

The siren launched into its maddening whine. This stretch of road was always a speed trap, something else the old man lectured her about ad nauseam and still she managed to earn her first 70-in-a-55-zone ticket the day after she got her driver's permit. He never let her forget that one either. Shoveling chicken shit in the hen house for two months to pay him back his lousy one hundred and forty-three bucks. Pissed, she floored the foot pedal like she was running from the hounds of hell, which some might argue she'd been doing for years.

"The cops found his body. They'll put us in jail!" Dante's voice escalated to a fearsome pitch.

"Calm down!"

He started thumping on the dashboard, bug-eyed and wild, like he was about to have another fit. God, he was a sensitive plant. Rock of Gibraltar one minute, bowl of mint jelly the next. They were alike that way.

Up ahead, the interstate turned into a two-lane black-top until Gideon. She remembered that much. Ginger made a fast exit. So did the highway patrolman, flashing his red light like he was chasing a serial killer, for Christ's sake. Usually, she respected perseverance, but not in this case. In this case it was her or him, and she made the decision in L.A. two nights ago that self-sacrifice was no longer an option.

Her speedometer climbed from seventy to ninety in a heartbeat. First she passed a rattletrap pickup, then a clunky station wagon. Ginger was riding high. Nothing could stop her, not even the big silver semi lumbering over the crest in the opposite lane, the same lane she was now traveling in order to scoot past a kid taking his dad's Corolla out for a spin on the right, the same lane the patrolman was also speeding along, still on her tail.

"Oh my God, oh my God, oh my God!" Dante was screaming now.

The trucker did not blink. He was king of the road, even here in this land of New World pharaohs. Kings, regardless of the century, should never budge from their rightful place. That's exactly what her old man used to believe, and look what happened to him.

Ginger veered out of the trucker's path back into her own lane, leaving the patrolman with two choices: collide with the kid in the Corolla or with the hard-nosed trucker who would give no ground. A third alternative proved more appealing. He sailed off the blacktop into Earl Hadley's cornfield and sideswiped a two-ton National Harvester at rest on the south forty.

Ginger looked at Dante, who was hyperventilating at her side. When she reached over, he tried to pull away. She held on, stroking his tense muscled forearm until he could breathe again.

Sundown. The pyramids, behind them now, were turning purple against the butterscotch sky. Only a couple more miles to go. Up ahead she saw a half-lit neon sign advertising Polly's Piece of Heaven.

A few minutes later she crawled into a gravel parking lot in front of the pie-shaped café, then circled round back. She hid the car behind a stand of weeping willows, thicker and taller than the last time she saw them, in case the patrolman called in her plates—although nobody would think to search here at the end of the world.

Turning off the key, she felt dizzy. It was time, whether she was ready or not. Time for her long river of regret to run into a greater sea.

She faced Dante. "You hungry?"

"No way, not in that nasty place."

"Regular meals, that's what the doctor said."

"I'll wait for Mickey D's." He stuffed a double wad of Juicy Fruit in his mouth.

The place looked deserted, not like the old days before the car crash took away her mother and left the drunk driver a bitter cripple. Ginger climbed out of her Corvette and walked up the cracked wooden steps. A tiny bell jingled like always when the door opened, but Polly did not exit the kitchen to greet her daughter. No hostess appeared to offer a menu. Johnny Cash's whiskey-throated baritone sang the "Folsom Prison Blues" on the jukebox. He seemed to be the only one around.

"Anybody here?"

"We're closed!" The owner called from the kitchen.

"Then why'd you leave the door open?" She looked around, thinking a good coat of paint would do wonders.

"Lock it on the way out."

"Not leaving."

An old man in a wheelchair rolled out of the shadows, cradling a shotgun on his knees. "Don't give me any trouble."

"It's your daughter."

The old man squinted behind his bifocals, raising the gun to ward off his intruder.

"My daughter's in California."

"Not anymore."

He rolled closer, staring at the woman in front of him like she was an apparition from the Indian burial mounds.

"My God," he croaked. "Julia Mae?"

The bell jingled. She stiffened then relaxed when she saw it was Dante. They would be safe here, she reminded herself again. Safe.

"Jesus Christ," Dante whispered when he saw the old guy with the shotgun.

"Robbing the cradle now?" Her father snorted in disgust. "And colored to boot. This the latest no-good bum in your life?"

"No, this is your grandson."

The two men stared at each other.

Shameless! That's what the old man had hissed over the phone after her naked picture hit the magazine stands. *You are a shameless woman!* He got that right.

The prodigal daughter felt a wellspring of laughter deep inside threatening to break loose. How could she help but take pleasure in bringing the first man and last man in her life together? Too long coming, but most miracles were. A "Biblical offering," her faithful mother might have called this moment, and that was good enough for her. No question her father used to be an asshole when he drank, but after he got religion to avoid the burning fires of Judgment Day, he learned a thing or two about charity. He would take them in. Dante would adapt. And she would be there to protect her son as he protected her. Just because the three of them were broken didn't mean they had to stay that way. All things considered, pride proved a pretty worthless substitute for solace.

"Dante, shake hands with your grandfather."

"Not while he's holding that thing."

She stepped to her father's side, lifted the shotgun from his grip, and placed it behind the counter. He did not object. His grandson's hand grazed his grizzled claw like a soft bullet taking mercy on its mark. The old man did not pull away. The grown daughter wondered how many more pages in the book of hours she and her father would suffer through together. Nobody ever knew, that was for certain. Here today, gone tomorrow. And never any warning.

When Mr. B ran off with the principal's wife during Easter break, nobody saw it coming. Least of all the sad sack principal. Before he left town, Mr. B encouraged his favorite student to join the drama club. *Julia Mae, we all got to role-play life when the occasion calls for it. That's the only way to get through.* And she was glad she took his advice.

Her fist tightened around the flash drive in her jacket pocket. If Herbie had his life to live over, would he do things different too? A hell of a memory, that bastard, up to a point. They had first met at a bachelor party in Rancho Mirage right after she landed in L.A., three years before she won her shot at immortality with the centerfold. Funny how he remembered the airbrushed goddess but not the teenage girl who sold her innocence on a desert night under a star-choked sky.

A pal of mine is having a shindig over the weekend, her agent said, honchos from the business. All you have to do is smile and be friendly. Trust me, this can be a big career move.

Julia Mae—she was still Julia Mae then—showed up as she was instructed. A curtain of smoke sucked the breath out of her lungs, but she stayed. Herbie told her she was special, so she stayed. He invited his friends to join the fun and still she stayed. She did not leave. She did not refuse. She did not deviate from the script she'd been given. She performed her part, and they paid her for the pleasure. Herbie promised he'd remember her name the next time he lunched with his buddies at the studio. He had a great memory, he said.

She had a great memory too. His Cuban cigars, the drunken cronies, their Scotch-soaked hundred-dollar bills. None of that mattered anymore.

She felt free now. Free as a bird.

BLONDE NOIR

DC DIAMONDOPOLOUS

Kit Covington sat on the sofa in her Pacific Palisades mansion with a cigarette lodged in the side of her mouth. A cloud of smoke floated around her head. She adjusted the oxygen tube in her nose, then brushed ash from her dog Muffin's champagne-colored curls. The miniature poodle dozing in Kit's lap startled when the camera crew from *The Great Morning Talk Show* banged equipment into Kit's antique furniture.

"Watch it! You scratch anything, you'll pay for the restoration." Since her left lung had been removed, Kit's husky voice had a rattle that lingered between words chaining them together like loose ball bearings.

"Sorry," the stocky, tattooed sound woman said.

Kit wondered if the all-female crew was a set-up—some kind of knife-twisting in the gut. She'd been anxious about the interview and now regretted it.

Her son, Robin, urged her to confront the nonsense. The 1950s blonde bombshell became notorious because of some damn YouTube video a pop singer made by super-imposing Kit's dance sequence from the 1956 movie, *I Was a Teenage She Wolf from Mars*, while he sang to her.

It went viral. Paramount capitalized on it with a box set of her films. The Screen Actors Guild sent her checks she hadn't seen in sixty years.

Kit would have laughed at the male juvenile obsession with her big breasts, platinum blonde hair, and erotic gyrations in her bullet bra and tight sequined space suit, but the video was made during a time when actresses came forward and named producers, directors, and actors who raped and assaulted them. The video ignited a firestorm of criticism from young women, who blamed her for their sexualization. She became the poster girl, Adam's Eve, the anti-feminist, the target for all the ills cast upon womanhood—making her name *Kit* into a verb synonymous with "fucks for favors."

What a load of shit!

Kit had had enough after months of headlines, *CNN* pestering her old studio for her telephone number, and the tabloids offering money to anyone who had a recent picture of her. Centerfolds, headshots, movie-posters, her sexy blonde images from the fifties were everywhere.

She chose *The Great Morning Talk Show* because Bridget Lundgren, the lawyer turned TV host, defended her on the show.

Muffin jumped from Kit's lap and wolfed a piece of jelly donut the beefy, spiked-haired, lighting woman had dropped.

"This isn't a barn! Use a napkin. That's a three-hundred-year-old Persian rug," Kit said.

"Sorry, Miss Covington."

Kit watched Lundgren scrutinize the pictures on the wall. She was a real fashion plate in a navy pantsuit, with her short blonde hair tucked behind her ears. Kit tensed when the woman took a photograph from her carnival days off the wall and examined it, revealing a yellow nicotine outline.

How dare she!

"Is this from the Gerling Carnival?" Lundgren asked.

"Could be," Kit said, surprised that Lundgren knew about her carny days. Lundgren replaced it and moved to the photo of Kit riding bareback in *The Barnum and Bailey Greatest Show on Earth,* where she performed flips until she fell from the horse and broke her ankle.

Above the walk-in fireplace, Lundgren gazed at the huge painting of Kit by Willem deKooning. It was Kit's favorite, by the artist who inspired her to take up painting. Completed in 1958, when she was twenty-five, the painting recalled the memory of sitting for hours, her back arched, her tits pointing to the North Star, pouty full lips, a halo of platinum blonde hair, and the moist come-hither look women still use to lure men into the bedroom.

"This is one of the few deKoonings I've seen that isn't an abstract," Lundgren said. "He did others."

"My favorite was the *Woman* series. I love how he broke rules," Kit said.

Kit puffed on her cigarette and flicked ash into a large serving dish sitting next to her. She wondered how much of the art world Lundgren knew. In person, Kit judged her as a cool and calculating woman, the way she inspected the pictures as if they hid the da Vinci code. Why not ask how all the hullabaloo affected her, how it made her irritable, critical, and bitchy. She wondered if Lundgren had gone so far as to play nice-nice on TV, knowing Kit would be watching.

Outside the sliding screen door, she saw Robin watering the rose bushes. Since the operation, he'd been pestering her to stop smoking. She cut back from four packs a day, to two and a half.

What the hell did he want? She'd been smoking since she was ten. When he tried to scare her with images on his phone of how the cancer could spread to the liver and kidneys, she grabbed the phone and threw it at him. She made him swear that when she died, he'd put her in a box, stick a cigarette in her mouth—preferably lit—and prod a lighter in her right hand.

"I can go without oxygen for four minutes," Kit said. "So break. I don't want these damn tubes on camera. I'll need a cigarette—"

"Your son told us," Lundgren said.

Miffed by Lundgren's rudeness, Kit said, "When do we start?"

"In five minutes. Do you need to use the restroom?"

"My legs are cramping." Kit struggled to rise, shooing Lundgren away when she tried to help. She stood and rolled the oxygen tank she called Sherman across the living room floor while pulling a pack of Winstons and a lighter from the pocket of her long flowing gypsy skirt.

"Aren't you afraid of the tank exploding?" the sound woman asked as Kit wobbled by.

"No, I'm not. If I could walk a tightrope while on my period, I can roll a damn dolly while smoking a ciggie."

The girl raised her eyebrows and turned away.

Robin saw her and slid open the screen.

"I don't want to do this," Kit said. "That woman's going to ambush me."

"C'mon Mom, you liked her."

"Not anymore. She snapped at me, '*Your son told us,*'" she mimicked.

Kit pushed past Robin and stood above her tiered English garden. Even with her fading sense of smell, she caught fragrances of her lemon and peach trees. Below the garden was a view overlooking Highway 1, Malibu, and the Pacific Ocean. She had bought the house in the fifties while pregnant with Robin and married his father, Daniel, soon after.

The April morning glistened as Catalina Island sat like a treasured cast-off from the mainland. Cast-off. When Kit hit her late twenties, it was over. No producer wanted to hire an old hag at thirty. Her agent got her jobs on TV, as a panel member on *To Tell the Truth, I've Got a Secret,* and her big whoop-de-doo, the center box on *Hollywood Squares.* In the 1970s, her agent dropped her.

"You signed a contract, Mom. Let people hear your story." Robin peered into the living room. "They're ready for your close-up."

Kit rolled her eyes. Robin was always quoting from *Sunset Blvd.*, *The Wizard of Oz,* or *All About Eve.* On occasion he'd dress in drag and perform dance numbers from *Cabaret, A Chorus Line,* and musicals she never heard of. Her boy knew how to make her laugh.

Kit counted five strangers in her house, eating, drinking coffee, moving her furniture, and using her bathroom. Well, at least they were women and wouldn't be pissing on the floor.

"We're ready, Miss Covington," the sound woman yelled.

"C'mon, Mom. It'll be fun."

"I look like an old beatnik."

"You are an old beatnik."

Kit's chuckle rumbled like a truck bouncing over potholes. She smoothed her long white hair with her ciggie hand. She hadn't worn lipstick or make-up in years. She lived in sandals and, before the operation, went barefoot.

Robin waited for Kit to enter, then slid the door behind him. Kit rolled Sherman to the couch and settled in. Muffin jumped in her lap and Jezebel the cat slinked around the sofa and nestled beside Kit.

"We'll open with the video," Lundgren said, "then cut away for the interview."

"Why show that again?"

"It's the reason for the interview, Miss Covington."

How sucky, Kit thought. She wasn't ashamed. She just didn't like having to defend herself. "Everyone in the world has seen it."

"It's a lead-in," Lundgren said.

Kit scowled at Robin. He came over and straightened the string of turquoise and silver beads that dangled from her neck.

"Qult fussing."

"Come out, come out, wherever you are and meet the young lady, who fell from a star," Robin whispered.

"Glinda the Good Witch," Kit mumbled.

Robin winked at her.

"Ready when you are, Bridget," the camerawoman said.

"Good morning. Today, we have a very special guest. Kit Covington. In case you've been living under a rock the last several months," Lundgren smiled, "we're going to play the video that's caused a sensation. Here's the Grammy-winning pop star, Walker, singing from the hit video, 'You're My Dream Girl in the Night' along with Kit Covington from her movie, *I Was a Teenage She Wolf from Mars.*"

The video played on a small monitor. Kit watched herself from the 1956 horror movie, dancing, spinning, cleavage bouncing, her generous ass stretching the satin on her sequined spacesuit. It was hard to imagine her wrinkled and shriveled body once had so much oomph and had been so sexy.

She took off the tube and laid it beside her.

The camerawoman pointed her finger at Lundgren.

"We're sitting in the home of Kit Covington, a movie actress known as the Queen of the Bs from the 1950s, who has become infamous for being the poster-girl for the sexualization of generations of women."

"That's a load of shit!" Kit said. "Why blame me? Women have always used their bodies to get what they want. As if women didn't fuck before 1956."

Lundgren's jaw dropped. Seconds went by before she made the throat-slash sign with her hand.

Kit coughed and hacked. Muffin jumped on the floor. Jezebel leaped from the sofa and ran around the couch. Kit took the tube and fastened the nasal cannula inside her nostrils, then lighted up a Winston. She inhaled and glanced at the stunned crew and Lundgren. Robin, with his eyes popping and mouth opened, reminded her of Joan Crawford in *Whatever Happened to Baby Jane?*

"You can't swear on TV," Lundgren said.

Kit glanced at Lundgren, looked away, and flicked ash into the dish. It was a knee-jerk reaction, a build-up from the last several months. Also, she wasn't convinced Lundgren was on her side. "You can't go off the rails like that, Miss Covington. It won't help you."

"Infamous. Sexualization. Men sexualize women. Who's head of advertising? They use sex to sell hamburgers, anything. Look at films! Who runs the networks?"

"It's a lead-in," Lundgren said.

"I've been assaulted and harassed like all those women. I don't blame anyone but the shits who hurt me." Kit blew smoke at the side of Lundgren's face. "How dare you judge me."

Lundgren waved away the smoke. "I'm not, Miss Covington. Not at all," Lundgren said. Jezebel arched her back and rubbed against Lundgren's leg.

Kit crushed the cigarette into the plate. She narrowed her gaze at the blonde. The way she furrowed her brow and gently stroked Jezebel didn't fool Kit. Behind Lundgren's look of compassion was a frozen dish of ambition.

"Would you like to try it again?" Lundgren said.

Kit caught the rapport—the way Lundgren and Robin shot glances at each other—and now her cat had turned traitor.

She took off the oxygen tube. "Muffin." The poodle ran to her and leaped in her lap. Robin sat at the far end of the couch.

"We're ready," the camerawoman said.

Lundgren looked into the camera.

"We're here with Kit Covington. Known in the 1950s as Queen of the Bs, she has made a scandalizing comeback—"

"Scandalizing! That's nothing compared to the shit I see on HBO."

Lundgren made the throat-slash sign and stood from the sofa. "We need to take a break."

"We sure as hell do." Kit attached the oxygen tube and rose from the couch. Muffin bounded to the floor. Kit wheeled Sherman to the screen door, shooing Robin away, opened it, and went outside.

"Mom?"

Kit ignored him. She wheeled Sherman down the ramp while lighting a cigarette. She and her boy had been snookered into believing Lundgren was on her side.

"Scandalizing," Kit mumbled. What did Lundgren know about the life of a girl in the 1940s? Those young punks don't know a damn thing about what life was like before they were born. She clamped the ciggie in the corner of her mouth and steered the wheels over the yellow bricks Robin had laid that led down to her studio. She'd shut the door, pick up her palette and brush, and lose herself as she disappeared into her painting.

The white stucco building, with red bougainvillea blooming against the side of the wall, inspired the artist in Kit. She painted color in splashes and dashes, mix-matching paint, blending oil, watercolor, and charcoal onto the canvases. Entering her studio was the closest thing to going to church. It was a place where her creativity transported and elated her.

She mashed the cigarette into the standing ashtray outside. The galleries complained of having to clean her canvases. To show her how the smoke diminished her work, Robin took a moist cloth and gently wiped a painting. The rag turned yellow. Without the cover of nicotine, the colors burst with vitality. It was a huge sacrifice not to smoke while she painted, but for her art, she would do anything.

Kit went into her sanctuary, the studio overlooking her cactus garden. Rows of tall windows allowed light to stream in. And where there weren't windows, her imagination decorated the walls. Robin had constructed built-ins for stacking paintings, nooks for brushes and paints, a worktable with drawers. Her boy built the studio exactly how she insisted. In the late 1980s, Robin went behind her back and entered her work in contests. Furious by Robin's betrayal, even when she won, she wouldn't talk to him for days. He adored being the son of a movie star, but being her art agent satisfied both his nurturing and dramatic nature. He arranged her exhibits at MoMA, the Whitney, and others, with as much flare as his once movie star mother. He made deals so her work hung in The Metropolitan Museum of Art and the Prado. From the beginning she signed her work D. L. Hawkins, after Robin's father, leaving off his last name, Sutton. He lived his forty-four years as an art form, free and spontaneous—he danced when other men walked. My God, how she missed him.

Kit made a fortune from her paintings, donating millions of dollars to art institutes. Who would take her seriously if they knew the esteemed D. L. Hawkins was once a second-rate sex kitten?

Kit shut the door against the world. It hurt having those young women wrongly judge her. She knew what women went through, especially young women. Mad at herself for being so sensitive, she hated to admit that she cared what others thought of her.

"I knocked, but you didn't answer."

Kit turned so fast the oxygen cannula pulled at her nostrils.

The blonde talk show host stood in the doorway, holding Muffin. Lundgren wore the same expression—open mouth, wide eyes—as when Kit dropped the f-bomb.

"Oh my God. I don't believe it."

"I'm not doing the interview," Kit said.

Lundgren gazed at the art on the walls. "Neither am I, Miss Covington."

"Then why are you here? And why are you holding my dog?"

"I followed Muffin," Lundgren said, releasing the poodle. "She brought me here."

"Fink," Kit said, glaring at the dog.

"I wanted to let you know I cancelled." Lundgren continued to stare at the art and the unfinished oil painting on the easel. "And to say goodbye." Lundgren shook her head. "I can't believe it," she said, looking at a pastel that leaned against the wall. *I'm standing in D.L. Hawkins's studio.*"

Kit hacked, "Th—This is," she stuttered, "*private.*"

"I'm sorry. I swear—*swear* I won't mention a word to anyone. Are you and Hawkins an item?" she said, glancing at Muffin's bed and water dish in the corner.

Shaking, startled by the intrusion into her secret life, Kit watched dumbfounded as Lundgren made a beeline to the easel.

"You, you're not supposed—" Kit stammered.

"A merry-go-round, where the horses are riding the people," Lundgren said.

Didn't Lundgren hear her? Just barged her way into D. L.'s studio as if Kit didn't exist. She shuffled across the wooden floor, shoving Sherman over to the easel.

Lundgren angled her head. "Animal cruelty. It's amazing to me how Hawkins takes an idea and turns it on its head. I saw his exhibit at MoMA when I did my post-graduate work. Blew me away."

"You know his work?" Kit asked.

"I majored in art. Didn't have the talent, so I changed to law." Lundgren leaned into the unfinished painting. "He tells a story with brush strokes. What a genius." She looked at Kit. "I know he's a recluse, but I'd be honored to meet him."

It reminded Kit of when Robin told her how critics and docents praised her work at exhibits. But to have someone stand in her studio and express how her art touched them, well, it made her—happy.

"He uses horses a lot," Lundgren said. "My favorite is the *Equine Series.* You can feel the movement, hear the hooves beating against the ground."

Kit was impressed by the woman's knowledge, her trained eye.

"Where did you meet? In the carnival, or circus? It must have been a hard life."

"Not as bad as home. Carnival came to town, and I ran away. Fourteen years old, a hoochie coochie girl. It was roughest on the animals and freaks. In 1948, no jobs for women, but I survived." Kit hadn't talked about her life with the carny for years. But like Lundgren said, it showed up in her work, often with horses. "The circus. Then the pin-ups and movies. I survived that too. Not like the other blonde bombshells. So many died—suicides, overdoses. Jayne Mansfield was killed in a car crash." Kit felt fatigued. "Yes," she nodded, "I survived that life, too."

Lundgren listened, but Kit observed her inching her way toward the collage series on the worktable.

"This is an incredible studio. The lighting. High ceilings. Skylights. Everything an artist could dream of. Makes me want to paint again." Lundgren glanced at Muffin lapping water from her bowl and then settling into her bed.

Kit flinched when Lundgren spotted her pink paw-patterned smock draped over the back of a chair and the unopened pack of Winstons on the worktable.

Lundgren turned slowly. She didn't look at her, just stared off. Kit experienced a shock of her own. She saw Lundgren putting it all together—amazement, then the revelation. Oh shit! What could Kit do about it? Kill her?

Lundgren tidied her short blonde hair behind her ears.

"I need a cigarette." Kit wheeled Sherman toward the door. "C'mon Lundgren. D. L. wouldn't want anyone but me alone with his work," she said, making light of a moment that changed both their lives.

Muffin ran out the door. Kit looked over her shoulder. "You coming?"

Their eyes met. Lundgren's were filled with tears.

"I'm tired. I need to sit down. Coming?"

Kit and Muffin walked down the path to the cactus garden. She figured Lundgren was somewhere behind. Tears. She knew them well. But when others cried, it put her at a disadvantage, made her feel mushy. And the young woman looked so beautiful standing in her studio with the sunlight catching every nuance of understanding that passed over her face.

Kit sat on a wrought iron bench, pulled Sherman close, lighted up, and surveyed her garden. On a lookout, atop the Palisades, her nearest neighbor somewhere below, she really was a recluse. At eighty-five, with death a kiss away, she'd been angry for decades, for her stepfather's abuse, Daniel's death, even the small slights, building on top of one another making her view of life a vista of loneliness.

Muffin whined. Kit looked up and saw Lundgren. Muffin jumped up on her hind legs begging Lundgren to pick her up. The woman crouched down, petted Muffin, and looked at Kit. She nodded.

"I have two silkies. I bet she smells them," Lundgren said.

"It's more than that." Kit's voice had the tired monotony of a flat tire. It wasn't even noon and she needed a nap. She coughed, hacked, and spit out a glob of phlegm. "Excuse me." Kit took out her handkerchief and wiped her mouth. "I'm not used to company," she said and continued to smoke.

"Hey, Mom," Robin yelled from the top of the garden path, "is everything okay?"

"Yes," Lundgren answered for her. "Tell the crew I'll be up in a few minutes." Lundgren handed Muffin to Kit and walked around the garden. Her hair was tousled by the breeze.

Kit preferred her like this—mussed. She wondered what the woman looked like at home, in jeans and a T-shirt. Lundgren walked through the narrow aisles, inspecting the plants.

"They're beautiful how they bloom," she said. "Like a miracle. I love the subtlety of the color, the shape, how the sunlight captures the unexposed side of the petals." Kit remembered how Lundgren studied the photos on the wall. She was sensitive, with an artist's eye. Maybe she wasn't going to exploit her after all. The pretty blonde with the slender build must have put up with a lot of sexual harassment. If so, Kit doubted she'd share any of it with her. She thought of Lundgren as quiet, low-key, except when she talked about D. L. Hawkins, then she herself bloomed.

"I understand why you had to choose a pseudonym," Lundgren said with her back still to Kit. She turned. "I can't imagine what you went through." Lundgren walked over and sat next to her. "Not just your generation. My mother had me young. My father ran off and the only way she could keep me and get an education was to dance in strip clubs. She made a good living. That was the 1980s. It's still hard."

The two women gazed at the garden with the Pacific as a backdrop.

"There's a way to make everyone forget about your video," Lundgren said. Kit took a deep inhalation of oxygen, closed her eyes, and savored her last moments as D. L. Hawkins. It was her little champagne-colored poodle who had pulled back the curtain and revealed her identity—Muffin, leading Lundgren down the path to her door, giving her away. Kit could see it now. Robin would take off her oxygen tube and dance her around the living room, overjoyed that his mom would be coming out of the closet. The thought of his endless euphoria exhausted her, but Lundgren was right. It would wipe that stupid video off the networks and change her name from a verb back to a noun.

She stubbed out her Winston. Leaning on Lundgren, she struggled to her feet. "I'm going to lie down. Run this by Robin. You guys work out the details. But tell him not to wake me until three. And I'll want my martini extra dry."

Kit shuffled along. She pulled Sherman as the wheels made clap-clap sounds over the yellow brick path, with Lundgren beside her and Muffin running ahead.

192

Acknowledgment
"Blonde Noir" by DC Diamondopolous was originally published in *Human Decency is Key* in 2018.

FIDELITY

JACK NICHOLLS

Joan Elvidge was dead.

My phone alerted me three ways in three minutes—text message, Facebook, and tweet. Time of death was 11:02 a.m. Pacific Standard Time, five hours ago, and I was stuck watching a permed starlet mangle Brittany Murphy's lines for the *Clueless* thirtieth anniversary refill.

"*You're* a virgin who can't drive," she said, posed sassily in front of the greenscreen. She delivered the line to an off-camera monitor, where Alicia Silverstone's performance played to give the timing.

"CUT!" yelled the director from his folding-chair. "Goddammit. Fidelity!"

That was my cue. The girl glared at me as I stepped forward. Talent always hated Fidelity.

"It's 'you're a virgin,' half-beat, 'who can't drive,'" I said. "Emphasis on *virgin*. And play up the Jersey accent."

I had a good memory for detail.

"I'm interpreting!" the girl complained. Her name was Jaslyn or Jasline or something.

"Nobody wants your *interpretation*, doll," said the director. "This is Hollywood."

My phone vibrated again. Jazzlynne was storming back to her dressing room now, and it was close enough to five that I guessed we weren't getting any more work done today. I slipped out the delivery door and ran up to the neglected roof garden. Joan Elvidge was dead, and so I had two calls to make.

Scratch answered on the first ring. "Pacific Edge Theater."

"Scratch, it's me. You've heard the news?"

"Elvidge? Yeah. I'm digging around the basement tapes now. We'll start the Deathwatch at six. Remember *The Roost?* Who else was in that?"

"Bud Sullivan. He's still around."

"Bud, yeah. Okay, we'll start with that, bit of classic T&A. You don't see curves like that no more, do ya?"

"Do you have *Beauty versus Beast?*"

"*Beauty versus Beast?* Of course. Anytime a star hits ninety you gotta be prepared. It's somewhere."

There was pause, emphysemic wheezing, a clatter of film stock being shifted.

"Yeah, we got it. I'll make it the centerpiece."

"We'll be there," I said, and hung up.

I had to call Dad.

★

Once, Dad would have been able to reel off the whole of Joan's filmography with critical commentary, but his sentiments at the news of her death seemed more polite than heartfelt. "It's a shame," he said.

The House in the Hills, with its confusion of staircases flanked by ornamental cacti, was hardly senior-friendly, but my parents had lived there since the '70s and had no intention of leaving now. I pulled into the drive beneath the eucalyptus and honked twice. Dad emerged in his old awards suit—it hung too large on him these days—and descended the steps with a shuffling, heavy tread. I swung open the passenger door and he eased himself onto the leather. Mom watched his progress from the portico and waved us off as I pulled away from the curb.

"How are you feeling?"

"Oh, all right. I had a couple of teeth taken out last week."

"What?" I glanced sideways, and he parted his lips in a feral snarl to show me the wet gap at the back of his mouth. "Why didn't Mom tell me?"

"She doesn't like you to worry. What would you have done, come watch?"

"Did it hurt?"

"Yes," he said shortly. We drove in silence for a minute, while I focused on sliding between lanes to push through the rush hour traffic. It had already been seven hours since Joan's time of death.

"You know, you really don't have to do this," Dad said. "It doesn't make sense for you to come out to pick me up, then go back down. I can just watch on the TV."

"We always do it together."

"I know. I know."

The quiet welled up between us, sharpening the outside sounds of the engine's rumble, the whistle of the air past the window, distant horns.

"Reading anything?" I asked, idling in the traffic. It was 6:15 p.m., and I was anxious about missing the show.

"Not much. How's the work?"

"It is ... good. We're expecting Pacino soon, so Paramount is finally looking for someone who can refill the Godfather. It's going to be the hottest part in Hollywood."

"Very morbid," he said.

We drove the last mile in silence and pulled up on the curb beneath the marquee, picked out in amber sunset. Scratch had dressed up the sign for the occasion. "DEATHWATCH: Joan Elvidge" it read, and in smaller lettering beneath: *The Roost, Beauty Versus Beast, Molasses*.

"A double feature," Dad said approvingly, if not quite accurately.

Scratch had our tickets ready to go. He perched on a barstool behind the counter with a black fedora slouched on his head. "Good to see you again, sir," he said to Dad, who grunted in assent.

Theater 1 was always on blockbuster rotation; Scratch used the smaller Theater 2 for Deathwatches. The fabric on the seats was torn, and the screen wasn't much bigger than a high-end plasma, but we were thankful Scratch kept the tradition at all. The multiplexes had given it up.

There weren't many people there yet, and we were able to take our usual seats in row D, 20 and 21; Dad liked to be close to action. We were a little late, but it hardly mattered. A square-jawed Bud Sullivan was saying to the surviving lab-coated scientists, "The radiation's been contained. There's nothing there but owls."

"I've never seen this one," Dad murmured.

"Yes, you have. We used to watch it together."

He shook his head slowly. "No. I don't think so."

Dad quickly dozed off, and I didn't blame him. As an adult, I could see *The Roost* was a cheap Harryhausen knockoff. Joan screamed with enthusiasm, but her performance wasn't going to be a great loss to mankind. The villainous Dr. Werther had passed decades earlier, so in the empty lulls of his scenes I studied Dad's face in the flickering light. Hair thinning on top, bristling mustache tinged with nicotine, the blotches and stains of old age forming around his temples. He'd been a large man, a hearty eater, but that weight had all fallen away since he'd got sick. His face had shrunk into his beard.

People trickled into the theater as the movie progressed, all much older than me. They slid quietly into the back rows like latecomers to church. Nobody spoke.

After the owls had been tricked into catching explosive mice and the world was saved, I went out to buy some soda and Reese's Pieces. Dad and I shared a sweet tooth.

Scratch rolled straight into *Beauty versus Beast*. The last time I'd watched it had been for Jack Lemmon's Deathwatch, and I'd remembered it as an entertaining throwback to the screwball comedy era. Now it was something more existential. The house party was anemic, the hubbub muted, and periodically Joan would flee to lock herself in empty rooms and chatter to the spaces where Jack had once lounged.

It was about 8:20, shortly into the second act, that she began to fade.

It was the hands I first noticed—Joan was very expressive with her hands. Then it was her dress: the color became washed out, then so translucent I could make out the garish wallpaper behind her. I had to strain to hear her dialogue, which had fallen to a whisper.

And then she was gone. Her soul lifted from the celluloid.

Someone in the audience sniffled. An emotional voice cried out, "Goodbye, Joan." The orchestra played on, but there was nothing left on screen but a succession of almost empty rooms, like establishing shots for an event that would never play again.

The audience began to file for the exits, but Dad and I stayed. The Deathwatch was about paying your respects. You waited until the end.

As always, my eye was drawn to the remaining faces on the screen. Children, a couple of young adults. In what was clearly supposed to be the climactic drunken argument, the film intercut between empty close-up and wide-angle crowd reaction shots. But there was only one woman left in the crowd now, unbalancing the composition at the left of frame.

You never really notice extras in the background until they are alone. She was more beautiful than Joan, hooded eyes evocatively framed by dark curls. She was pantomiming her expressions; I could count the beats of the humor from her reactions to unheard dialogue. I wondered what she had been thinking during the filming, if she had been resentful or scornful of the woman—slightly younger, more conventionally attractive—who was going to become a star.

"I know her," Dad commented.

I shot him a dubious glance. Dad was fond of reminiscing about the romantic conquests of his Hollywood days, but he would have been a teenager when this was filmed.

He saw my skepticism. "She's in quite a few of the classics," he insisted. "I've been rewatching them."

The violins swelled, the credits rolled. Some tenacious actors held on for up to eighteen hours after death, so Scratch had scheduled the New Hollywood-era *Molasses* to round out the Deathwatch. But without Joan's Oscar-nominated turn as the mother, there didn't seem much point. Dad started to worry that Mom would worry, so I bought a bottle of water for him to take his pills, and then we headed out to the streetlights. Scratch waved at us from his booth.

We listened to public radio as the car slid through the darkness. Dad stared into the windows of other people's homes and hummed to himself. It was much later than he usually stayed up these days. I racked my brain for something to say. Had he enjoyed it? It was hard to tell. He used to be a man of booming laughs and bellowing rages, but now his emotions remained beneath a placid surface.

We pulled up outside the house. I could see my bedroom window on the upper story, darkened now. But the front light was on, and Mom was waiting there wrapped in a dressing gown. She gave us a smile.

What if he fell, tonight, and that was the end? What if he fell, and I'd had nothing to say?

"I love you," I managed.

"Love you too," he said automatically as he got out of the car. Mom met him at the base of the steps and held his arm tenderly as they shuffled up to the door. I sat in the dark beneath the eucalyptus tree until they were inside, then turned for home.

★

My next week was spent knee-deep in Paul Newman look-alikes in anticipation of a new *Sundance Kid*. First round was surface fidelity, using a Newman's Own Sauce bottle as a convenient comparison. Second round was screen and drug testing. Talent was an investment, and the studios had come to appreciate clean living since Heath Ledger's death and fadeout had bankrupted Legendary Pictures. Apparently, *The Dark Knight* had been a hell of a movie, briefly.

I never had a lot going on after hours, so I was back at the old house for Sunday dinner. I tried to keep my parents company as much as possible; they didn't have a lot going on socially either. Poor Mom. Marrying a man twenty years her senior must have seemed exciting at the time, but now she was in the downswing of that bargain.

Dad was smoking in his screening room, sunk into a collapsing leather couch, lit by the flicker of his little 35mm projector. He called a greeting as I padded past. I moved to the well-lit kitchen, where Mom stirred dinner with one hand and held a tattered Chandler novel in the other.

"How are you guys?" I asked, sneaking a spoonful from the pot.

"I'm well," she said. "Enjoying studying again. It's keeping my brain trained."

"And Dad?"

She shrugged. "He has good days and bad days. The doctor says that it would be dangerous to increase his medication much further, so we'll have to make do with what we have. But we're fine. You're the one we worry about."

"I'm fine too," I protested.

She raised an eyebrow. "Go say hi to your Dad," she said.

I stepped into his den and wrinkled my nose from the blast of cigar smoke. Dad patted the seat next to him without looking round.

"*Psycho,*" I said instantly, taking in a few frames of monochrome taxidermy. If Dad was impressed, he didn't show it.

"An oldie but a goodie," he said, instead.

The camera cut between two empty chairs, silent.

"You know Gus Van Sant shot-for-shotted this, right?" He snorted.

"Jesus, Dad, do you just sit here watching empties now?" I couldn't convey how depressing I found that idea.

He tapped ash into the misshapen clay bowl I'd made for him two decades ago. I sagged down beside him. Dad's den hadn't changed since the bowl's arrival, though it had accumulated more dust. The oil painting of him and Mom on the wall. Film reels stacked higgledy-piggledy. Piles of script books lumped on the shelves, with the half-dozen he'd written himself displayed on the mantle. His two hawk-shaped WGA awards served as rather fascist paperweights. And on the glass table in front of us, a slew of photo albums.

Most of the guys Dad had run with back in the '60s and '70s were now dead of drink, overdoses, heart attacks, or boredom with the twenty-first century. Most of the women were holding on. The photos showed Dad in his hedonistic period: a grinning black bear, rampant chest hair loosed from unbuttoned shirts, arms around aspiring actresses with flat-ironed hair. He kept an eye on the albums, as a way to mark the passing of people he'd fallen out of touch with. More and more of the photos were empty these days.

Blood swirled down the plughole. The reel behind us unspooled, and dead light flooded the room. Dad swore and got up to fix it.

"That's the best bit anyway," he said. "Here, I've got something else to show you."

He fiddled around for a minute, and then a new film started. A noir? Stark shadows and light shining on puddles. I was too young to have seen these. The camera panned over an empty, rain-slick street and came to rest beneath a streetlight. A striking woman in a fur coat lit a cigarette and glanced up through her lashes for a moment, then walked out of shot.

"What did I tell you?" said Dad, coming back around to the sofa. The camera was tracking an empty car now.

"What?"

"The girl from the other night."

I stared at him in confusion, then it clicked. The extra from *Beauty versus Beast*. That had been her again, a little younger but the same curls, same mysterious eyes.

"I told you I'd seen her around," said Dad triumphantly. "You thought your old man was bonkers."

"When was this made?" I asked as the title came up: *The Devil's Kiss*.

"Around 1950 or so."

I surreptitiously checked on my phone. It was 1939, fourteen years before *Beauty versus Beast*.

"And you've seen her in lots of films, you said?"

"Oh yes, way back. One of those faces made for black and white, don't you think? Cheekbones."

"That's too weird. She looked the same."

Dad's retort was lost in a coughing spasm and my pounding him on the back. The mean streets of long ago rolled through the projector, empty now.

★

Scratch looked at me over his sunglasses. "That stuff's gone, man. Nobody wants empties."

"That's why it's cheap," I said. "Don't tell me you can't get it."

"You know, real customers come here also. This is actually a business."

I counted out six fifties onto his ticket tray and pushed it through. He sighed and pocketed them. "I'll call you," he said.

He knew a guy who knew a guy, and over the next week we came to a deal. Scratch would let me use Theater 2 after the eight o'clock showing ended. In return, I bought a ticket for each night and promised to keep him in mind if and when any suitable casting calls came along.

I brought a notebook and a beer and settled in. These were the films too long forgotten to be profitably refilled, from a golden era I'd only heard about. Capra, Hawks, early Hitchcock. *Casablanca* I'd heard called a contender for the greatest movie ever made, but I could barely keep awake through the tinkling piano and empty soundstages. I guess Bogart must have made it away on the plane in the end.

The past had always seemed to me a cold and empty place: drained of color, drained of life. Decomposing imagery of a decomposing world. *The Wizard of Oz* was a revelation. I'd seen the '80s version, of course, but nothing prepared me for the explosion of Technicolor that washed over me in that lonely theater, like a Van Gogh come to life.

And a few people did still pop up, now and then. Children, mainly—sometimes only a twitch in a baby carriage, sometimes a toddler marooned in an empty living room. The last survivors of a receding generational wave, who had lived through World War II, television, the internet, the Towers.

Then there was our mystery woman.

1934: *Cleopatra*, she danced around waving a palm frond in empty Egypt and cheered in the streets of Rome. 1937: *A Star Is Born*, she played a waitress and actually had a line; her voice had a Transatlantic flatness to it, so I couldn't even swear she was American.

And how old? How old? I couldn't be sure. She was always so full of life. A life I watched out of order, in decaying silver slivers. When I found an appearance, I borrowed the film reel from Scratch and surreptitiously cut out her sequences. Like he said, nobody else wanted it.

Each afternoon I rang Dad, and we compared notes. He seemed happy to have an excuse to keep rewatching his old favorites without disapproval, and for my sake he noted down her appearances in his own viewings. She appeared a lot.

"What are you doing this for?" Scratch asked, joining me for ten minutes of *The Adventures of Robin Hood.* "So out of all the background of the '40s, some are still alive. Ain't that just statistics?"

"Maybe. I've got to look back further, Scratch. Can you get silents?"

"Silents? That stuff was all nitrate. You want to burn my place down now?"

"You know, Scratch, I see you stepping into the shoes of a beloved character actor. Perhaps Danny DeVito after he passes, God forbid."

"I see you as an asshole," he said. But he called his guy.

Some of the cans Scratch sourced smelled of rancid butter. Some were encrusted with brown mold. The ones that still worked unreeled in grainy sepia, the only sound the clicking of the projector. It reminded me of those space telescopes. The further you look, the further into the past you go, until there's nothing but flickering background radiation forever and ever.

We found her in 1923.

Younger, for sure, though it was hard to tell how young in her pancake makeup. She danced a lone chorus line, arms clutched around the vanished supports to either side, wriggling painted eyebrows and mouthing a silent song. The motion was jittery, like a cockroach scurrying, and darkness crept in around the edge of the frame.

We watched from the projection booth.

"How old do you think she is there?" I asked Scratch.

He squinted at the flapping images. "I dunno, sixteen?"

"Bullshit, that's a grown woman."

"If you say so."

I did say so. She didn't age. And she was still out there.

★

"So what's the point?" asked Dad at the kitchen table.

"The point? It's incredible! She must be well over a hundred years old. She must have some blood protein or something, like that guy who had natural resistance to AIDS, and when they gave his bone marrow to an HIV positive recipient, he recovered from the disease."

"Getting old isn't a disease."

"Of course it is, Dad! Telomere degradation, transcription errors. But genetic biology is right on the edge of this breakthrough, Dad, on the edge! Maybe it's already there, maybe this woman is a secret test case. You can't give up this close—" My knee jittered under the table.

Dad shook his head, but Mom put a hand on his shoulder and shot him a meaningful look.

"I think it would do you boys good to look into it," she said, pouring me more wine. "What can it hurt?"

He looked exasperated, but at least seemed focused on what I was saying. "Okay, let's say she's out there. How are you going to find her?" he asked.

I gulped the wine. "I'm working on it. I've been comparing the credits for all the films she's been in, but I'm not finding names in common."

"Of course you're not. She was an extra. Those girls come and go like fireflies."

"Well, I thought I'd call some film historians … maybe track down the paperwork for the movies."

Dad dismissively waved away that idea, but his eyes lit up as he started thinking about it.

"The Hollywood Studio Club," he said. "If she was Old Hollywood, she'll be there."

★

We wound down Outpost Drive to Sunset Boulevard, Dad resplendent in a Panama hat and cream suit.

"Alright, six degrees."

"Come on, Dad."

"Six degrees," he repeated loudly. "Kevin Bacon to Jane Fonda."

"Kevin to Donald Sutherland, *Animal House.* Sutherland to Fonda, *Klute.*"

I knew Kevin's filmography. You had to, growing up in my house.

"You're supposed to take six," Dad said peevishly.

"All right, show me Kevin Bacon to Tom Hanks," I said, tossing him a lowball.

Dad stayed silent for a long time and stared into space.

"Hey, don't worry about it," I said awkwardly.

He began to chant. "Tom Hanks was in *The Burbs,* which was a Joe Dante film, so had Dick Miller. Dick Miller was in the original and best *Little Shop of Horrors,* which was a breakthrough for Jack Nicholson. Nicholson gave a passable Welles imitation in the shot-for-shot of *Citizen Kane,* with Diane Keaton, and *she* was with Sarah Jessica Parker in *The First Wives Club,* and SHE starred in *Footloose* with Kevin Bacon. So, there's your six degrees."

"Jesus," I said, glancing sidelong at him.

"You think I've got no brains left. I'm still *compos mentis* for now."

"I don't know what to think. You barely talk to me anymore."

"Maybe you don't listen," he said shortly.

We crawled through the traffic of Sunset Boulevard for half an hour, watched sardonically by the Hollywood sign above. Dad stared out the window at the succession of Starbucks, acupuncturists, and divorce lawyers and shook his head.

The Hollywood Studio Club boasted a grand Art Deco façade, now in very poor repair. We rolled to a halt in front of it, where a rockabilly girl about my age waited beneath three cream archways, arms crossed over a clipboard.

"Hello, Mr.—" she began.

"Indeed," Dad said grandly, extending his hand to shake. "This is my son and amanuensis."

I straightened up and introduced myself as well. She had a sleeve tattoo of Jessica Rabbit entwined in celluloid.

"Sienna," she said. She smiled at me with intensely red lips, then turned back to Dad. "On behalf of the YWCA, it is an *honor* to have an Oscar-winning screenwriter show such an interest in our history. You're researching a movie, you said?"

Oscar nominated, actually, but Dad took the compliment.

"That's right. You know how Hollywood loves celebrating itself. Award-bait piece for one of today's starlets. Sworn to secrecy about the name."

"Well, I can understand why she would be interested, it is *certainly* a fascinating place!" she continued, unlocking the door. "From 1918 to 1975, thousands of girls looking for stardom came through here. Imagine what they must have got up to." She gave me a wink.

"There's no business like show business," I deadpanned.

Blank cream walls, faded green carpet. I thought it was hideous. Our voices echoed among the high ceilings as Sienna took us for the full tour around the inner courtyard, where dying palms drooped in their pots.

"It was fifteen bucks a week back then for a twin room, can you imagine? What a golden era. In some ways a much more inspiring time for actresses. Now, this is a sketch of our most famous resident, who I'm sure you'll recognize," she said, gesturing to an angel-faced chiaroscuro.

"Marilyn?" I guessed. I recognized her from cartoons of the billowing dress.

"She was an old pal. I knew her through Miller," Dad said, stretching a two-second adolescent introduction to its breaking point, but it impressed Sienna and got them chatting away. I lagged behind, trying to imagine the faded corridors ringing with laughter. It was a stretch—it felt more like the Overlook Hotel now.

"Hey, so would Marilyn's admission records be here?" I asked.

"They sure would, we've kept all the archival material. Just through there." She gestured to an office lined with empty pigeonholes and flaking filing cabinets.

"Wow, mind if I have a look?" I said. "I'll catch up."

I knelt by the filing cabinets, picking through cardboard folders. There were hundreds of them, dating from 1919 all the way to the club's closing. But, as I'd hoped, each file was set up like a college admissions profile, with a headshot paperclipped to the inside cover.

Dad was charming Sienna now, even if he misheard half the things she said. She'd taken his arm when he'd stumbled on a step and was now chaperoning him down the hall like he was royalty, listening to his story about being trapped in a lift with Mick Jagger.

Before 1940, most of the photos were blanks—gradations of silver shadow, like an inkblot psychological test. I flipped through file after file, wondering if we were wasting time.

Then, there she was: 1923, sporting a nervously hopeful smile and little-girl curls. *I want to join the Studio Club to become a star like Mary Pickford*, was written in faded ink at the bottom of the page. Her name was Ruth Mercer, and she was born in 1907, when Teddy Roosevelt was President, making her 116 years old.

I slipped the file into my satchel, emerged, and gave Dad a nod. He pretended not to notice, since he was enjoying having an audience again. At last his stamina gave out, and we emerged into the hot buzz of the street.

"Let me get a photo with you guys," Sienna said, sliding an arm around my shoulders and raising her phone. "Proof for when the film comes out!"

"Paint a picture, it'll last longer," suggested Dad. She smiled uncertainly and clicked.

"Well, if you have any more questions for the script, here's my card," she said, proffering it to me. Sienna Lake: Agent and Entrepreneur.

"We will," I said, impatient to be on our way.

"The woman as temptress," remarked Dad as we climbed back into the car. "Nice girl, though."

"Bit young for you, perhaps," I said.

"Nohow," he said, puffing his stomach out. "Contrariwise."

His laughter turned to another coughing fit, and we remembered he was an hour late for his pills.

★

There was no Ruth Mercer on Wiki's list of American centenarians, which furthered my certainty that there was something uncanny about her. I had been planning to hire a private eye, but the next bit was so easy we didn't have to. Five minutes on Google found an elderly Ruth Mercer in the church newsletters and local records of a Bay Area town called Hollister.

"Try the nursing home," said Dad.

"She might not need a nursing home," I said.

"Try the nursing home."

I did, and asked to be put through to Ms. Ruth Mercer. There was nobody of that name at Angel Falls Care Home, but the nurse at Whispering Oaks said, "I'm afraid that Ms. Mercer isn't very good on the phone. Can I take a message for her?"

I hung up, mouth dry.

"Well let's go then," said Dad. "No time like the present."

★

It was a five-hour drive to Hollister, and after we'd finished arguing over whether or not to use the GPS, we got a lot of talking done.

"*2001: A Space Odyssey* will be immortal. When Keir Dullea dies, the audience will just take Bowman's place as observer. Kubrick was a genius."

"I agree, Dad, I'm just saying—"

"If you refill that movie, I will rise from my grave and torment you."

"Stop it; you're not in the grave yet."

"So, what are you planning? Drain her blood and pump it into me? Very Hammer Horror."

"We're not assaulting anyone with a needle," I said. "But if this is as big as I hope it is, we could cut some sort of deal. Get a gerontology team to look at her in return for you being put on a trial programs."

"Oh, I see … a *program*."

"Look I'm trying, all right? Just because you goddamn gave up on everything, I don't have to."

He went still and looked at me. I focused on the road awhile, and he kept on looking.

"I'm sorry," I said.

"That's how you see things, is it?" he asked. "Cancer behind, Alzheimer's on the way, but I'm giving up?"

"Well, you know, most days you seem all right to me."

"I'm not."

"Okay, so you're not. What happened to not going gently into that good night?"

"Do you think your mother would prefer it if I raged all day?"

"I mean you could channel your feelings somewhere. You could write an autobiography. You could try watching some new films."

"New? Reenacting is not acting."

"Christ! I'm just trying to salvage something. Why shouldn't my generation get the same enjoyments yours did?"

"At least our generation knew how to enjoy ourselves. You and your friends drink three cups of coffee, you book yourselves into rehab." He lit a cigar in reproach.

We drove in silence for a while, the strong scent of garlic wafting through the windows as we turned inland. The Whispering Oaks Retirement Community sat on the edge of farmland just outside Hollister. We crunched along a gravel path lined with apricot trees and pulled up outside a flat, pink-roofed building.

"The descent to the Underworld," Dad stage whispered as we approached the door, me lugging his battered projector case behind him.

"That's insensitive, Dad."

Please wash your hands read an A4 sign printed in Comic Sans by the front doors. Dad grudgingly pumped some antiseptic ooze onto his fingers, and we walked inside. Lavender scent wafted from plastic canisters on the walls. A nurse smiled at us and pushed a clipboard across her desk. Half a dozen seniors sat in a lounge watching a flat-screen television, but the nurse said that we would find Ruth in her bedroom. She didn't get out much these days.

She led us through blue carpeted corridors that felt like a mirror-image of the Studio Club where Ruth had stayed a century ago. Dad glanced at me, and I felt my excitement rising as we came to a door with "Ruth Mercer" etched on a bronze nameplate, like a dressing room.

We knocked, then opened the door.

The shrunken woman in the bed didn't look like a movie star anymore. She didn't even look well preserved. She looked like what she was—a very, very old woman, with gray skin and a head drooped low between her shoulders. But when she turned her face uncertainly toward us, I could still see those beautiful lashes framing her clouded dark eyes.

"Good afternoon, ma'am," Dad said softly, doffing his hat. "You don't know us, but my son and I have been looking to meet you. We've been watching your films."

"My ... films? That's a long time ago."

"A lot of water under the bridge, eh?"

I cut in. "Ms. Mercer, we've watched you perform from 1923 to 1948. You didn't age!"

"That's mighty kind of you to say. I was always very proud of my face."

"No," I said, shaking my head. It couldn't be only makeup and healthy living. "That's not what I mean, Ms. Mercer. It's not normal to reach the age you have. Have you spoken with the doctors here? What have they said about your health?"

She clutched nervously at the sheet that covered her, shrinking away from me. "I don't understand," she said.

Dad coughed sharply and waggled his eyebrows at me, breaking my flow. My knee was jittering again. I leaned against the wall to cover it.

Sinking into the visitor chair and fanning himself with his hat, Dad took over. "What my son means to say, Ms. Mercer, is that you are a magnificent actress. You hold the screen."

"I never amounted to anything … wasted my youth."

"That's what youth is for. We brought my projector along. Do you mind if we set it up?" He gestured at me and pointed me to his case.

Ruth laughed hoarsely as I opened it up. "Oh my," she murmured.

We pulled down the blind and set up the projector facing the blank cream wall at the foot of her bed. I loaded in the reel of film I had cut together at Scratch's, and we opened a window to her past. Where, for the first time, she was center stage.

Ruth on the range. Ruth on stage. Ruth in the harem— Dad smiled at the latter. The film spooled through the projector with a whir, snatches of mismatched soundtrack and isolated conversation flitting around us as the light played over her mushy face. I couldn't connect the woman in the bed and the woman on the wall. I felt claustrophobic and slipped back out to the front desk.

"How is Ms. Mercer doing? Is she healthy?"

"She's had a very good run," said the nurse. "But there's not much time left now, poor dear."

"She's had an astonishing run. You must have her medical records. Has anyone ever looked over them?"

The nurse stiffened. "All matters pertaining to our guests' records are confidential."

"What if Ms. Mercer gave her permission?"

"Well, unless you are a member of the family, we would advise her strongly not to do that."

I drummed my fingers on the desk. "I see. Thank you."

I crept back in. The lights were back on, and Ruth was more animated now, sitting upright and drinking from a plastic cup.

"I got off the train at Pasadena, covered in soot, and there was this marvelous smell. Someone told me it was orange groves."

"Do you remember working with Robert Wise?" asked Dad. "I used to play ping-pong with Rob."

"I do. He was a gentleman. Is he still working?"

"No. Dead, I'm afraid."

"Everyone's gone, now, aren't they?" she said. "I lost my friends, and my family. Everyone from the papers and everyone from the pictures. Shirley Temple, did you know she died? Little Shirley. The whole world empties."

"Well, we have to make room," said Dad.

Ruth turned to me. "Your pop said … you wanted my help with something."

I stared at her and then at Dad, who watched me neutrally from the corner.

Once when I was six, I'd packed three apples, a juice box, and a book into my Teenage Mutant Ninja Turtles backpack and run away from home. I don't remember why anymore. But I was going to go live in the Los Angeles Zoo, and I remember how carefully I planned the trip, and how confidently I set off down the hill. Until I reached the end of our street and saw the city stretching out to the horizon. Then I realized my plan wouldn't get me that far, and stood there bawling until someone found me.

I remembered that because it's how I felt now.

"It's all right, Ms. Mercer," I said, and swallowed. "We just wanted to meet you."

"Would you mind playing those pictures again? It's just so funny to see them after all these years."

We did. And then again. Gradually Ruth began to drift, and soon she was in a doze. We sat in dimness behind the pulled shade, listening to a robin test its voice somewhere outside. The film ran out, and the projector shone its blank white square against rose-petal wallpaper.

Dad glanced at his watch. "Come on," he said. "It's time for my pills."

"That was very kind of you gentlemen to pay an old lady a visit," said the nurse as we returned to the desk. "There aren't many who care."

"You look after her. She's a movie star," said Dad.

"Really? Well, the things you learn."

As soon as we stepped outside, Dad reached for his cigar case and lighter. His thumb slipped a few times on the wheel, so I lit it for him. He nodded his thanks, and we stood a while quietly drinking in the sunlight, the projector case hanging loosely from my hands.

"Home again, home again, jiggety jig," he said at last, stubbing out the cigar against a tree.

The coughing overtook him again as he was trying to do up his seatbelt, struggling to twist himself enough to click the metal teeth in place. He leaned forward in his seat, handkerchief to his mouth. When he removed the cloth, there was blood on it. He sighed and put the folded fabric back in his pocket.

"Jesus! Fuck! Aren't you angry?"

He looked at me quizzically through his horn-rimmed glasses. "Why would I be angry?"

"She wasn't exactly what we'd hoped."

"Of course not. There's no such thing as anti-aging antibodies, or whatever it was you were looking for. But you know, atonement with the ..."

He lapsed into silence, searching for the word. Apparently, he couldn't find it, because his expression gradually reverted to neutral. "She was a nice woman," he finished vaguely.

I rested my head on my hands, then howled, and slammed it against the wheel, sounding a plaintive bleat on the horn. Dad jumped.

"I don't want you to die," I sobbed, digging my fingernails into the sticky rubber of the wheel.

"What?"

"I don't want you to die!"

"Oh shit," Dad muttered, and patted me on the shoulder. "You know, everyone dies."

"Not yet. It's too soon. I want … I want you to see what's going to happen next. My career … your grandchild …"

"What grandchild?"

I laughed through tears. "I don't know yet. I'm working on it."

"People fade out, new people fade in. That's how it is. Who wants to be surrounded by ghosts anyway? Besides," he added, "I don't need to see what happens next to know how proud I am of you."

"Yeah right, except you hate refills."

"Well, not always. I liked it when you did *Stand by Me*."

"We haven't refilled *Stand by Me* …"

"When you were ten. Kneeling down beside the TV."

It had been my birthday present to Dad, who had never forgiven River Phoenix for dying in '93. A classic deserved more than seven years, he said. So, I'd bought the script book and learned River's part. I'd crouch beside the television delivering that school monologue to Will Wheaton onscreen while Dad looked on, cigar clamped in mouth, and applauded at the end.

"'It's the way people think of my family in this town. It's the way they think of me. Just one of those lowlife Chambers kids,'" I quoted.

"That's right. You all right to drive?"

"Yeah."

"Hit it," said Dad.

He slept for most of the return journey, nodding face bronzed by the sunset light. We drove quietly through the dusk. I nudged his knee as we turned into his street, and he jerked awake, blinking.

"We're home," I said.

"Back across the threshold," he murmured as we rolled up the drive.

He opened the door and tentatively swung his legs out to the gravel. After levering himself to his feet, he bent back down to check on me again.

"You know I might have three years left, if you want to get moving on that grandchild. Call that hippie girl from the Studio Club," he ordered.

"All right."

"Thank you, for what you were trying to do. That was a good little trip."

I nodded. "Love you."

"Love you too," he said, and closed the door, fading into the night and leaving a lingering scent of sweat and cigars.

MILLIE'S GAME

KATE MARUYAMA

(Excerpt from the novel THE COLLECTIVE, from Writ Large Press)

Los Angeles, 1918

Millie was at the end of her rope when Simon found her in a bar on Sunset drowning her sorrows in her last dollar of whiskey. Later she would wonder if he'd known she was exactly ripe for the plucking. She'd heard of him, but she couldn't get a bead on him. He had a Howard Hughes type interest in films. He seemed to have a lot of money but didn't have a job anyone could put a finger on. People knew him and wanted to be with him, and famous people seemed to flock to him. Those not yet famous emerged from his crowd well on their way to fame.

But here was Simon in a bar, not at some important party, but sitting by himself at the end of the bar over a club soda. He had the accustomed slouch tall men took. His blond hair was slicked back, and his reddish-brown beard well groomed. His eyes were a piercing blue, but he was slightly left of handsome; something not sharp enough in his face.

Millie said, "What, you goin' to church after?"

He smiled. That smile lit up like some sort of hope in her—a hope she hadn't felt for a few years now. He thanked the bartender, stood up, and walked down the bar. "This seat taken?"

She said, "You sure you want it? I got failure coming off me like a stink."

He chuckled and sat down next to her. It was hard to explain his charisma, given his looks, but Millie felt a pull the moment he sat down, as his elbow brushed hers and he folded his hands on the bar.

Millie had gotten a few jobs as an extra, but couldn't seem to land a role to pay the rent. In the meantime, she'd gotten mouthy with a patron at the Formosa Café and was summarily fired from her waitressing job. A guy had grabbed her behind, *right there*, and she was supposed to put up with it? Hell no. Her mama raised her better than that.

But apparently her mama didn't raise her right to get by in Hollywood. This place had different rules from anywhere else.

Simon extended his hand, with its long, gorgeous fingers. "Simon Raithe."

She said, "I know who you are. Millie, Millie Burgess."

"Pleasure, Millie." He didn't take her hand in that half-baked way gentlemen did at the time, halfway between a shake and I'm gonna kiss it. He shook her hand firmly like she was *someone*. Like she mattered. After feeling increasingly invisible in this strange sunlit paradise of shifting earth, it was quite a change. They got to talking, and he told her of her hidden talents, her cleverness, her *power*. It wasn't creepy, it was bolstering. He told her if she joined his acting troupe, she'd be able to develop those talents, form connections, and her career would be on its way in no time.

And it was. It started with an invitation to a party. Crazy house atop a hill in Los Feliz with rooms bigger than her apartment, babbling fountains, and those quiet rooms tucked away upstairs ...

Well, a lady doesn't tell, but she took advantage of those rooms.

Then the classes with the acting troupe that called themselves The Players—so exhilarating! All of them actors chosen by Simon, with classes led by Charlie Chaplin of all people! She learned so much of the craft from this terribly handsome man. She didn't know how he could hide all that gorgeous under greasepaint and that awful suit.

Millie knew she'd been dealt a winning hand. Thanks to the classes and whatever juice The Players provided, she was finally getting traction in her acting, in her place on the planet. She was introduced around and started getting auditions. Sure enough, she started getting roles. Supporting roles—the kid sister, the best friend, the nosy neighbor—but steady work. She got herself a sweet little apartment on Curson in Miracle Mile. It wasn't the Hollywood Hills, but it was a good start. She was energized by wanting *more, more, more.*

But—and she only noticed this later—she wasn't invited into the Conclave. There was this chosen group of Simon's who were the inner circle. She had plenty of invites, but the parties she found out about secondhand, where she showed up breathless and expectant, were part of this circle she couldn't get into. Not for want of trying; she spent serious time sucking up to those insiders. Mary Pickford, Doug Fairbanks, Miriam Davies, and Charlie Chaplin were all amused by her sense of humor, charmed with the way the girl could dance on a tabletop, the way she could mimic popular songs on the radio in her warble. But there was always a wall up, a time when the smile faded—a line she couldn't cross. This drove her nuts.

Maybe that's why she did the stupid thing, the thing she got punished for. But now, as she sees what's going on—and she's seen *plenty* over the years—she wonders if she wasn't punished for doing the stupid thing, so much as set up in a situation that would put her in this predicament. Wasn't she more useful to Simon in her current situation than whatever he got out of the Fatty Arbuckle situation?

★

The thing is, she was *at* the party. And she *knew* Roscoe Arbuckle didn't rape anybody.

Roscoe was the best. He was always good for a party, had a wicked sense of humor, and seemed genuinely tickled that his fame surpassed his looks as far as getting women was concerned. Roscoe was a player.

At the turn of 1921, Roscoe "Fatty" Arbuckle was the king of Mack Sennet comedies, and America saw him as a star. He was as big as Chaplin, no pun intended. Lord knows that guy was plagued by fat jokes. The large, affable fellow who started as a Keystone Cop had just signed a two-million-dollar contract with Paramount.

Maybe that was the deal-breaker, that two million dollars.

On top of it, Roscoe was the sweetest guy. Seriously. That inner circle Millie couldn't break into? Roscoe was the only one of them who talked to Millie like she was a person. He'd crack her up with a joke when she'd been rebuffed by the bigwigs. He always checked in on her: "Millie, how's tricks?"

She'd say, "Still breathing, still acting, can't complain."

He'd wink and click his tongue and say, "Attagirl."

So, when it happened, well, she *couldn't* keep quiet.

★

All she knew is that night, Virginia showed up stumbling and deathly pale. Millie walked her back to one of the bedrooms and sat her down, went to fetch her some water. Virginia was blubbering but finally came out with it. She'd been to an abortion doctor, and she knew something had gone wrong, but she just wanted to get out of there. She was in a lot of pain, but it was only when she saw the blood that she started screaming.

Millie went to get her some wet towels to clean her up. Why did these girls trust these quack doctors? Surely there was an easier way to get rid of a pregnancy. When she came back into the room with the towels, Virginia was still screaming, but now she was pointing fingers at a baffled Roscoe, who backed out of the room. He was fully clothed. Like he'd taken his tie off and his shirt was unbuttoned, and his hair was a bit of a mess, but nothing else was out of place: his belt, his shoes, nothing.

Someone came to the door, someone said, "Rape." There was blood everywhere and people watched and murmured. Something had switched, and it took a while before Millie could make sense of it. The energy in the room shifted, and Roscoe was railroaded so swiftly she couldn't keep up. The murmurs said, "Rape." Someone else added, "Brutal rape." Everything just followed.

Simon was there immediately, consulting with folks in corners. Millie thought he was there to help. He always looked out for his people, and Roscoe was part of the Conclave. She didn't know about the police reports and what they'd said until later. She felt like Chicken Little screaming that the sky was falling, but nobody cared.

She volunteered to give a statement to the police that she knew about the abortion, that Virginia was lying, but she kept getting shoved aside. Soon a well-meaning friend offered to drive her home.

Two days later, Virginia died in the hospital of a ruptured bladder and internal bleeding. From the *abortion*. Then the roof caved in.

It was awful to watch. One trial, lickety-split, then a second, when Roscoe wouldn't even take the stand. She couldn't bear the way the light had left his eyes. She'd never seen a person so instantly decimated, nothing but a sad shell sitting in his best suit in that courtroom. He'd given up. She went in every day and sat in the gallery. Someone had to be there for him. She wanted to stand up and holler, but she could only bear silent witness to the awfulness.

And the language around it! The first trial and the second. They had to attack him for being fat. Everyone painted an image of this large fat man raping a young, innocent girl. Millie couldn't take it. Plenty of that garbage went on, and she knew so many girls ruined by men in so many ways. Virginia's false claims cheapened their reality.

People tried to pin the burst bladder on Fatty's weight. "Killed her with his weight." It was awful. Those quack abortion doctors were the ones oughtta be put away. Charging an arm and a leg to do an operation they had no certification for.

Millie went to Simon. He was the only one she knew who had the cachet to fix this. She drove her little jalopy out to his house in Los Feliz. The driveway was steep and ran alongside a fake concrete waterfall that trickled down the hill. It took a lot of shifting and grinding to mount that hill. She pulled up in front of his enormous Craftsman and stopped the car, looking up in awe. She'd been to the house at night and it was gorgeous, but here in the daylight, when you could really capture the size of the thing … it looked as big as a grand hotel back east.

Serena, or whatever his new assistant's name was, showed her to where Simon sat in the garden, Indian-style of all things. He had the most peculiar clothes on: trousers that looked more like pajamas, but they were made of the wrong material. Millie waited a full half-hour for him to talk to her.

"Millie. How are you?"

"I'm good. I'm good. I came to ask a favor."

He breathed in and rose to his feet. The guy was so limber. He gestured over to a table and chairs that sat on a mini patio alongside the house. Extra sitting areas, that's what the rich had.

It was a gorgeous afternoon, the sun having retreated enough to make it pleasant to be outside in the warm. This place was so green, so far removed from the bustle of Hollywood Boulevard, that it felt like a different planet. Birds chirped in the surrounding trees and bushes, and the distant sound of that waterfall made the city right beneath them disappear.

"Are you in trouble?" he asked, gliding into a chair opposite her.

"I just. Can you do something to help Roscoe? Simon, he's dying out there. Dying for something he didn't do."

In that moment something clicked over in Simon's eyes. She should have known it and backed off. But she had come all the way here, resolved to make a difference. She had to keep on. Nobody else was speaking up for Roscoe. Nobody.

"I was there, Simon. I *know* he didn't do it. Virginia got back from the doctor, if you could even call him that. Not to speak ill of the dead, sir, she was in a bad way. She'd just had an abortion. The guy was a hack. A quack. A …"

Simon stared at her steadily and spoke carefully. "Millie, you are to speak no more of this."

"But I can't just sit by …"

"Do you understand me?" His voice was terrible. It jolted her right in the chest and forced her eyes to down to her shoes.

She said, "Yes. I understand."

That was it. She was dismissed.

After the second hung jury, Millie knew it was time to take her chance. She went to the lawyers.

Simon wouldn't know her involvement until she took the stand.

She tried to enjoy the drive all the way up to San Francisco for the trial, staying over in a coastal town so small, she didn't catch its name. It was her first time along those winding ocean roads, and her first time in the city. She tooled along in her brand-new shiny blue roadster, bought with her contract money from United Artists. She was one of their first contract players, and although her roles would be supporting, it was nice to have a steady salary. Despite her growing fear that doing the right thing might somehow be the wrong thing to do, she breathed in the cold air and sunshine, ate up the ocean, and rejoiced in the sun on her face and the knowledge she was going to set things right.

The courthouse, only six years old, was of European size, its dome supposedly the fifth largest in the world. Her heels clicked on the marble floors under a ceiling so high it felt like she was outdoors and very small indeed.

Someone had to speak up. And from what she could see, she was the only one volunteering. On the stand in that enormous space, her voice quavered at first, but it grew stronger as she told it straight, from beginning to end, exactly what happened. She told how Virginia was in a bad way when she arrived, how the crowd had turned on Roscoe, how Simon had greased those wheels. It flooded out of her with the flow and freedom that only real truth can supply. And that moment where the light came back into Roscoe eyes? That hope? That's when she knew it was the right thing to do.

At some point, she can't remember when now—and when she replays the day in her head she wonders if the *when* was important—she noticed Simon sitting at the back of the courtroom. This dynamic, buoyant soul who had welcomed her into The Players, made her what she was, those clear blue eyes in which she thought she could see her future—see forever—had turned. He stared at her with the same control and self-awareness as always, but what she saw in his face scared her to her bones. It wasn't anger or worry. What she saw in him was resolve.

When she left the stand, she walked past Roscoe, who smiled that goofy, grateful smile. Simon had left. His absence made her more afraid than his presence. She was now playing against the house. Her keys were shaking in her hands when she went to her little roadster, parked down the street.

It was nearing sunset when she got back to the Palace Hotel, her grand indulgence. She passed the Victorian greenhouse-topped fern-lined dining room, where ladies in ridiculous hats assembled over rich cakes and tea. She took the too-slow elevator up to the tenth floor, and rushed down the hall about two miles too long. She gathered her stuff, threw it in her suitcase, and left.

She drove down a windy stretch of the Roosevelt Highway, not yet named the Pacific Coast Highway, which teetered at the edge of a cliff overlooking the ocean. The curved, freeing road she had driven up now seemed fraught with peril. Driving on the right side of the road going south put her closer to the edge and, in the dark and fog, the turns were hard to see. But she steeled herself, determined to get back to her comfortable apartment, even if she had to drive all night. Yes, it was dark. Yes, it was hard to see. But *something* took control of her wheel. *That* she remembers. A sudden curve made her turn her wheel to the left, but it was jammed somehow. She tugged at it, and it would not turn. She can't have been going more than twenty miles an hour when the car hit dirt and went straight off the cliff.

There was an absurd moment of quiet, of ocean breeze, of peace, before she crashed onto the rocks below. There was a sudden ripping pain in her side. Was it the gear shift? There was a cacophony of metal and waves and rocks and the feel of cold and hot wet spray. Everything went black.

★

Millie was standing on the winding road again, looking over the edge at her car, the flames of the initial explosion abating. She was here, and she knew what she saw, but she somehow *wasn't* here. She watched her car just long enough to think about things, but not long enough to figure it out.

There was a burning warm hand on the small of her back, and it was Simon. Her living self would have been afraid and angry. She should be so *angry*. Clearly, he made this happen. Her dead self thought, *Of course*.

She said, "Hello."

He said, "I'm sorry."

She said, "No you're not."

He said, "And neither are you, so we'll call it square."

She held her arms out in front of her. The ugly bruise acquired from bumping into the dresser in the hotel room in search of the bathroom the night before was gone. She spread her hands wide and wriggled her fingers, which would not crack in their accustomed way. She said, "How does this work?"

Simon laughed softly. He said, "I should have thought of this weeks ago. What amazes me is that no matter how long I stick around, there is more to learn." He sounded genuinely surprised. He put his arm around her and things went black.

She came to in the Conclave, which, it turns out was more than a collection of people. These recognizable luminaries were all dressed in robes, surrounding her in some sort of cavern, and as they bound her, she lost consciousness.

★

And, like that, she was home, in her bed, in her apartment. Only there was no confusion this time. She knew what had happened. She knew she was alive. But she wasn't. She had this body. No one, aside from those in the Conclave, acted as if anything had happened. She didn't know how she got from there to here. Her apartment was her apartment, and her clothes were her clothes, and she could eat. She *loved* to eat. But she never, ever got full. She craved and she tasted, but she was never satisfied. And her body couldn't feel—cold, hot, pain, pleasure. It was a numbness, a numbness to her emotions, her thoughts. The way she used to be able to piece things together was missing. It was like that one time she tried opium, only without the pleasant feeling. Everything was distant.

Roscoe was acquitted. He took her out to lunch to celebrate. Now that she was *back*, everything tasted different, everything looked different. She looked at her club sandwich like it was some kind of miracle. This was a hundred-year sentence. She didn't know what came *after* the hundred years, but she figured she'd better take advantage while she was here. She ate her sandwich in large bites.

Roscoe said, "Did you get in trouble?"

She had to focus really hard to realize she was meant to be in a conversation. "For what?"

"For testifying."

"With who?"

"With *Simon*. You know. I got in trouble with him when I talked to a biographer doing his life story. It's not like I even knew much, but Simon was pretty furious."

What a strange reason for a setup like that rape story. Or maybe because the opportunity presented itself? Simon wasn't behind Virginia's set of woes. Was he?

"Millie …" The worry in Roscoe's voice nagged at her.

She remembered his question. "Oh no, we're pals, we're fine." It's not like she could condemn this man she was now tied to. People would see them around. She'd have to stay on his good side.

This appeared to trouble Roscoe.

There was a finality in his eyes that day when he said goodbye to her and hugged her for too long. He was grateful, but it was obvious this friendship wouldn't continue. She was stuck with Simon and everyone else would step away.

She was pleased to see Roscoe get a little bit of a life back. Eight months after he'd condemned him, even old man Hays stepped forward and said that Fatty Arbuckle had been acquitted on all counts. It was time for the public to forgive him as well. He had just been offered a role in a movie when he died in his bed of a heart attack. Millie wasn't sure Simon didn't have something to do with *that* also.

★

When Simon's hand closed on her back, on top of that winding hill against the sea air she could no longer feel, she was his. There was no choice but to serve, and there was no escape. She was cute, personable, and good at recruiting souls. She'd get them in with her guilelessness and charm. Simon and that *pull* would clinch the deal. She felt a little bad for these kids, but they were getting a better career than she ever had.

Every once in a while she'd ask Simon, "So, how long is this going to go on?" Was there some point in her servitude when she'd be released? Done? Was a hundred years a real number or was it figurative?

Simon only laughed that warm laugh she'd loved so much when she first met him. The laugh that now made her ghost blood run cold. Because he knew all, held all the cards, and she held none.

MULHOLLAND DRIVE

SOPHIE FRANK

That summer, we felt united in our singular urge to fuck around. After long days scooping ice cream or babysitting snot-faced kids, one of us would text in the group: *Meet up on Mulholland?*

We discovered our spot the night of graduation. We were headed to a party at one of those houses in the hills with walls of glass, the kind of place where we could cosplay wealthy, pretend we'd grown up driving Teslas to high school. Kash picked us up one by one, in Burbank, North Hollywood, Van Nuys, and Studio City. The engine shuddered as we cruised up Laurel Canyon Boulevard and turned right onto Mulholland Drive. Kash drove the curves for two minutes and then jerked into a turnout along the northern edge of the scenic route, inertia knocking Jay's forehead into Ace's temple.

"What the fuck, man?" Ko grunted.

Kash parked the car and jumped out; we hesitated and then followed, relaxing our cramped bodies as we flooded from the car. Dust floated in the air, a dry wind stirring the earth. Kash led us toward the mountain's edge.

The Valley spread out beneath us, the San Gabriel and Santa Monica Mountains trapping the light in the bowl. Arterial freeways ran north-south and east-west, parallel curves of red and white, blurred heads and tails racing nowhere. Down there, my city glittered brighter than anything I'd seen.

Ace leaned against the steel guard rail, their waist-length hair blowing ethereally. Jay crouched in a deep squat, their hands in prayer. Ko grabbed Kash's hand, and the two of them stepped back, away from us, into each other. I spread my feet and shoved my hands in my jeans pockets.

"Fuck the party," Kash called out. "This is where it's at."

Our spot had a name, officially: the Nancy Hoover Pohl Overlook. Ko laughed the first time they saw the sign. "What do you think Nancy did to get this place named after her?"

"She probably was into saving the trees," Kash said.

"Nah, I bet she fucked someone," said Jay.

"I'd fuck someone to get this spot named after me," Ace said.

"You'd fuck someone just to fuck someone," Jay replied.

Nancy Hoover Pohl, eco warrior or slut or whomever else she may be, became the sixth in our fivesome that summer. We spent our days tying up the loose ends of childhood; we spent our nights at the overlook.

Although sometimes we sat in silence, more often we talked. We talked about weed and plastic dicks and eyeliner and the wool socks Ko would need in Vermont. We talked about top surgery and Joni Mitchell and childhood dogs and if Jay should buy pepper spray when they got to New York. We talked about bank accounts and lemon meringue pie and dead grandparents and whether Kash's little sister would steal their car when they were gone. We talked about fluoxetine and divorce and doughnuts and whether Ace should live at home in Burbank or try to get an apartment near Santa Monica College. We talked about friendship and longing and change, and I wondered if our fivesome had a future beyond that summer.

At the end of August, we met up on Mulholland for the last time. We sat in a line on the edge of the mountain and watched the world below. That night's conversation seemed shrunken, relegated to the minutiae of going away to school. Class registration. Bed Bath & Beyond. New roommates. On-campus jobs. After a while, I looked down the line at my friends' faces and noticed Ace was gone.

I found them a hundred feet away, sitting on a bench at the trailhead. A black sage bush blocked the view. "I can't listen anymore," they said, when I sat down next to them. "You all are going away and starting your lives. Some day you guys might even buy one of those glass houses up here in the hills. All I've got going for me is SMC." The sage bush blurred as I reached down and squeezed their hand.

That fall, I spent many nights wandering around rural Ohio. The earth was flat. My campus was surrounded by cornfields. The landscape felt muted compared to the bright lights of L.A. One night, as the daylight waned and the cutting chill of winter settled into my toes, I felt my phone buzz. Up popped a picture of the Valley, taken from our overlook. Not in the group chat. Just for me.

Miss you, Ace.

MOVING SALE

ELIZABETH ALICE GRAY

Emily Johnson looked at the remains of her forty-nine years in Los Angeles scattered on the tarps on her front lawn. Not much was left at the end of her moving sale, and what was left could be easily taken to Goodwill without much of a Marie Kondo goodbye. All except for the small antique mantel clock. It was the one thing she took from home, tucked into her suitcase on her one-way TWA flight to LAX decades ago.

Her small house was empty without its sound, but now that her house had been literally emptied, it was time to let it go. She was moving on while there was still time left in her aging-yet-healthy body and mind to pursue other adventures.

A production gypsy, she had moved from show to show in the entertainment business at a time when filling in the dry spells with savings and temp work had been possible. It was tough being a freelancer all those years, but she had learned the hard way how to live beneath her means and to prepare for recessions and impending strikes. That was until the day she realized she had vanished from the workplace. She had become like the people who disappeared before her. *Obsolete.* She, like them, had become what everyone feared most. *Old.*

Her life, once full of work and social commitments, was now reduced to funerals and fifteen-minute doctor appointments. Many of her friends had either moved back to their families, suddenly died, or developed some form of dementia. Others moved up the ladder and never bothered to look back down, or traveled incessantly and boasted about it. All this left Emily feeling even more out of place than usual.

What pushed her further into detached loneliness were the last remnants of her social circle. They seemed to be stuck in one-sided conversational loops, endlessly complaining about their health and lack of money. She had lost her community and felt like she did all those years ago before moving to Los Angeles. *Isolated.*

At that time, she had recently graduated from college, returned home, and was asked the never-ending question, *What are you going to do now?* She kept that answer to herself, as she had learned dreams come true faster if you don't share them with the peanut gallery.

Back then, she watched her friends slowly drift away, settling into their grown-up lives of marriages, relation-ships, jobs, and graduate school. But she couldn't "settle" where she was. It wasn't the right place to turn her dream into a reality. Working in show business had been her life's purpose since she was a teenager.

But that was then, and this was now.

Her landlord of thirty-five years died, and his daugh-ters sold her small bungalow. The new owners didn't want her as a renter; they wanted the house. So, when she got the Owner-Occupied Eviction Notice, it was her "inciting incident," as screenwriters would have called it. In everyday lingo, it was a change she could do nothing about, except use it to pull herself out of fear's inertia into action.

After the initial shock and learning that there would be no "relocation assistance fee," she viewed the eviction as an opportunity to check off something on her bucket list: to live in a foreign country. She just didn't know which one yet. She had always been careful with money and had enough of a cushion to do it, for a while at least. But, as adventurous as the unknown future promised to be, the present was unsettling and uncomfortable. Everything was up in the air. One thing was for certain. She had to get out in thirty days.

And she was ready to go. She had grown tired of listening to leaf blowers and looking for a parking space. Emily was weary of the drive-by friendships based on short-term interests. She longed for the emotional intimacy she had with good friends now long gone, who listened more than they talked and who had earned her trust.

Once she made the decision, she was energized and started by sorting all her belongings into four piles: keep, sell, throw away, and donate. It was a painful process, but she was determined not to be held hostage any longer by her stuff. Things she no longer used, wore, or needed she could now finally part with. What lay on her lawn of her moving sale was the last of it, and she was ready to let it all go.

All except the clock. There had been some interest throughout the day, but no sale.

"Well," she said as she picked it up, "guess I could make room for you in my suitcase one more time."

A beat-up Toyota pickup truck with North Dakota license plates pulled up in front of her house. In its back was a secondhand couch that had clearly seen better days. The tall, stocky, young woman who got out looked like she could do an oil change on anything with four wheels, even though she wore heavy makeup, false eyelashes, and form-fitting jeans. A large handbag was slung across her white T-shirt. She had an intense air about her, and she gave a cursory nod as she stomped up the front lawn in her brown work boots before she bent down to scrutinize the items on the tarps.

"Have any cooking stuff?" she asked in a strong Midwestern accent, barely glancing at Emily.

"Yeah," said Emily. She put the clock down on the tarp in front of her, then led the way to another in a far corner. "Over here."

"Oh, great!" said the young woman. "How much you want for these?" She picked up the very first and only set of measuring cups and spoons Emily bought forty-nine years ago.

A twinge of unexpected grief went through Emily as she recognized these household objects, which had been in her life for so long, were about to leave her. She pushed through loss and started the negotiation. "Oh, I don't know. How about two bucks?"

"I don't have much cash. Do you take Venmo? Zelle?"

"Well, how much cash do you have?" Venmo and Zelle were a pain in the ass to Emily.

The young woman put the measuring utensils on the tarp, fished around in her large purse, then pulled out a dollar bill and some change. She counted it then offered, "A dollar fifty?"

"Deal."

Emily took the money and, as the young woman put the cooking stuff in her purse, got the feeling they were going to a good home.

"Do you have any chairs?"

"No, sorry. Got sold earlier." Emily could sense the young woman's disappointment but also sensed she was a kindred spirit just starting out on the same path she did decades ago. "How long have you been in L.A.?"

"Eight days," said the young woman.

"Well, welcome," said Emily, offering her hand to shake. "I'm Emily. I'm a transplant, too. Or was one."

"Oh! I'm Sharon," she said, shaking Emily's hand. Instantly her demeanor went from all business to friendly. "Where you from?"

"Originally?" Emily asked. She had thought of herself as a Californian for so long. "Just outside Philadelphia. You?"

"Fargo. Way outside of Fargo. A farm. My family has a farm."

Sharon's wistful tone of voice struck a deeper chord in Emily, and her mind flashed back to her first few months in Los Angeles. No air conditioning. No heat. No furniture in a bare basement flat. How hard it was. She had nothing, yet she had everything—everything she needed to make the best start in her life, and do it her own way. She had never been filled with so much energy, excitement, adventure, and terrified joy.

"I just graduated from Morehead," said Sharon. She went on to explain, reacting to Emily's inquisitive look. "Minnesota State University at Morehead. It's kind of near Fargo." Sharon seemed to read Emily's thoughts about what brought her to L.A. "I'm an editor. A video editor."

"Ahh," said Emily. *No pink-collar ghetto for you! Nice!* Emily thought of all the typing tests she had taken in temp agencies on IBM Selectric typewriters and all the bottom-feeder assignments she worked on that went nowhere. She wouldn't wish that on her worst enemy. "Come out by yourself?"

"No, I have my cat with me. And I'm sharing an apartment with friends from school. There's five of us. Pretty crowded, but the rent's not too bad."

Good, thought Emily. *She's not alone. And she has a cat.*

Sharon paced between the tarps, taking one last look at everything. She stopped, pointed, and asked, "How much do you want for that?"

Emily bent down and picked up the clock. "Oh, I don't know."

"Could I see it?"

Emily handed it to her. Sharon's face softened as she held it carefully and examined it. "Does it work?"

"Sure does," said Emily. "Put it back down on the ground, open its front, and start the pendulum."

Sharon followed the instructions, and the clock started ticking. It was like a heartbeat that had been in Emily's life forever. Its steady rhythm unconsciously calmed her and connected her to the unseen love she left behind. It was a connection Emily never completely understood yet felt completely.

The clock suddenly chimed four times. It was four o'clock.

"Oh, wow!" said Sharon as she looked up at Emily. "This is exactly like my grandmother's!" Her *I've got it all together* guard went down and her body relaxed.

Emily looked at the young girl gently holding the clock and felt her homesickness and fear. It was the price Emily paid all those decades ago by leaving home to chase a dream. A price finalized by hope.

There was no bargaining strategy when Sharon boldly stated, "I have to have it!"

"Yes, you do," said Emily.

"I can go get cash and come back. How much?"

"Nothing."

"What? Really?"

"Really. Take it," said Emily, who could tell it had been a while since Sharon had been on the receiving end of kindness without an agenda. "For some reason," Emily continued speaking out loud her feelings in a way that rarely happened these days, "I needed to hang onto it today. Now I know why. It was to give it to you. It was my grandfather's."

"Oh, wow," gasped Sharon. "Sure you want to give it to me? I mean, won't someone in your family want it?"

"Positive. I've already checked," said Emily who had reached out to her nieces and nephews to ask if they wanted it, but they all said no. She had no other surviving members of her immediate family and no children of her own.

"You'll need this," Emily said. She reached into her pants pocket and handed the clock's key to Sharon. Sharon looked at it in her hand then up at Emily who advised, "Don't wind it too tight. It's bad for its insides. It's kind of like a person that way."

"Thanks," said Sharon, who took it and carefully put it in her jeans pocket. There was an awkward pause between them, and then she asked, "Can I help you in some way? Help you put your stuff away?"

"No, thanks. There's not much left. I can handle it."

Sharon looked at Emily again for a longer time, hesitant to leave. Finally she asked, "I feel like we have met before. Ever been to Fargo?"

"No. Never," said Emily smiling. Emily decided not to admit she was feeling the same familiarity. It might open a whole can of metaphysical babble that L.A. seemed to draw out of people.

Sharon stood still on the lawn, still not wanting to leave. Emily didn't want this younger version of herself to leave, either. Suddenly Sharon put down her purse, grabbed her phone out of her back pocket, turned it on and posed.

Amused and amazed, Emily watched Sharon do something she would never do. Effortlessly and shamelessly, Sharon took selfies holding the clock then posted them on her social media. There everyone could see her story of the clock, and it would live in the digital universe forever.

While Emily's story was more personal, and soon to be only a memory.

"Want me to send these to you?"

"Sure."

"What's your handle?"

"Let's do AirDrop," said Emily, who hated social media but wasn't a total luddite.

Afterward, they were both ready to part.

"Good luck to you, Sharon from way outside of Fargo," said Emily as she shook Sharon's hand again.

"You, too ..." said Sharon, blanking on Emily's name.

"Emily," said Emily, patiently well-versed in the short-term memories of the digital generation.

"Emily, from ...?" said Sharon, blanking again.

"From outside Philadelphia," prompted Emily.

"From outside Philadelphia!" said Sharon. "Good luck to you too, Emily." Sharon suddenly embraced Emily like a long-lost family member and said, "Thank you so much again."

"You are so welcome," said Emily, breaking the embrace.

Sharon stood staring at her, again hesitant to leave.

"Go on, go! You'll make it!" Emily echoed the words her grandfather gifted her when she left home and when he gave her his clock. It was the last time she saw him in person, but she recalled the scene many times in her mind, especially when she needed encouragement.

"Thanks," Sharon whispered. She turned away, got into her beat-up pickup, and started its engine. Then she smiled, waved at Emily, and drove off.

Ding, ding, ding, went Emily's phone with a series of texts. She looked down and smiled as she scrolled through the airline notifications about great deals to foreign countries.

BIOGRAPHIES

SERIES EDITORS

SARA CHISOLM

Sara Chisolm is a speculative fiction writer based in the Los Angeles area. Her urban fantasy short stories "Serenade of the Gangsta," "The Fortune of the Three and the Kabuki Mask," and "We Found Love as the Undead" were featured in the second and third volumes of the Made in L.A. fiction anthology series. Her story, "Selkies Among the Pines," was published in *Fiyah* literary magazine. Another story, "Anansi and the Hot-Lanta Flow," can be read in the anthology, *Anansi: New and Ancient Tales* by Flame Tree Press.

GABI LORINO

Gabi Lorino is a founding member of Made in L.A. Writers and serves as a co-editor for the Made in L.A. fiction anthology series. Her articles and short stories have been published in newspapers, websites, newsletters, magazines, and books. She has self-published one novel, *A Magical Time Called Later*, in addition to a journal series.

ALLISON ROSE

Allison Rose is a novelist, screenwriter, and visual artist born and raised in Los Angeles. While Rose's stories vary in genre, the city often acts as a diverse backdrop for complex stories about female and LGBTQ+ characters and the deconstruction of tropes about women. Rose has worked in the entertainment industry in varying roles, including television production and music engineering. She is a founding member of Made in L.A. Writers and has used her twenty years of graphic design experience to create her own book covers, including every volume of *Made in L.A.* Recently, Rose has turned the lens onto herself in an upcoming memoir, which promises to be as darkly compelling and controversial as the figments of her imagination.

CODY SISCO

Cody Sisco is an author, editor, publisher, and literary community organizer. His LGBT psychological science fiction series includes two novels thus far, *Broken Mirror* and *Tortured Echoes*. He is a freelance editor specializing in genre-bending fiction. He is a founding member of Made in L.A. Writers and the publisher of the Made in L.A. fiction anthology series. His startup, BookSwell, is a literary events and media production company dedicated to lifting up marginalized voices and connecting readers and writers in Southern California and beyond. He serves as a co-chair of the Board of Directors for the Editorial Freelancers Association and as a board member at APLA Health. Find him online at codysisco.com.

CONTRIBUTORS

MELIZA BAÑALES

Meliza Bañales, aka Missy Fuego (she/they), is the author of six books, a Lambda Literary Finalist, and a Slam Champion. She has written for the *Washington Square Review*, *On Our Backs Magazine*, *Razorcake*, *Ladybox*, and *Encyclopedia Brittanica*. Along with being the 2024 Los Angeles Erotica Slam Champion, they were a founding member of the championship West Hollywood Slam Team. They completed 2024 summer residencies at Tin House and the LA LGBTQIA Center. They co-produce the acclaimed L.A. event, the Harold & Belle's Slam, monthly and are the co-founder of CULTURE Slam Team. They live, write, and cause radical trouble in their hometown of Los Angeles.

JACQUELINE BERKMAN

Jacqueline Berkman is a fiction writer and screenwriter based in Los Angeles. The short film "Panofsky's Complaint" based on her short story "Picking Locks" was screened at the Cannes Short Film Corner, the Brooklyn Short Film Festival, and LA Shorts Fest, and her short fiction has been published in *The Coachella Review*, *The Write Launch*, and *The Writing Disorder*, among other publications. Check out her work at jacquelineberkman.com

PAULA BERNSTEIN

Paula Bernstein is a physician, a scientist, and the author of the medically-themed series Hannah Kline Mysteries. Her short stories have been included in the anthologies *LAst Resort*, *Avenging Angelinos*, *A New York State of Crime*, and *Angel City Beat*. They have also been published on *Short-Story.me*, and *Fiction on the Web*. She has been an active member of Sisters in Crime and served as President of the Los Angeles Chapter and Chair of the California Crime Writers Conference. Her nonfiction publications include *Carrying a Little Extra, A Guide to Pregnancy for the Plus-Sized Woman* (Penguin) and *Woman to Woman, A Gynecologist's Guide to Your Body* (Bantam).

DUNCAN BIRMINGHAM

Duncan Birmingham is a writer and filmmaker based in Los Angeles. His short story collection, *The Cult in My Garage*, was published by Maudlin House and the title story was chosen for the *Selected Shorts* radio show. His fiction has appeared in *The Oxford Review*, *Volume 1 Brooklyn*, *Joyland*, and *Mystery Tribune*, among other publications. He's worked as a writer/producer on TV shows that include *Maron* (starring Marc Maron) and the Jonathan Ames comedy *Blunt Talk* starring Patrick Stewart. His short films have premiered at various festivals, including Sundance, and his feature film directorial debut *Who Invited Them* was named one of the best horror films of the year by *The Hollywood Reporter*.

DC DIAMONDOPOLOUS

DC Diamondopolous is an award-winning short story, and flash fiction writer with hundreds of stories published internationally in print and online magazines, literary journals, and anthologies. DC's stories have appeared in: *Progenitor*, *34th Parallel*, *So It Goes: The Literary Journal of the Kurt Vonnegut Museum and Library*, *Lunch Ticket*, and others. DC has two published collections of short stories, *Stepping Up* and *Captured Up Close* (20th Century Short-Short Stories). She was nominated twice for the Pushcart Prize and twice for Best of the Net Anthology. She lives on the California coast with her wife and animals. dcdiamondopolous.com

SOPHIE FRANK

Sophie Frank is a writer and teacher who grew up under the shade of oak and eucalyptus trees in Laurel Canyon. She has spent her adult life in cities up and down the East Coast but is always called back to her native Los Angeles for inspiration.

KEN FUNSTEN, CFA

Ken Funsten, CFA, has been a librarian, English teacher, punk-rock journalist, stock analyst, corporate executive, and hedge fund manager. And yet his most life-changing event took place before all this, at age ten, when he crashed his bike into a tree and lay in a coma for a week, then bedridden for most of a decade, during which time often all he could do was listen to Vin Scully or read in bed. As his body atrophied, his mind grew. He absorbed Homer to Heller, Freud to Tolkien, Melville to Miller, Updike to Spillane. His first published fiction is in *Angel City Beat: A Mystery Anthology from Sisters in Crime* (2024). He likes writing about financial fraud and white-collar crime, using his professional designation Ken Funsten, CFA, so when readers see this they'll know to expect a story set in the wider world of business and finance. His website is yourfunsten.com.

M. LOPES DA SILVA

M. Lopes da Silva (he/they/she) is a polyamorous, bisexual, and non-binary trans masc author and artist from Los Angeles. He writes pulp and poetry, and lectures about the political power of desire. Their short fiction has been published within *In Somnio: A Collection of Modern Gothic Horror Fiction*, *Stories of the Eye*, and at *Electric Literature*. Weirdpunk Books released his collection of heartbreaking and exquisite trans and queer horror stories, *Infinity Mathing at the Shore and Other Disruptions*, in March of 2024.

ELIZABETH ALICE GRAY

Elizabeth Alice Gray has decades of working on television documentary series and feature documentaries and is a Primetime Nonfiction Emmy Award-winning producer and a Best Documentary nominee from the National Association of Minorities in Cable. A long-time resident of Los Angeles, she also writes for radio, television, and film, and is a published and produced playwright. A multimedia writer, her words can even be found in Playboy Centerfold rejection letters from the late 1970s and early 1980s. She is always on the hunt for a good book and loves cats. This is her first short story publication with Made in L.A.

CHRISTINE HERIAT

Christine Heriat is a fiction writer intensely interested in the everyday magical, the fantastical, and the adventurous. Her work has been published in *Baltimore Gothic* and the University of Alabama's *Al Dente Journal*. When not writing, she is an avid traveler, cook, and hiker. She lives in Venice, CA, crammed into a small house filled with too many books and cooking gadgets.

GEORGIA JEFFRIES

Georgia Jeffries is the author of *The Younger Girl*, a Midwest noir based on a true crime of family murder and deception crossing three generations. Her short story, "What would Nora Do?" appears in the Mystery Writers of America *Odd Partners* anthology and was praised by the *Los Angeles Review of Books* as "domestic tragedy brilliantly segueing into comic farce." A writer of Emmy and WGA Award-winning television, she is a professor at USC's School of Cinematic Arts where she created the first undergraduate screenwriting thesis at an American university. Born in the Illinois heartland, she came of age in the San Francisco Bay Area and the wilds of Los Angeles. Read more at georgiajeffries.com.

KATE MARUYAMA

Kate Maruyama is the author of *Alterations*, *The Collective*, *Bleak Houses*, and *Halloween Beyond: A Gentleman's Suit*. Her novella *Family Solstice* was named Best Fiction Book of 2021 by *Rue Morgue Magazine*. Her short work has appeared in numerous journals and anthologies, and she is a two-time Pushcart Prize nominee and winner of the Uncharted Short

Story Prize. She served on the working Board for Women Who Submit, and the Board for the Shirley Jackson Awards. She writes, teaches, cooks, and eats in Los Angeles.

LAURA MCGHEE

Laura is an alumna of The Second City Theater, with an Honors Bachelor of Arts Degree from The University of Western Ontario and a Master of Education Degree. Laura has written and performed on CBC RADIO and at the Just for Laughs Festival. Her play, *Joyride*, won the Special Merit Award in the 7th Annual National Playwriting Competition. Another play, *Reservoir Dogs*, received a Canadian Comedy Award Nomination for Best Play. Laura's television writing credits include the 2001 Canadian Comedy Awards, nominated for a Gemini Award. A retired airline pilot, Laura is now a STEM instructor.

JACK NICHOLLS

Jack Nicholls is a British-Australian writer based in Melbourne, but with many fond connections to the United States. Their speculative fiction has been published in a variety of anthologies and internet corners, including in *Grist*, *Aurealis*, and *Tor.com*. Jack's father Peter Nicholls was the Hugo award-winning author of the *Encyclopedia of Science Fiction* and, for a time, a Hollywood filmmaker. He has since faded out.

A. J. PAYLER

Author A. J. Payler's novels include *The Killing Song, Lost in the Red, Terror Next Door*, and *Bank Error in Your Favor*; his short writing has been published by *Suspect, Twenty-Two Twenty-Eight, Flipside, Black Cat Weekly*, and *Flash in a Flash*. He has also released several albums of original music including *That Says It All* and *Apocalyptic Sunsets*, performing live as often as time permits. Born in Hawaii, he lives in California with his family. He has shaken hands with both Kurt Vonnegut and Lemmy from Motörhead, but not at the same time. Learn more at ajpayler.com.

THEA PUESCHEL

Thea Pueschel is a writer, multimedia artist, and the Chapters Liaison for the literary nonprofit Women Who Submit and a repeated Dorland Arts Colony Resident. Thea has been published in *Short Edition*, *Perhappened*, and *Made in L.A. Vol. 5: Vantage Points*, among others. Thea is known for drinking copious amounts of iced tea, random acts of binge creation, taking people through subconscious journeys, and teaching people to make shapes with their bodies.

AMY JONES SEDIVY

Amy Jones Sedivy grew up in Los Angeles and has lived in many of L.A.'s neighborhoods. She admits that the best was her childhood home a block from the beach; sadly, it was torn down for the LAX expansion. Amy currently lives in Northeast L.A. Recently retired from years of teaching high school English, she spends her time reading, writing, and exploring the rest of Los Angeles. Her most recent stories have been in *The Write Launch*, *Chiron Review*, and *Roi Fainéant Press*. She also proudly had a story in *Made in L.A. Volume 4: Beyond the Precipice*.

KATHERINE TOMLINSON

Katherine Tomlinson is an award-winning fictionista, a Pushcart Prize nominee for her short stories, and a screenwriter and editor. She began her career as a writer/editor for city magazines in Virginia, Hawaii, and California before transitioning to writing features for Copley News Service. She has worked in the entertainment industry as a development executive, researcher, and script doctor. An inveterate traveler, she is currently a digital nomad living in northern Portugal. She is fond of cats, train travel, and dark chocolate.

RAYA YARBROUGH

Raya Yarbrough is a singer-songwriter, and a writer of poetry and prose, based in Los Angeles, California. Although she may be most recognized for her musical work in TV and film, such as her featured vocal on the theme song for *Outlander* on Starz, Raya has written and produced five albums of original, eclectic music. Most recently, she released *North of Sunset West of Vine*, a concept album, based on Yarbrough's original staged musical of the same name, and *Artifacts of Grace*, which is her poetry converted to song, based on a series of paintings and sculptures by artist Pam Douglas that explores the way female-bodied experiences intersect with larger issues of race, justice, and equality. In addition, Raya writes creative nonfiction about growing up as a multiracial human. She lives with her husband and children and is finishing a humorous memoir about her first five years of being an artist while parenting. Yarbrough is also preparing for a month-long art/poetry/music installation at the TAG Gallery in Los Angeles with artist Pam Douglas. This installation will include both musical and spoken word versions of her poetry, performed by Raya Yarbrough.

VOLUNTEER EDITORS

CHRISTINA HOAG

Christina Hoag is the author of novels *Law of the Jungle, The Blood Room, Girl on the Brink,* and *Skin of Tattoos,* and co-authored *Peace in the Hood: Working with Gang Members to End the Violence.* A former journalist for the

Miami Herald and Associated Press in Los Angeles, she reported from Latin America for major media including *Time, Business Week, New York Times, Financial Times*, and *Houston Chronicle*. Her short stories and essays have been published in numerous literary reviews, including Toasted Cheese, Lunch Ticket and Shooter, and have won several awards.

JOVON C. JOHNSON

Jovon C. Johnson was born and raised in Compton, California. Educated at San Diego State University, Oregon State University, and Antioch University Los Angeles, where he received an MFA in Creative Writing. He is a Kimbilio Fellow and the author of a poetry collection, *Keep Striving*. He assisted in the creation of the Kuumba Journal at San Diego State University. His work has appeared in *SoMa Literary Review, Caesura Journal*, and *Elsewhere Lit*. He is an avid outdoorsman who spends most of his time getting lost in nature.

THEA PUESCHEL

Read Thea's bio above in the contributor section.

MADE IN L.A. WRITERS

Made in L.A. Writers is a collaborative of Los Angeles-based authors dedicated to nurturing and promoting indie fiction. While our styles, themes, and story locales differ, our work is both influenced and illuminated by our hometown and underpinned by the extraordinary, multifaceted, and often surreal culture and life in the City of Angels.

As indie authors, we face formidable challenges: fragmented audiences, intense competition in a crowded market, and traditional publishers' deep pockets.

If you enjoyed this book, please leave a review. Rave about us to your friends. Find us online and tell us how our stories made you feel. We're looking for connection; we hope to hear from you.

www.madeinlawriters.com

www.ingramcontent.com/pod-product-compliance
Lightning Source LLC
Chambersburg PA
CBHW031441200726
48289CB00007BB/2060